TERRI MACKENZIE

To Marry the Devil

For anyone who has ever felt unloved

Contents

Prologue

14th May, 1802

"Enter."

Jacob Barrington pushed open his father's study door with more than a little trepidation. The room was a forbidden one, although he sometimes stole inside for fun, snapping his father's quills and emptying his ink. A rebellion against the inevitable.

Even at fourteen, he knew there was only one possible reason he had been called to this study. He had been punished for no shortage of sins over the years. Most he had deserved— he *had* stolen his brother's precious poetry book and dropped it in the pond, he frequently stole food from the kitchens, and he took considerable delight in causing mayhem.

The thing he did not deserve was his father's unrelenting, blazing hatred. He received that, anyway.

As always, his father was sitting behind his desk. It was an old desk, made of rather fine mahogany, with papers piled high. Jacob had once rifled through them when he had broken into the study through the window, but he had found nothing interesting. Nothing that warranted his father being locked up in this room for so many hours every day, avoiding everyone

1

in the house except Cecil. Jacob's perfect older brother.

He took his time advancing into the room. A carriage clock ticked ominously on the mantel and a fire burned in the hearth despite the heat of the day. The room was swelteringly hot, although there wasn't so much as a bead of sweat on his father's pale, iron face.

Demons were used to the heat. When Jacob was little, he'd fantasised about his father being an instrument of evil, sent from Hell to terrorise everyone except Cecil. As a child, that had been his favourite explanation for his father's bouts of cruelty and violence.

Now he was older, he knew better. His father was just a man who fed on pain, and Jacob's was his favourite flavour.

He stopped just before the desk. His father's grey eyes narrowed.

"You called for me, sir," Jacob said stiffly.

"That was five minutes ago."

"I came as soon as I received your summons." Jacob paused long enough for the insult to sink in. "Sir."

His father's lip curled. "Your insolence has no bounds, I see. I presume it was you who entered this office while I was in London?"

Jacob didn't break his stare. Not yet, but soon, he would be old enough to fend his father off, and he counted the days. "That was me, sir."

"As I supposed." His father took one of the broken quills and twirled it in his fingers. "Cecil informs me you have not attended your lessons this week."

Jacob clenched his fists. He had never understood why Cecil, superior only in his bookishness and age, was so revered while he was so reviled. In his father's eyes, Cecil could do no wrong.

Cecil was the heir, the golden boy, the apple of his father's eye. Jacob, as soon as he had come into the world with his mop of dark, unruly hair and deep brown eyes, had been deemed a disappointment.

It had not taken him long to learn that, if he wanted anything for himself, he would have to take it. His mother had never shown him any interest and the servants, scared of his father, had ignored him. Cecil only paid him attention to tease or lecture him.

Or, apparently, to tattle to their father.

"He told me I was not required to attend," Jacob said stiffly. He, unlike Cecil, had never been bookish, but that did not mean he didn't enjoy his lessons. At least his tutor treated him with a modicum of respect—a rarity in this house.

"So," his father said in a deceptively quiet voice, "when faced with your shortcomings, you would choose to blame your brother."

Jacob's back stiffened. "It's the truth."

"What would you know of the truth, boy? You were born a lie." Eyes glinting with an anger Jacob had never fully understood, his father planted both fists on his desk and pushed himself to his feet. "It would have been better if you had never been born at all."

Jacob could smell sherry on his father's breath, but the words still ricocheted deep inside him, lodging in his chest like broken glass. He had long known that his father would have preferred him not to exist, but he had never understood *why*.

His father's thin, cruel mouth puckered in distaste. "Turn around," he ordered coldly. "Take off your shirt."

Briefly, Jacob considered rebelling. He was almost as tall

as his father, though nowhere near as wide. It was likely he could have put up a small fight, but in the end his father would win. And then he would be that much angrier.

His father's eyes narrowed into grey, endless slits. They reminded Jacob of the time he had shorn slivers off the lead drainpipes with his pocket knife. Just as sharp. Just as poisonous.

He turned, shrugging out of his waistcoat and tugging his shirt over his head. His breath came too fast and his chest was tight. Afraid, even though he would never have confessed to fear, his muscles bunched in anticipation of the pain.

"You are a disgrace," his father said without inflection as he brought the cane down hard. Pain lashed, a visceral, unsteady thing that filled his veins with fire. His free hand curled into a fist as he fought not to cry out.

"Father," he began. "I—"

"Do *not* call me father." For the first time, rage coloured his voice. The cane swished again and lightning flared across Jacob's back. Despite the lip caught between his teeth, he made a mewling sound of agony. "You're a coward," his father continued, tone biting, the words falling almost as hard as the cane's metal tip. "And you are unworthy of the name of Barrington."

A different kind of hurt settled in Jacob's chest—not the sting of pain, or the aching sensation of being beaten, but something colder that wrapped around his heart with frosty fingers and ate away the last of his desire to belong. He had known for a long time that they would never accept him, but this beating was the final straw, and his desire for acceptance was the camel's back.

If they would refuse to love him, he would not love them.

If they thought he was bad, he would be worse; if he was to be hated, he would give them something to hate.

And he would make them all regret every day he carried the name Barrington.

Chapter One

January 25th 1814

Lord Jacob Barrington crawled out of the ditch that held his curricle and took stock of the situation. Groaning, Mrs Clarissa Bentley also extracted herself from the splintered wood, and he extended a lazy hand to her.

"How gentlemanlike of you," she said with a trace of irony.

"For you, my dear? Anything."

"You could have not taken the corner too fast and upturned the carriage," she said impatiently, but he was already striding towards the horses, examining them with a critical eye marred slightly by the fact he was, as it happened, somewhat drunk.

"Damn," he said as he noted one of the horses had twisted its fetlock. "Riding home is out then, I suppose."

Clarissa sighed. "I suppose I should have known better than to accept the Devil's offer of company."

"You should," he agreed. People often said that about him. He was known as the Devil of St James, which meant that most who involved themselves with him grew to wish they had not.

Two years ago, Clarissa had been unfortunate enough to

marry a gentleman many years her senior, and fortunate enough to see him buried within six months. Now, she was a rather fast widow, and Jacob offered her company and entertainment with no expectations. Both things she provided, to an extent, in return.

"And yet," she said, "I still chose to accompany you."

"A poor decision."

"I should have known better."

"I quite agree." He freed the horses and looked at the curricle again. One of the wheels had detached entirely and the other had shattered spokes; the seat was, regrettably, pierced by a shard of wood they were lucky had not impaled them too. All in all, the chances of getting this particular carriage fixed were small. Especially at the side of an empty country road.

Of course, it was unfortunate they had crashed. But considering he'd stolen Cecil's horses and carriage, he didn't feel burdened with the cost of replacing them.

He would, however, arrange to have the remainder of the curricle towed back to his brother, as a token of goodwill. That would be sure to get a reaction. After twenty-six years of less-than-cordial rivalry and being the inferior brother, baiting Cecil was as much habit as inclination.

"Well?" Clarissa asked, her arms folded and her eyebrows raised. Her bonnet had all but fallen off her head and her gloves were muddy. "What are you going to do?"

"Regretfully, I am not going to ravish you on the blanket I had procured specifically for the occasion."

"Regretfully?" She looked at him in exasperation. "If you had thoughts of ravishment in mind, you would have done better to visit my house. Where there is a bed."

"Then where would be the adventure?" he mocked.

"Between the sheets. Or perhaps on the floor. Against the wall. There are plenty of places the more adventurous of us might look."

"And yet it lacks a certain something," he murmured, looking at the empty road. London was not far away, but they were surrounded by green hedges and fields, with not another soul in sight. "I believe we are going to have to avail ourselves of a stranger's generosity," he said. "We passed a farm a mile or two back."

"My shoes," she said in resignation.

"How unfortunate," he said, not giving a damn about her shoes or any other aspect of her appearance. In addition to being a widow, she was fabulously wealthy, which was more than he could claim. His income came from the generosity of his brother—which was to say, he had little income except for when he won it at the card table.

"If they ask, I shall claim to be your wife," Clarissa warned as he cut the horses free and took hold of their reins.

"Certainly, so long as you have no aspirations in that regard."

She gave an unladylike snort. "I most definitely do not. You, Jacob Barrington, would make a very uncomfortable husband."

He gave her a glittering smile. "I'm glad to hear it."

"But it truly is a shame that the best lovers make the worst husbands."

"I'm flattered you consider me your best lover."

"One of," she emphasised, rubbing at the smudges of dirt on her gloves. "And that is hardly the point."

Jacob stifled a sigh. Now there was no prospect of gratification, he found her presence wearying. "It is to me. But, Clarissa, I am *one of* the best lovers you've ever had only because you require nothing else from me."

"How flattering," she said dryly, but there was no offence in her voice. Jacob knew as well as she did that he was not the only man to warm her bed. "I do believe you're drunk."

"I'm always drunk."

She raised an eyebrow. "Why is that?"

He smiled, though he did not feel like it. "So, my dear, I can forget."

* * *

Once Jacob finally returned home, he arranged for the curricle and bill to be delivered to Cecil's house and promptly went to sleep. When he woke, it was to a summons. Cecil enjoyed summoning him. It was his prerogative as the older brother turned marquess; he could require Jacob's presence at any time he chose, and he seemed to take great pleasure in doing so. Mostly, it was so he could lecture Jacob about his lifestyle choices and threaten to cut off his allowance.

In their twenty-six years of being brothers, little had changed except Cecil had grown ever more pompous. He had been just nineteen when their father died, but he had taken up the mantle with a characteristic seriousness. They were born and bred to be opposites: where Jacob was wild, Cecil was restrained; where Jacob was impetuous, Cecil was measured; where Jacob was irresponsible, Cecil took his duties extremely seriously.

One of those duties, of course, was disapproving of everything Jacob did. An easy feat, given Jacob did everything in his power to tarnish the Barrington name. He was known as the black sheep of the family; he was the embarrassment that had to be covered up. He prided himself on excess.

Thus, sensible Cecil had a bee in his bonnet about Jacob finding a vocation.

Jacob had no intention of going into the army or politics or training as a lawyer. And there was nothing that would suit him less than taking up a living, preaching to his parish about the evils of licentious living.

Although, he allowed, he was an expert on the subject.

Therefore, once receiving his brother's summons, he chose to delay until after his leisurely day, which culminated at the new gaming hell that had opened on St James's Street. As a result, he was somewhat inebriated by the time he finally made his way to Cecil's house. Or, rather, the Sunderland London house, the one Cecil had inherited when he had become marquess and wasted no time appropriating for himself.

Smythe, the austere butler, answered the door. "I'm here to see my brother," Jacob said with a swagger he knew the butler hated.

Smythe looked down his nose. "I'm afraid his lordship isn't here."

"Not receiving me, is he? Well, it wouldn't be the first time." Ignoring Smythe's protestations, he forced himself inside, glad of the warming effects of the brandy as he looked around the large, arching space. His family's London home was not a place he had often visited, even as a child, but there were memories etched here just as clearly as the scars on his back.

He strode through to Cecil's study, which was, for once, empty. No fire burned in the grate. Jacob frowned.

"As I informed you, sir, Lord Sunderland is not at home,"

Smythe said, taking great pleasure in the words. "He asked you to come by this morning."

"I was busy then."

"He is busy now."

"Sensible Cecil going out? It must be an occasion indeed."

"I believe it is a notable occasion, sir, yes," Smythe said.

Jacob spun on the slightly worn carpet to face the butler. "Well? Where is it? And don't tell me you don't know, Smythe, because I shall call you out for being a liar."

Smythe hesitated. Obviously he knew exactly where Cecil had gone; equally obviously, he was reluctant to tell Jacob lest Jacob do something foolish.

A reasonable precaution. Jacob was feeling especially reckless tonight.

"Well?" he demanded. "I could insist on staying here, but then I would be tempted to read through my brother's correspondence to see what secrets he's hiding from me."

"Very well, sir," Smythe said haughtily, his voice so frosty Jacob's fingers almost numbed. "He is at the Norfolk Ball to celebrate Lady Annabelle Beaumont's coming out."

Jacob blinked. Cecil was at a ball? Unusual—if there was one thing the brothers had in common, it was that they both reviled balls and ballrooms and dancing. Cecil because the idea of fun was an alien one, and Jacob because his idea of fun encompassed vastly more interesting things.

As for Lady Annabelle Beaumont . . . Jacob racked his brains to think of a girl under that name. He could think of none. She had probably been told to keep well away from him; most well-bred young ladies were—his reputation as a rake and ruiner had been fixed despite the fact he hadn't entertained himself with unmarried ladies since Madeline.

11

He shut away the thought and the accompanying shot of pain. Cecil had a decanter of whisky somewhere, and Jacob found it, pouring himself a glass.

So his brother was intending to marry, then. There was no other reason for him to attend this ball. And logically, it shouldn't have come as a surprise; Jacob was surprised he had waited as long as he had. Still. If this was Cecil's plan, it behoved him to ruin it. Revenge of the best—and worst—kind.

"Thank you, Smythe," he said as he drained the last of the glass and placed it hard on the table. He had a ball to get to.

* * *

Unusually for a girl of nineteen, Annabelle Beaumont detested balls. Equally unusually, she had no wish to be married—a stance which won her no favours with her mother. It was not that she had any moral objections to the institution; her sister was married, and happily so. Rather, she disliked the process. To be married, one had to talk with strange gentlemen, and as she'd discovered when lavish balls were held in her honour, that was extremely taxing. Then, one would have to be *married*. Manage a household and please one's husband and present themselves willingly in Society. Annabelle shuddered at the mere thought.

The issue was, and she felt churlish for even considering it an issue, Nathanial Hardinge, the Duke of Norfolk and her sister's new husband, had bestowed upon her a large and exceedingly generous dowry. In the space of a few weeks, she had gone from no one to someone, and her desirability as a conversationalist and dance partner had increased exponentially.

No matter that she flushed red as a beet whenever a stranger directed a word to her. Or that the noise of the crowds made her feel uncomfortable and overwhelmed. Being around so many people, constantly required to be smiling and polite, was intolerable and exhausting, and she hated it.

Unfortunately, her mother and the Dowager Duchess of Norfolk, both keen to see her married at the first possible moment, were not sympathetic to this argument. Thus, Annabelle had curled up in her favourite spot in the ballroom: a small space concealed behind two potted plants. Before the ball had begun, she'd stowed a book there, and after squeezing through the narrow gap, she settled herself on the floor, skirts spread across the cool wood. The novel she'd selected was named *Fanny Hill: Memoirs of a Woman of Pleasure*, and the main reason she had chosen to read it was because she suspected it was salacious—and she had never read something of that nature before.

Usually, Annabelle read romances. This was something different, and just what she needed to alleviate her boredom.

She thumbed through to the beginning of the book, and had just begun to read the heroine's overwrought emotions when Theodosia, her sister and the new Duchess of Norfolk, squeezed between the plant pots into the tiny space with her.

"This is extremely undignified for a duchess," Annabelle informed her without looking up.

"And reading at your own ball is crass," Theo retorted, making herself as comfortable as she could. "How long have you been here?"

"Not long." Annabelle eyed her sister with resigned irritation. "What are *you* doing here?"

"The Dowager is looking for you. It's only a matter of time until she checks this hiding spot."

Annabelle closed her book with a snap. The Dowager Duchess of Norfolk was Theo's new mother-in-law and one of the most terrifying women Annabelle had ever met—something the Dowager was well aware of. The only person to ever occasionally defy her was Nathanial, her son, and even then he chose his moments.

"Does she know about this hiding place?" Annabelle asked.

"It's well hidden but not invisible, dearest," Theo said sympathetically before her gaze fell on the book Annabelle was still holding. She gave a little gasp. "Annabelle Lydia Beaumont, do you know what sort of novel this is?"

"I know it's more interesting than the ball," Annabelle said, although strictly speaking she had not reached the interesting parts yet.

"That sort of interesting is . . ." Theo trailed off. "I presume you know precisely what you are letting yourself in for?"

"I think so," Annabelle said carefully. In truth, her understanding of these matters was slim at best, but she was looking forward to opening her eyes to a whole new world.

"Well, I won't stop you if your heart is set on it, but Anna, if you were curious about—that nature of things, you would probably be better placed asking me than reading this."

"I think," Annabelle said dryly, "I would prefer the book."

"Yes, but this is not how it goes in reality."

Annabelle eyed the novel in her lap with renewed interest. "It's not? I thought, as it was about a prostitute, it would be—"

"Heavens, Anna, don't say those words out loud." Theo clapped a hand over Annabelle's mouth, smothering her words. "Take it from one who has read it—it is not even remotely realistic. You see, it was written by a man from the perspective of a woman. Don't you see how that changes things? And," she added significantly, "it was a book written by a man about a woman for man's pleasure. Read it if you will, but do not take it as fact."

Annabelle rolled her eyes. If she succeeded in her goal of remaining unmarried, which was seeming increasingly unlikely with every passing day, she would never have a chance to experience whatever pleasures were outlined in the book. "I won't."

"And do not let Mama see you've been reading such a thing."

"I won't," Annabelle said again, tucking the book in the corner. She sighed, resigned, as the sound of her name cut through the air. "I suppose I should see what she wants with me."

"You mean who," Theo said.

"Spare me," Annabelle muttered. "How did you persuade your suitors not to propose?"

"I didn't," Theo said heavily. "Remember the Earl of Whitstable?"

Annabelle fell silent. As it happened, she did remember the Earl of Whitstable, the elderly gentleman who had wanted to marry Theo for her childbearing hips. If it hadn't been for Nathanial intervening and proposing instead, their lives would look very different.

At least she did not have childbearing hips. Although it appeared her dowry was sadly large enough to offset that particular defect.

"It's like she's trying to marry me off before I turn twenty," Annabelle said heavily.

"Well that does only leave her four months," Theo said, and squealed as Annabelle pinched her arm. "Just reject all your offers. The Dowager and Mama can't do much about that."

"Easy enough for you to say," Annabelle said, taking a few deep breaths as she prepared to leave her refuge. "You'd have married Whitstable if Nathanial hadn't come along and proposed instead."

"I would have done my duty by my family," Theo said primly, "but now I've provided for us all, and excellently I might add, you have more freedom of choice."

More freedom to choose a man she liked, Theo meant— Annabelle was still expected to take a husband. Even her sister, sympathetic to a fault, didn't really believe she would go through with her plan to remain unmarried.

No. A romantic at heart, Theo believed Annabelle just had to meet the right man and fall in love and everything would slot into place. What she didn't understand was Annabelle struggled to talk to strangers, and the chance of her meeting a man she cared about, who also shared her aversion to Society and London, was deeply unlikely. The very thought of spending the rest of her life with someone she despised was enough to make her skin prickle.

And, frankly, Annabelle would rather read a good book.

"Oh no," Theo whispered as a nasally voice went past. "Wait a moment. That's Lady Tabitha."

Annabelle had met Lady Tabitha enough to know two things: she was an insatiable gossip, and she didn't respect personal boundaries.

They waited until she'd gone before emerging from their hiding place, brushing down their dresses and hoping no one had seen them.

16

Objectively, Annabelle knew the ball was a success. Hot-house flowers were wound around the pillars and overflowing from copper bowls. Lamps and chandeliers sent merry, flickering light across the room, and the floor was elaborately chalked.

It was also loud, hot, and crowded, and she hated it.

Nathanial hailed Theo from where he stood with a large circle of his friends. Annabelle could have gone too, but she didn't particularly enjoy trailing behind her sister like a lost puppy. For a moment, she was tempted to flee to the double doors at the end of the room. Escaping via them would mean traversing the entire ballroom, but once she was there, she could easily make her way to her bedchamber. Or, failing that, the library.

"Lady Annabelle," the Dowager Duchess of Norfolk called, coursing through the crowd like a ship in particularly full sail, a gentleman following in her wake. Young ladies scrambled to move out of the way, and Annabelle couldn't blame them. She felt like a butterfly pinned to a board.

"Your Grace," she managed, sinking into a curtsy.

"Where have you been? Your own ball and you have only stood up twice." The Dowager sniffed, piercing Annabelle with a glare that went straight through her, and lowered her voice to a harsh whisper. "Don't look so nervous, girl. It's not becoming."

As far as the Dowager was concerned, nothing Annabelle did was becoming, which was probably why she was determined to get Annabelle married off so quickly.

"No, ma'am," Annabelle said quietly.

"Good. Now"—the Dowager slapped her closed fan against her gloved hand—"I have a gentleman who wishes to be acquainted with you."

Annabelle reluctantly glanced at the sandy-haired man to the Dowager's right, who had remained silent for this entire exchange.

"This," the Dowager said with no little excitement, "is the Marquess of Sunderland."

Chapter Two

Annabelle froze, still debating the merits of sprinting wildly for an exit. Her mother waded through the crowd, resplendent in a blue dress that showed off her trim figure to advantage, beaming in delight when she saw Annabelle. The Marquess of Sunderland. Well, as titled gentlemen went, he was one of the best catches of the Season. No doubt her mother was thrilled.

Annabelle was considerably less so. She took him in slowly. Sandy hair, blue-grey eyes, cheeks that were a trifle hollowed, pale skin. There were bags under his eyes. Thankfully, he wasn't overly tall, and despite the very slight sickliness that clung to him, he contrived to be handsome enough. No doubt he was rich, too, in case the rest were not enough.

"Lord Sunderland," the Dowager said. "Meet my daughter-in-law, Lady Annabelle Beaumont."

The Marquess bowed. Annabelle curtsied, her tongue stuck, as usual, to the roof of her mouth. Now the Dowager had introduced them, there was absolutely no chance of fleeing without causing some kind of scandal, and considering her dowry alone was enough to make people look at her when she crossed a room, she didn't think she could bear a scandal.

No, she was going to have to dance with him. It was inevitable.

The Marquess's eyes sparked as though he could sense her thoughts, and his thin mouth pressed into a line that was either suppressing a grimace or a smile. "Lady Annabelle," he said. "Would you do me the honour of this next dance?"

Her card fluttered at her wrist as, with an internal sigh, she accepted the Marquess's proffered hand. "Of course, sir," she said.

Yes, sir. Of course, sir. My pleasure, sir. All phrases designed to placate a gentleman. She'd come to hate them all.

The music began and the Marquess led her out into the middle of the ballroom where everyone could watch them. Not that this was unfamiliar to her—every dance so far had felt as though she was a trophy being paraded around the room. Her only consolation was that, if she could avoid marriage, in another couple of years she would probably be able to quietly retire from London Society. Then she would be able to sit and read in peace without any expectations she'd marry.

Another two Seasons of this. Her head pounded. The music was too loud, sawing on her open nerves with bows of jagged steel. The thought of enduring two more years of Society felt intolerable.

The Marquess looked at her as they linked hands and began the dance. His palms were warm and sweaty, unpleasant even through his gloves, and she knew the inevitable small talk was coming. They would discuss the same things she had discussed with every partner: the weather (cold), the number of couples (far too many), and how much she was enjoying the evening (she would be forced to lie through her teeth).

Perhaps she would accidentally step on his foot and he

would leave her alone, concluding even her dowry wasn't enough to overcome her shortcomings.

Perhaps she would step on his foot deliberately.

"I see you enjoy dancing as little as I," he said.

Annabelle began to give a vapid agreement before his words penetrated. She frowned, glancing up at him. "You do not enjoy dancing?"

"I much prefer a good book."

She was speechless. This was not an uncommon event, but usually it was because she had nothing to say. Now, too many things sprung to mind. Instead of empty, her mind was buzzing with the improbability of a gentleman saying such a thing to her, and what the correct response would be.

The dance parted them, and by the time they came back together, his hand limp around hers, she had almost gathered her wits.

"You like to read?"

"In my opinion, it is one of the greatest pleasures in life."

Annabelle thought back to Fanny Hill and her face flushed tomato red. "You like novels, sir?"

"I do. Do you?" He looked down at her with a serious expression. "I have seen you often at Hatchards."

"You were watching me?" she blurted, then clamped her mouth shut. This was why she was better suited to the peace and quiet of a library.

"I confess I was," he said. "It is not often I meet a young lady quite so interested in reading."

"What is your favourite novel?"

"A charmingly difficult question. Do you have a favourite novel, Lady Annabelle?"

Again, she thought back to the book she had been reading,

and tried not to let her thoughts show on her face. "Perhaps *Evelina*," she said. "Or *Sense and Sensibility.*"

"Ah yes, I'm familiar. You enjoy novels, I presume, that reflect on the position of women?"

"And that are written by women." Annabelle tilted her head as she looked at him. Now they were on her favourite subject—books—she found she was far less tongue-tied. "Do you value lady authors, sir?"

"I think to write a book is an admirable thing whether the author is a man or a woman."

"But to write a book as a woman, when ladies' education is far more genteel and they do not have the same connections as men in the business world, seems a harder task."

He raised his eyebrows at her, a light igniting in his eyes. "You have strong opinions on female novelists. Fine, let us agree with you on one point: it is not considered genteel for a woman to author a book, and thus ladies have more opposition. But it is becoming more common."

"I hope it will become very common in the future," Annabelle said seriously. When he smiled, as though in approval, she felt some of her nerves loosen. This was the first time she had conversed with a gentleman about something she was interested in, and the novelty excited her.

"I have a large library," he said eventually. "I believe you might take quite some enjoyment in it. I add to it whenever possible."

"You do?" Annabelle could not stop herself beaming. Nathanial's library was well-stocked but he was not assiduous in keeping it fully up to date, which necessitated her many visits to Hatchards, spending what little pin money she received on books instead of bonnets and ribbons.

She was not like her sister, dreaming of romance at every turn. Love could not be death-defying—death was the one constant. And marriage, trapped with a man she did not like, sounded akin to torture; the idea of managing a house filled her with nothing but dread. But books—they were her true love.

Books truly were death-defying.

"I wonder," the Marquess said as he looked down into her face, "whether I might have the honour of calling on you in the next few days."

She could hardly refuse. "I am always at home in the morning, sir."

"I shall be sure to bring a book I think you might enjoy."

Well, this was new. And not entirely unpleasant. Although she was not sure if she looked forward to conversing with him or merely the prospect of another book to add to her collection. Had she done the unthinkable and found a man she would be interested in spending time with?

The irony that he had appeared just after she had resolved it was impossible did not escape her. Of course, she still had no intentions of marrying, but . . .

One day, she wanted a library of her very own.

The dance ended and the Marquess bowed over her hand. She expected him to follow her across the ballroom, but he glanced over her shoulder and his eyes narrowed.

"Excuse me," he said, his voice clipped and angry. "There is something I must attend to. Until next time, my lady."

Confused, Annabelle stared after him, but only for a moment. When she turned, she saw her mother searching for her with yet another gentleman in tow, so she skirted the edges of the room. Her mother was standing close to the plant pots, so Annabelle finally took her chance and escaped through the double doors. Talking about reading made her want to read, so she hurried along to the library. It would be quieter there, too.

There was no dancing in libraries. Books demanded nothing from her but her enjoyment.

The room was dark as she slipped inside, and she did not alleviate it, though she knew there were candles and oil lamps she could light. Her favourite place was on the window seat, looking out into the chilly night beyond. Across the lawn, she thought she saw Theo and Nathanial emerge from the hothouse. It was the wrong time of year for them to be admiring the flowers, given that none were growing, but she knew Theo had ambitious plans. Perhaps they were discussing them.

She tipped her head back to the moon, pale and distant. "What will it take to persuade Mama I don't want to marry?" she asked no one in particular.

She received no answer.

* * *

Jacob watched his brother march across the ballroom to him, and he almost smiled. The moment he had entered the ballroom, whispers had fanned out in all directions, and dowagers held onto their daughters a little tighter.

If there had ever been a time he wasn't notorious in Society, he couldn't remember it.

"What the devil are you doing here?" Cecil demanded,

taking Jacob's arm and steering him towards the patio doors. Jacob paused along the way to pick up a glass of wine. He tossed it back in one and put it on a footman's tray.

"A pleasure to see you too," he said, leaning against the wall. "You wished to see me?"

"Not here."

"Gracious. Could it be that I, your esteemed brother, am a disappointment?"

Cecil's jaw tightened, looking remarkably like their father. To his relief, Jacob bore no resemblance to the man who had raised him. "You stole my carriage and had the nerve to deliver the remnants to my front door," Cecil snapped.

"You're welcome."

"I would like to know how you are going to pay for its repairs."

"The damage is too great. You will have to have a new one made," Jacob drawled, rolling his signet ring around his finger. When he'd reached his majority, he'd had one made in the style of Cecil's—which he had stolen for the endeavour—to annoy him, and to remind the world that he was a Barrington.

Cecil's fury had been worth the effort he had gone to.

"And how, pray, are you going to pay to have a new one made?" Cecil demanded.

"I have no intention of paying for it. Your fortune is far greater than my paltry allowance."

Cecil's nostrils flared. "I pay your paltry allowance!"

"Then you ought to be aware of its insignificance."

"Perhaps I should cut you off."

"That seems somewhat churlish when you own four houses." Jacob gave a sharkish smile. "Though I'm sure none of your closest friends would think anything amiss with casting your only remaining family member to the wind."

"Few who know you would question it, I think," Cecil said coldly. "You take no responsibility for your actions."

Jacob glanced across the room, marking every person who was subtly watching their argument past fluttering fans or glasses of punch. "Why would I take responsibility for my actions when you have always done so, and so admirably?" Rarely acknowledged bitterness sharpened his voice. "You are the perfect son, are you not, and I am your wild, sinful younger brother who makes you virtuous by comparison. Has that not always been my role? Why throw it away now?"

Cecil glowered at him. "You can't taint me with the sins of our father."

That was the first time Cecil had criticised their father's behaviour, and Jacob tilted his head, smile fading. "I don't," he said. "I judge you purely according to your own sins, dear brother. But fear not, I won't tell anyone."

"You're being ridiculous." A muscle in Cecil's jaw jumped. "You need a vocation, Jacob. Something to keep you out of trouble."

"On the contrary; I already have one."

"Dissipation is not an occupation."

Jacob gave a lazy smile he knew his brother detested. "Unfortunately, I find myself extremely busy."

"Fleeing vengeful fathers and cuckolded husbands? Or perhaps just taking widowed ladies on inappropriate excursions?"

Jacob glanced across at Clarissa, who was laughing with another gentleman, her eyes sparkling. Truth be told, she had already started to bore him, but he would never have confessed that to his brother. "Is she not delightful?"

"The whole of London knows your affairs." *As they have for five years.* The words were unspoken but angry. They had never openly addressed what had happened with Madeline five years ago, but he doubted Cecil had forgiven him. No doubt now he was worried Jacob had come to stand between him and this Lady Annabelle.

Of course, Jacob knew he would never seduce and ruin an unmarried lady again. But Cecil did not.

To reinforce that thought, he raised his eyebrows at Clarissa. "I suppose I should dance with her, then. Or make the most of this vast house. How many unoccupied rooms are here, do you think?"

"In the Duke of Norfolk's home?" Cecil spluttered. "You would not dare."

"Watch me." With a wink, Jacob sauntered over to where Clarissa was procuring herself some lemonade. She glanced up at him, lips curving into a smile.

"Speaking to me in public, Jacob?" She popped a strawberry in her mouth, biting seductively. "You must be intending to pique your brother."

"And if I am?"

"How flattering you chose me," she said dryly, and he laughed.

"I can make it worth your while."

"Am I such a certainty you have dispensed with manners entirely?"

"Why, do you need wooing, Clarissa?" He raised an eyebrow at her. "Find an empty room and I shall show you just what sort of wooing I am capable of."

Her eyes sparkled with mischief. "In the Duke's house? How scandalous."

"Luckily for both of us," he said, leaning past her to select a strawberry of his own, "you delight in scandal."

She slowly drew her fan along his arm before strolling away. "Don't come after me too soon, darling," she said over her shoulder. "I have some semblance of a reputation to maintain."

In answer, he merely picked up a glass of champagne and tossed it back. Then he picked up another, turned, and raised it to Cecil. It was petty revenge, he knew, and barely worth his time, but his life had become a study in how best to embarrass his brother. Especially after his father had died.

Especially after Madeline.

After the appropriate amount of time passed, he made his way unobtrusively from the room. The hallway beyond was large, with a stairway leading to an overlooking gallery in the shape of an L, and a corridor to his left led back, he suspected, to the main body of the house.

Where would Clarissa have gone? Would she have dared find an unoccupied bedroom upstairs? That seemed a dangerous venture. Downstairs, therefore, she must be; he followed the gallery into the main body of the house. The first door he came across had well-oiled hinges, allowing him to peer inside soundlessly. It was a library, large and cast in shadow. Here, the sound of the ballroom had faded, and he could almost believe he had not just come from music and light and dancing.

Jacob had not, over the years, spent a great deal of time in libraries. Given Cecil was the bookish one, and Jacob had resolved to be as little like Cecil as possible, this was easily done. Added to this his father's propensity to beat him in the library when the mood took him, it had become a matter of survival.

Still, there was a considerable chance that Clarissa, who

knew nothing of his past other than his feud with his brother, was hiding at the darkened end of the room.

His scars burned as he prowled across the soft carpet, gaze fixed on a shadow by the window. She was gazing out across the gardens, no doubt bored and waiting for him to arrive. Without giving her any warning, he took her shoulders and spun her around, barely giving himself time to take in her expression of shock before he kissed her.

Her lips parted under his, soft and surprised. A small noise escaped her throat and she placed both hands against his chest as though to push him away, but when he licked her lower lip to encourage her mouth open, she stiffened then softened. Never quite returning his kiss, but not ending it, either. For a reason beyond his understanding, desire kicked in his belly. Usually, Clarissa kissed differently—expertly, as though it was an exercise in pure skill rather than passion.

He came to the conclusion at the same time as she shoved him back, and he looked down into a face he did not immediately recognise. Dark eyes he suspected might be blue, a full mouth different from Clarissa's pert lips, and an expression of outrage that didn't belong to any lady he dallied with.

"How dare you," she gasped, fully confirming that she was not who he had thought she was. "Do you know who I am?"

He allowed his gaze to travel across her face, amused by the way her throat worked as she swallowed. "You," he said, his voice low and rough, "are not Clarissa."

Chapter Three

Annabelle had been kissed once before. He was the son of the local baronet and he had been besotted with her. When she was fifteen, he had pressed his damp lips against hers, and after it was over, she had cried, believing for certain that kissing was not something she would ever enjoy.

Now she was nineteen, and a stranger had done much the same thing to her. Except his mouth had been warm and dry, and his tongue had brushed against hers in a way that had, briefly, made her body stop responding to all commands. Even now, staring down at her with his face half crafted dark, she could see enough to know he was ludicrously handsome— his eyes were pools of ink and his mouth a wicked slash that made her heart beat altogether too fast when she looked at it.

Stop looking at it.

His smile grew and he tilted his head, casting more of his features into the moonlight; the curve of his cheek, the strong, hard line of his jaw. He looked familiar, but she couldn't place him.

"No," she said as tartly as she could. "I am *not* Clarissa. Why are you walking around my sister's house without invitation?"

He blinked, the smile turning from amused to predatory.

"Your sister?"

"The Duchess of Norfolk. This is her house and her library." Annabelle drew herself up and glanced at the door. If she was to make an escape, it would have to be past him, and she did not fancy her chances. "You are trespassing."

"What makes you think I didn't receive an invitation?" the man asked. "But I am more intrigued by you, little bird. What did you say your name was?"

"I didn't."

"And yet if your sister is the Duchess of Norfolk, that can only make you one person." A gleam entered his eye, as cold and unfeeling as the moon above them. "You are Lady Annabelle Beaumont."

"And what if I am?"

He moved, boxing her into the corner. His breath smelt like wine, and panic burst over her like fireworks. If he was inebriated, she could only guess at what he was capable of. After all, her father had drunkenly gambled away her dowry. Anything was possible.

"If you are," he mused, looking the very vision of ease while her heart fluttered like a trapped bird, "that would make you the person I was looking for."

"I've already said I am not Clarissa."

"No indeed." He chuckled. "You are something far better."

"Leave," she said stiffly. "If you do, I will tell no one of this."

With one hand, he reached out and tweaked her curl. The familiarity of it made her want to scream. "I don't think you will tell a soul no matter *what* I do to you tonight."

"Then you are mistaken."

"It happens," he acknowledged. He *still* had not moved back. Annabelle's fists clenched impotently. She had never struck another person and unfortunately she doubted she was capable of starting now. Although he did make the prospect seem remarkably appealing.

"Who are you?" she demanded.

"I? I am the last man in the world you would wish to meet, little bird." He leant forward, studying her face. "For you are good and virtuous, are you not?"

Ridiculously, she thought back to the book she had attempted to smuggle into the ball and read. Good and virtuous young ladies were not likely to choose a novel based on their assumption it was salacious. But he was no doubt referring to her practical experience, which was very little.

How best to get rid of him?

"No need to dance around the truth, sweetheart," he said after a moment of agonised silence. "I think we both know the answer."

"You don't want me," she said with an authority she didn't feel. "Leave me alone."

"I don't want you?" He tilted his head and another ruthless smile curved his thin lips. "Why?"

"Because I don't like kissing, and I especially don't like kissing you."

A mistake.

This man was a predator, and she had just issued him a challenge. The gleam of amusement sharpened into something wolfish, and he reached out to take her wrist, pinning it beside her. His mouth hovered a heartbeat above hers.

"Fly, little bird," he whispered.

She remained motionless, unable to move, not *wanting* to move.

His mouth encountered hers with what should have been

bruising force—but wasn't. Oddly, against her every expectation, his lips were soft, gentle, and that thought alone disarmed her. His hands cupped her elbows and drew her into his body as he kissed her with deliberate slowness, crumbling her defences until there was no fight left in her body.

Annabelle did her best to remember that she hated him, and that she did not like kissing. But that proved difficult when all she knew was this moment and his hands, his mouth. She could not even remember her name.

First you move your lips, he seemed to say. *Taste mine. Slide our mouths together until they fit. Pressure, pressure, breathe.* He showed her what to do, a palm against her cheek as he turned her face to better fit against his, and she obeyed.

They parted, briefly, to breathe, and he trailed his mouth along the line of her jaw as she struggled to hold onto one logical thought. Just one would be enough.

Only then he was kissing her again, the hand on her cheek urging her still closer, sinking into the silken mass of her hair, and she lost herself once more. His other hand rested lightly on her waist, hot and urgent, and although he did not move it, she was aware of its burning presence. At any moment, he could choose to bend her body further into his or push her more firmly against the wall.

There were a thousand things a man this powerful could do to her if he chose, and yet he still just kissed her.

That was, if *just* was a word that could be used to describe the magnitude of this kiss. Her body opened before him like a flower, and she felt the first tendrils of warmth move through her with lazy intensity. It felt a lot like wanting.

After poor Ronald's kiss, she had never thought she could ever want a man. Yet here she was, sighing in pleasure as his tongue flicked lightly across her bottom lip.

Her mind, clearly, had been neatly taken from her body and disposed of somewhere, because no logical train of thought indicated that she should either enjoy this gentleman's kiss or be kissing him back. To be doing either, never mind both, lost in the dancing oblivion his kisses wrought, implied insanity of the highest order. She should confess her affliction to Theo at once and be locked at the top of a tower for the rest of her days.

The man broke away, a triumphant smile on his face. Cold air rushed between them, finally restoring a modicum of sense. Annabelle pressed a trembling hand to her mouth, recovering her faculties—and her anger.

Usually, when she was angry, she found herself at a loss for words. But this man had thwarted propriety and she found herself no longer bound by its restraints. Reaching her arm back, she leaned forward and slapped him across the cheek as hard as she could, her chest rising and falling.

The man rocked back on his heels, one hand cupping his cheek. The sound of her slap still hung between them, and his smile, for one moment, seemed to her genuine, rather than mocking. "A good blow," he told her, a trace of surprise in his voice. "Well made. I'll wager your hand hurts."

"Yes," she said, bewildered, before remembering that she was furious at him. Outraged. Horrified. Something warm and liquid she didn't want to think about. She scowled. "I hope it hurt."

He nodded, showing no sign of pain. "It did. Now, little bird, can you tell me in true faith that you have still never enjoyed a kiss?"

Lying was her only possible avenue, and she did not hesitate.

"There is nothing I enjoyed less, sir. Now let me pass."

To her surprise, he did so almost immediately, stepping back and giving her room. She took the opportunity to flee, thankful for the darkness concealing her, and thankful still more that no one had stood witness to what had happened.

"Lady Annabelle," the man called when she reached the doorway. "When my brother courts you, as we both know he will, you will look at him and see me. Do you think you could marry such a man?"

The final piece of the puzzle fell into place and Annabelle's jaw dropped. She blinked. Dread replaced her anger. This man was no stranger: he was a rake so vile she had been warned against him. A deflowerer of virtuous ladies.

He was the Devil of St James—and she was his latest victim.

* * *

Cheers erupted around Jacob as he paced the boxing ring, sizing up his opponent. This was his favourite place to come when he needed a break from the vapidness of Society. A place where beer sloshed over tankards and no one gave a damn whether you were a lord or a knight or a butcher. In the ring, you were equal.

Few gentlemen truly fought, the sport being dangerous at the best of times. But Jacob had been told all his life he was not a gentleman, and what better way to prove it than in the most violent of sports? There was not a time when he felt more alive. After all, he was no stranger to pain. Pain merely proved a man still lived; pain was the measure by which he tracked his existence.

His opponent was a smaller man, but that merely meant he would be faster. Daniel Mendoza, famous boxer from the past century, beaten only by Gentleman John Jackson, had been small, and he was fast and vicious with it.

Jacob's blood hummed with the anticipation of the attack.

It happened almost before he could blink. His opponent lunged, and had Jacob not been ready with his fists, he might have been taken down by the sheer force and speed. As it was, he struck like a tiger. Five blows in quick succession, aiming for his ribs, his jaw, the delicate bones he knew a man could break.

Again.

You can't taint me with the sins of our father.

Again.

The whole of London knows your affairs.

Again.

Anger rippled through him—a dark thing that indulgence and dissipation alone could not temper. He needed this rawness, the feeling of his knuckles splitting against another man's bone. His mind cleared as his fists worked, his muscles burned, and the cold February sun gazed down at the scars on his bare back. The only time he ever removed his shirt was here, when no one knew, or cared, who he was.

You are a coward. And you are unworthy of the name of Barrington.

The hurt had gone from that statement; it was a reminder of who he was and who he had vowed to be ever since his father had beaten him in front of that roaring fire.

His opponent fell, looking briefly like Cecil, briefly like his father, and the end of the round was called. Jacob walked in a tight circle between the ropes staked into the hard ground, steam rising from his skin. His knee-man took a knee in case he wanted to sit, but he waved him away. The only thing he wanted was water. An orange. To go again until every thought in his brain smoothed into emptiness. The feeling of nothing—that was what he craved.

Lady Annabelle's face flashed in his mind. The way her lips had felt against his own; the horror in her eyes when she finally understood who it was who had kissed her.

Irritated, he brushed the thought aside as the whistle blew and he walked again up to the scratch. His opponent's brows were lowered, his fists rising a little, and Jacob felt the mad, wild thrill of a challenge.

"May the best man win," he said, and they set to it again.

* * *

Jacob did not return home until late, drinking in the tavern until he could forget the way seeing Cecil made him feel: as though he was and always would be inadequate. A disappointment.

He had crafted his entire life into a disappointment to his staid, surface-respectable family, and still he felt the burden of their disapproval in those quiet moments when his mind refused to sleep.

That was the reason he had kissed Lady Annabelle, knowing Cecil wanted her. But it had been a mistake: he did not kiss virginal young ladies, and especially not ones who looked at him as though he had committed a cardinal sin (not a reaction he was accustomed to). If he had one rule, one moral guideline around which his life revolved, it was that.

He would not approach her again. If Cecil wanted her, he could have her—and good luck to him. Jacob did not make the same mistake twice.

When he finally stumbled back to his lodgings, he found his brother waiting in his drawing room, and more of that coldness descended on him. Ice in his veins.

Cecil, as usual, was glaring at him. Jacob, as usual, was roaring drunk and with none of his usual patience.

"So you found me," he said, sinking into his favourite armchair and looking up into Cecil's familiar face with a sneer.

"You're drunk," Cecil said, wrinkling his nose.

"I am aware."

Cecil's jaw flexed at the sight of the fresh scabs on Jacob's knuckles. "You've been boxing again. Don't think I am unaware of your activities."

Jacob yawned. "Distasteful are they, brother?"

"You know they are. If you have an interest, take lessons with Gentleman Jackson. Bet on the outcome of the matches if you must, but don't participate like a commoner."

The corner of Jacob's mouth ticked down. "Don't tell me you're ashamed of me *now*. And here I thought we had such a good relationship."

"You are my brother," Cecil said coldly. "I would rather not be ashamed of you."

"Is that so?" Jacob cocked his head. "Is that why you did everything in your power to ensure Father took out his anger on me and left you alone?"

Cecil's reddened cheeks paled. For a moment, he looked like the boy Jacob remembered from his childhood. Always trying, trying, trying—and for him, trying went somewhere. He excelled at his studies, was moulded into the perfect heir, and inherited young. That, of course, had not been part of the plan, but perfect Cecil rose to the occasion.

The only thing Cecil had failed to do was protect Jacob.

"I am not . . . proud of what I did as a boy," Cecil said falteringly. "But you have become a liability, Jacob. You have gambled away people's fortunes at the card table. Won everything from one man and lost it to another."

Jacob raised a brow. "Then they should have played better. And so should I."

"Last year, you fatally shot that man when you were travelling to Hungerford."

"A highwayman," Jacob corrected. "An important distinction, I'm sure you agree."

"Do you know how many strings I had to pull to ensure you could remain in the country?" Cecil demanded.

Jacob tilted his head in surprise. "I would have thought you'd want me gone."

"And how would that have made me look? I want you to be the man we both know you could be."

"On the contrary." Jacob gave a lazy smile that he knew would irritate his brother. "I have become precisely what you made me. You and Father both."

Cecil rose and paced around the room, his hands behind his back. Jacob ran a hand down his face, wondering whether, if he asked his brother to leave, he would go.

Unlikely. Cecil had not made a name for himself by respecting Jacob's opinions and preferences.

Eventually, Cecil turned, his hands still clasped behind his back. His cravat was crooked and his eyes were a little too bright. "I intend to marry," he said, and though Jacob pretended they didn't, the words hit him like a brick to the chest. All the brandy in the world was not enough to keep the familiar pain from wrapping around his heart.

He would not make the same mistake again, but he could not bring himself to forget.

"I know," he said, letting his words slur together. "The girl."

"Jacob—" Cecil advanced two steps then, when Jacob slitted his eyes, remained in place. "We should discuss this. It's been five years."

"Which part would you like to discuss?" Jacob asked conversationally, the hard, angry edge to his words a throbbing undercurrent. "Are you concerned your new choice will fall for my charms?" He fixed Cecil with a cold smile. "Or, perhaps, you're worried she will die in her attempt to flee your cruelty."

Cecil sucked in a breath, and Jacob could not find it within himself to feel guilty. Not for this. Once, he might have been able to forgive his brother for any childhood crimes. He had not been an easy brother to manage. But he could not forgive Cecil for turning a desperate Madeline away from his door, only for her to perish on the darkened streets of London by some degenerate's foul hand.

Just as he could never forgive himself for seducing her while she was engaged to Cecil, ruining her piece by piece, and not being enough for her to love in return.

"I could never have predicted the outcome," Cecil said through a tight throat. "And if you had not betrayed me by—"

"You did not love her." The words were sharp, digging into him like broken glass. Jacob almost felt the blood well in the aftermath.

"Marriage is not always about love."

"Presumably that is also why you are marrying this Lady Annabelle Beaumont. For the same reasons you chose Madeline?"

Cecil was pale now, sweat beading on his forehead, but he held his ground. "I need to know you won't stand in my way, Jacob. Let me have this one thing."

Jacob snorted. He was too drunk for this. The world spun around him and so many things he had once kept inside him finally broke past the dam. "Let you have this one thing, Cessy?" He tutted. "You have had everything since the day you were born. But me? There was just one thing I wanted, dear brother, and that was Madeline." He bared his teeth in a smile that was more like a snarl. "But as always, she chose you over me. I asked her to marry me, you know. Once I realised I loved her."

Cecil's cheeks seemed to hollow. "You did?"

"Yes, I asked her to break it off with you and choose me instead. You would find someone else, I knew, but she was the only girl I would ever love. And she told me no." He pushed himself to his feet, swaying a little. "She told me she would rather have your riches and your position and *you* than someone like me."

Cecil was silent, his throat working, and Jacob wanted to hate him. He hated the world. His hatred was a dark thing inside him that consumed everything good, that he could only tame with his boxing and his drinking, and even now he could feel it swelling inside him, demanding he hurt. Demanding he break something.

He thought of Lady Annabelle and the sweet, innocent way she had kissed him back. And that disgust in her eyes when she had come to her senses.

"And then her father discovered her affair with me," he continued, "and he threw her out of the house. I would have taken her in, protected her as far as I was able, married her, but she still ran to you first. You could have had her, Cecil, if you'd wanted, if you hadn't been so proud. So don't tell me I should give you this one thing."

"I'm sorry—"

"For what? For ruining my life?" Jacob laughed harshly. "Fear not, brother. I've made it my mission to ruin yours too."

Cecil's throat bobbed. His eyes glistened. Five years they'd been pretending they hadn't hurt one another and Jacob was tired. The darkness inside of him had been released, and there was nothing he could do to force it back inside again.

"I thought you seduced her because you hated me," Cecil said eventually. "Because I am . . ."

I am our father's and you are not.

Jacob did not know if the rumours were true that he was a bastard, begat of some unknown, but he knew his father believed it. In the end, it had been a relief to think he might not belong to the man he had learnt to hate.

Cecil had belonged, and Jacob had never quite forgiven him for it.

"I approached her to spite you." Jacob gave a careless shrug. "I never expected it to get so far, and then it became about far more than just you. But after you turned her away?" His nostrils flared. "I despised you as much as our family name." And himself. Because even for Madeline, who had lain in his arms and let him plot their future like constellations in the sky, he had not been enough.

Cecil stared at him as though he was seeing him for the first

42

time. And Jacob had never, not once in his life, wanted to hate his brother more.

From the location of Madeline's body, she had been on her way to Jacob after Cecil had turned her away. All this could have been prevented if she had come to him first. Or if Cecil had shown a morsel of mercy and allowed her to stay even one night.

"I should leave," Cecil said, taking his hat from the side table. "But for what it's worth, Jacob, I would have wanted to be your friend if you would only let me."

"A little late for that, don't you think, brother?" Jacob asked, turning to his drinks cabinet to pour himself a scotch. When he turned back around, Cecil was gone.

Chapter Four

"He has not come," Annabelle's mother said, directing her words at Annabelle as though she was personally responsible for the Marquess of Sunderland not calling. It was now three days after the ball, and though she had received other calls from other gentlemen she had done her best to repress, there was no marquess. Despite his promise.

Annabelle wasn't sure if she was relieved or disappointed.

Relieved because she had never wanted to marry, and one conversation had not changed that, even if he did like reading and books and, presumably, libraries. Disappointed because he had promised to bring her a book and she was keen to see what it was.

And, of course, it would be nice to have *someone* to discuss her love of books with, seeing as the rest of her family didn't quite understand.

Then again, after finishing *Fanny Hill*, Annabelle was not entirely sure she could count herself as a proponent of literature any more. Certainly, the book had been . . . illuminating. In several areas. Some she thought were distinctly more realistic than others, although she would certainly not be running to Theo for clarification. *That* would just have to be one of those never-ending questions that existed within her.

But it was not, categorically not, *literature*. It was a gaudy pretence, flimsy once one stepped behind the bindings and looked at the words and content. Not literature. No.

But enlightening, in its own way.

She controlled her blush. The book was stored under her bed until such a time as she could return it and never speak about it again to any member of her family.

She would, certainly, never think about the way a certain dark-eyed man had briefly made her feel a little like Fanny was described as feeling in the book. On fire.

Briefly. As in, before she was reminded that he was a stranger and she wasn't supposed to be kissing and *definitely* was not meant to be kissing him.

"He has not even sent flowers," her mother said, and Annabelle recalled with a guilty jump that they were talking about her stranger's brother. His *brother*. A distinctly more gentlemanlike, polite, eligible man.

Who had not, notably, come to visit her. Or sent her flowers.

She did her level best not to prick herself with her needle as she applied herself to her embroidery again. "He has not," she said calmly.

"But he seemed *so* very determined to court you," her mother said sadly.

"He danced with me once, Mama." Annabelle was in a losing fight with her needle. "And you have at no point asked me if *I* wished for him to court me. Or anyone, for that matter."

"Of course you do, dear. He's very eligible."

Annabelle ground her teeth together and, battle lost, jabbed herself in the fleshy part of her thumb. She would have preferred to read, but her mother insisted that spending all day with her nose in her book was detrimental to a lady's health.

Sometimes, spending time with her mother was almost enough to make her consider a husband.

Almost.

"I don't want to be married," she said.

Her mother sniffed. "Nonsense. All ladies wish to be married."

"Not me."

"That is only because you have given no gentleman the *chance* to get to know you." There was a distinct note of impatience in her mother's voice. "If you did, you would understand the appeal. And the Marquess is very charming, I've heard."

His charm, no doubt, was his fortune and title. Both of which, in her mother's eyes, made up for any other deficiencies.

"I would rather be useful, Mama," Annabelle said, "than married."

"You would be useful as a wife."

Annabelle glanced pleadingly at Theo, who was chewing her lip over a letter in the corner. "Do you think you are useful?" she asked Theo.

"Not at all," Theo said brightly. "I leave all matters of managing a household to my housekeeper, and the only thing I ever do is plan parties and social events. But I'm happy, and I think that counts for something."

"There you go," her mother said. Annabelle cast Theo a dirty look, and Theo shrugged as though to say *it's the truth*. "You would be happy if you were married."

"That's not the lesson at all!" Annabelle said in exasperation. "Theo is happy because she has a man she loves."

"Who is also a duke," her mother said. "And a marquess is only one step down from a duke." She frowned at her embroidery, and Annabelle stuck her thumb in her mouth, sucking away the blood.

"*Sorry*," Theo mouthed across the room.

"*I hate you*," Annabelle mouthed back, and Theo grinned.

* * *

The constable that Rogers, Jacob's valet, showed into the breakfast room was a man verging on middle age, with a shiny bald head and an officiously sympathetic expression. Jacob disliked him instantly.

His head ached. It was noon, but after his brother had left yesterday, he'd continued drinking until the early morning, at which point he'd passed out in the vicinity of his bedroom, and had crawled to bed at some later time. Now, he was barely functioning.

"I'm sorry to disturb you, sir," the constable said.

Jacob winced and waved him to a chair. "No need to talk so loud."

He frowned. "No, sir."

Jacob surveyed the breakfast table and eventually selected a slice of dry toast. "Well?" he asked caustically. "What has compelled you to come and disturb me?"

"It's about your brother."

"Cecil sent you, did he?" He held out his wrists in mock surrender. "Throw me in gaol if you wish, but I assure you I

47

was here all last night."

The constable took a breath. "It's not that, sir. I regret to inform you that . . . your brother is dead, sir."

Jacob stopped what he was doing and looked at the man. The light seemed to dim and he blinked several times. This was impossible. As impossible as the world being flat—scientifically absurd.

"What do you mean he's dead?" he demanded.

The constable shifted uncomfortably at Jacob's glower. "I mean to say he's dead, sir."

"But he can't be. I saw him yesterday." Jacob scowled. "And I assure you he was quite alive then."

"I regret to inform you he has perished in the time since."

Jacob blinked. Drew in a breath. Blinked again. "Impossible," he said, more to himself than anyone else. "How?"

"The physician said he had a weak heart," the constable said, wiping his forehead with a spotted handkerchief. "I understand it's not usual for a heart to give out so young, but this is not the first time he has suffered."

Jacob's head shot up sharply. "What do you mean?"

"The physician mentioned he had tended to your brother in the past, my lord."

Tended to Cecil in the past? For a moment, Jacob didn't move. Cecil had been suffering from a weak heart? Of course, that was hardly something he would confide to him about, but it put a selection of things into perspective. Cecil's paleness, the way he had never been particularly good at the physical activity Jacob excelled in.

He had been pale last night. When they'd argued, he'd looked almost sickly, and Jacob had assumed—of course he had assumed—that it was out of guilt. Regret. Perhaps even fear, because everyone knew Jacob was volatile, and hell, everyone knew Jacob and Cecil hated each other.

Although at their last meeting, Cecil had sounded as though he wanted to make amends.

"When?" he forced out, his voice hoarse. "Precisely when?"

"It's not entirely certain, sir," the constable began. "It's believed he passed shortly after reaching home last night, according to his butler. The physician thought it was a shock that strained his heart. Bad news, perhaps." The constable squinted. "Or a confrontation."

The words came from very far away. There had certainly been a confrontation, and about a subject they had never discussed before: Madeline. Jacob had said he would never forgive Cecil for his cruelty.

But never was such a long time when it was fulfilled in actuality. Cecil was supposed to be a permanent fixture in his life. A person against whom he could fight with their parents gone. Exacting revenge, especially over the past five years, had been his purpose.

Now Cecil was dead. And Jacob, directly or no, had killed him.

Just as he was the reason, indirectly, Madeline had died. If he had not seduced her, she would never have found herself roaming the streets at night.

Cecil was dead.

In the garishly bright light of the room, he saw his mother's dimly lit bedchamber. She'd fallen ill and died when he was seventeen, a matter of months before his father also passed from heart failure.

"You should never have been born," she said tenderly, cupping his face. It was the most softness she had ever shown him, there in her incense-heavy room, curtains drawn, light straining through the material. The hollows in her cheeks were almost skeletal. Jacob looked down at her and tried to remember what grief felt like.

To grieve her, he should have once loved her.

"All you will know is misery," she continued, her hand falling away. "That is your curse, Jacob. Bear it well."

Now, staring at his hands and the white tablecloth, he could hear her words as though they had been spoken directly into his ear. All he would ever know was misery. And those around him would soon know nothing at all. First his mother, then his father, then Madeline. That had been love, and that had been loss. Sorrow the likes of which he had never known before or since. *Would* never know.

Sorrow and guilt.

And now Cecil.

"My brother is dead," Jacob said again, testing the words. They settled as cold as freshly fallen snow.

"Yes, sir."

He rang the bellpull. "Rogers," he said as soon as his valet appeared, "some brandy please. Would you like brandy, my good man?"

The constable shook his head, a crease forming between his eyes. No doubt he believed it was too early for drinking.

Well, let him cast his judgement; Jacob had withstood enough of that to be indifferent. It was past noon.

Another thought occurred to him which necessitated the gulp of brandy, when it came. "There is no other heir," he said shortly. "I am the one to inherit."

"That's a matter for your lawyer, sir, but I doubt anyone would oppose your claim to the title."

"A pity," Jacob muttered, staring into the amber liquid. He was the next Marquess of Sunderland. A peer of the realm, bound to a name he despised for the rest of his life.

This was not what he was made for—he was not cut from the cloth that made dukes and marquesses and earls, and he had never aspired to be.

His head gave a stab of pain. "Please tell me this is a prank," he said as he finished his glass. "A joke in poor taste. I will forgive its perpetrator."

The constable gave him a look of sympathy. "I'm afraid not, sir."

He poured himself another glass and tossed it back. "Well then," he said. And again: "Well then."

The constable bowed. "I'm sorry to be the bearer of such bad news, my lord."

Jacob waved a dismissive hand at him. "Rogers will see you out."

The constable nodded and turned for the door. Jacob remained where he was, his mind spinning. There was the burial to think about, and mourning.

I am to be Marquess.

Cecil is dead.

No doubt he would be expected to move into Sunderland Place. Pick up all the slack of owning an estate.

Or, now he was its head . . . he could let the whole place go to hell.

Cecil is dead.

He leant back in the chair and closed his eyes, breathing through the strangely tight sensation in his chest. It couldn't be grief—he certainly hadn't grieved when his father had died, and Cecil had been little better. Ratting him out to his father so he could collect beatings like pretty rocks, the scars on his back roping together as he grew older. Pointing out Jacob's flaws in that supercilious way of his. Always being *better*. Better loved, better respected, better listened to.

Being the man Madeline chose, and casting her out into the night regardless.

Jacob had hurt Cecil in every way possible after that.

But now there were no more second chances. Cecil was dead. The words might as well have been a tolling bell. That was the end of it.

"For heaven's sake, Cecil," he said, speaking into the empty air of the room. "Could you not have waited? Could you not have remained alive even just to spite me?"

The room gave no answer. The brandy was finally hitting his system, and he let the alcohol soothe the absurd disappointment that his brother was no longer here to provide a retort.

"I will not grieve you," he warned. "You gave me no reason to."

A log fell lower on the fire, sending a flurry of sparks into the air. Jacob took another drink, willing himself to believe his own words—but even to his ears they sounded like a lie.

Chapter Five

Three months later

Annabelle tried not to wince as the musical recital she had been forced into attending reached new heights of excruciating. She was, she was almost certain, the only member of the audience to feel that way. Everyone was smiling, nodding, talking in low voices to their neighbour, or in the case of her father, slowly falling asleep.

Then again, no one else was sitting beside Lord Helmsley. She could only conclude this was punishment for severe misdemeanours in another life.

It was not that, on first glance, there was anything *wrong* with Lord Helmsley. Her mother and the Dowager Duchess, both keen to see her married to another peer of the realm following the death of the Marquess of Sunderland, approved of him. He was in his early thirties with a swarthy, handsome-enough face, brown hair neatly brushed back, a smile that *almost* dissolved into a smirk, and, crucially, a fortune.

Unfortunately, Annabelle was forced to suffer more than just a first glance. The recital had been going for almost an hour now, and his hand had been steadily making its way up her leg. At first, she'd thought it was an accident and shifted away. But his hand had always found its way back. First her knee. Then higher, higher, draping her shawl to cover the movement, knowing no one else would be looking at them.

Now, as his hand crept further up her thigh, she imagined interrupting the recital to make a scene. A vivid, stomach-curling daydream that had no happy resolution. Everyone's attention would be on her, and everyone would know what had happened. *If* they believed her; Lord Helmsley was bound to play her off as a hysterical woman and claim it was a misunderstanding. The *ton* would believe him.

This was not the first time a so-called gentleman had touched her without her permission. For one, Jacob Barrington, the new Marquess of Sunderland, had done so. But oddly, she had felt safer with him—she had known intuitively that if she had pushed at his shoulders and told him no, he would have stopped. He had kissed her in the full—arrogant—knowledge that she would enjoy it.

Lord Helmsley did not care.

She wanted to expire on the spot.

The musicians were excellent, she was sure—their host, Lady Cavendish, would not have settled for less than the best. But she was not a musical connoisseur no matter how well she could play the pianoforte.

Lord Helmsley had still not taken his hand off her leg, leaning closer to whisper in her ear something about the players. Probably. She wasn't listening. All she could hear was her rather ragged breathing.

To her relief, he removed his hand when he leant back.

The quartet finished on a grand note that seemed a trifle overplayed, and they rose to applause. Annabelle clapped quietly, plotting how she might escape. Next was dinner, and she had not secured anyone else as escort, but surely she could just approach a gentleman and ask him to walk her in. Unless he had already pledged to walk another young lady to dinner.

The potential humiliation in the idea made her stomach flip.

As the audience rose and Annabelle was still looking for an escape, Lord Helmsley took her hand and placed it possessively in the crook of his arm. "Allow me to escort you to dinner," he said, leaving no room for argument. Before she could protest, he had manoeuvred them so they were almost at the very back of the queue.

Where was Theo when she needed her?

"You are beautiful," he pronounced. Annabelle felt as though she was being slowly suffocated. "How charming it is to spend an evening in this way."

Perhaps there was a convenient window she could jump out of. Perhaps she would run away and join a convent. Would she be allowed to read as a nun? At least she would not be expected to marry.

"Do you not agree?" Lord Helmsley said. Annabelle stuttered, tripping over her words until her face flamed, and he moved on. Clearly her response was not required. "The charms of a good partner make every evening worthwhile."

Her only charm was her dowry and both of them knew it. Where *was* Theo? Annabelle strained, searching for her sister, and instead encountered him. The Devil of St James.

The new Lord Sunderland's tight, brooding face, rose a full head above the lady beside him. He surged through the crowd, moving with purpose she envied, until at the door, he paused and glanced back.

His eyes locked with hers.

It was as though three months had not passed at all. Instantly, she was back in the library being ruthlessly kissed, all hot mouth and firm hands, and the memory of it was so shockingly vivid, she gasped.

His eyes glinted and she knew he recognised her. There was no reading his expression because a moment later, he had disappeared through the doorway and vanished.

Something touched her backside. With no small amount of horror, Annabelle realised it was Lord Helmsley. He kept up his steady stream of conversation, all the while allowing his hand to brush her rear. She squirmed away, but he just inched closer. Positioned at the back of the crowd as they were, there was no one behind them to see.

Speak, she urged herself. *Convince this man you do not want him.*

Nothing had ever felt more impossible. Her eyes burned and her fists clenched and her tongue remained silent, frozen by the same ineptitude that always seemed to ground her.

If she vomited, would she be allowed to leave this dreadful party?

"You have such lovely eyes, Lady Annabelle," Lord Helmsley continued, and her chance of vomiting increased dramatically. "They could send a man to his grave."

I wish they would.

Her mouth refused to open, not giving vent to any of the thoughts inside her head, and humiliation crawled over her skin as his hand slid to her backside again, this time giving her a squeeze.

If she were Theo, she may well have slapped him, or at least demanded in a loud tone that he keep his hands to himself.

But she was helpless, encouraging him by her silence, and she despised herself for it. Nausea rose up her throat and her head throbbed and she wished, she *wished*, that she could tell him where to put his unwanted attentions.

The dining room came into view—had they really only been walking for a few minutes? It had felt like hours—and that was Annabelle's moment to escape. His grip on her arm loosened, sensing victory, and she took advantage of his lapse in awareness to yank her hand free.

"Excuse me, my lord," she muttered, turning away and practically running blindly through a nearby door. Although her stays were loose, her chest felt constricted. She couldn't breathe.

Out. Away. The library was out of the question, given what had occurred before, so she made the only choice she could: outside. The house was both cavernous and unfamiliar, so when she saw a small side-door leading into the garden, she took it.

Cool air chilled the damp sweat on her skin. Panting, disgusted with herself and with her skin shuddering from Lord Helmsley's touch, she wandered off the patio and onto the lawn. The grass was wet, soaking through her slippers, but she hardly cared. Cloaked by darkness, she moved through the garden like a shadow, a wisp of thought.

She had almost made it to the end of the garden, where fruit trees loomed above her, when she heard it.

"Lady Annabelle?" It was Lord Helmsley, his words sliding together like pebbles down a hill. "Are you waiting for me, sweetness?" His laugh was unsteady, and she shrank back into the shadows. "Fear not, I shall find you."

She surveyed the tree to her left. It was large and well-established. Perhaps she could climb it and escape that way.

"I wouldn't recommend it," a voice drawled from behind her. "You'll quite ruin your dress."

Chapter Six

Annabelle whirled, reticule dangling from one wrist like a feeble weapon. Her eyes widened as she took in the man standing before her, a black armband on one arm—the final signs of mourning.

Lord Jacob Barrington, the new Marquess of Sunderland, smiled down at her. There was something restless in his eyes, caught by moonlight, like he was on the verge of turning into a wicked fae prince. Despite everything, she was captivated— and she shook herself. This man was just as dangerous as Lord Helmsley. Perhaps more so.

If only she had climbed the tree earlier.

"I see I am not alone in seeking the obscurity of the night," he said, giving a mocking bow. "A rendezvous or an escape?"

Annabelle stood frozen, trapped between the devil and the deep blue sea, knowing that she was in danger no matter where she turned.

"Don't worry," he all-but purred as he stepped closer. "I don't bite."

That she didn't believe.

"What are you doing here?" she asked in a whisper, finally finding her voice.

"I could ask you the same question."

She winced as Lord Helmlsey called her name again. "You know why." *Escape.*

"Well, then my reasons are similar to yours, although perhaps for different causes." He glanced over her shoulder towards the house and Lord Helmsley. "Tell me, little bird, is that bumbling idiot after you?"

"What gave it away?" Annabelle asked, her heart pounding even as her tone was unusually dry. "The fact he called me by name and is visibly searching for me?"

"Ah, so the cat *does* have claws," he murmured, one hand coming to touch the same cheek that she had slapped all those months ago. "I remember now."

"Leave me alone."

"The temptation is there, believe me." His smile dropped as he looked down at her, eyes glinting with more of the wild danger she'd seen in them before. "Why are you running from him?" he asked, his voice low. "Did he touch you?"

As though you are one to talk. She held the words back. Somehow, there had been something different about the way he had touched her. Less invasive, though it had been a kiss. "What do you mean?"

"Lord Helmsley, your illustrious companion." The Marquess's lip curled. "I presume that is the reason you fled him so abruptly."

"And if he did?"

"No need to be coy with me," he said sardonically. "I have no interest in compromising you tonight."

"How reassuring." Annabelle shrunk back into the relative safety of the trees. "Can you distract him?"

"I? Why would I give myself such a task?"

She gritted her teeth. "So I can escape. Unless you were lying about your intentions for being here, in which case let me assure you, I am not that sort of lady."

"To be sure you are not," he muttered, running a hand through his hair. "I know that well enough. I believe my cheek is still bruised from our last encounter."

"You deserved it!"

His smile was entirely devoid of humour. "Perhaps I did."

She shrank back until she collided with a tree. The moon came out, drifting light across the garden like snow. If Helmsley came any closer, he would see her.

She closed her eyes.

There was a sigh of resignation, then the Marquess stepped closer, positioning himself so his body was directly in front of hers. And close, so close, one hand braced against the tree, the other up by her waist. Not touching, not quite, but still close enough that she could *sense* what his touch would feel like. The searing heat of his palm.

"Do not make a sound," the Marquess whispered, bending closer. "If you value your reputation at all, that is."

Her entire body vibrated from the force and speed of her heartbeat.

"Come out, Annabelle," Lord Helmsley called plaintively. "Enough is enough. I will find you."

For a moment, darkness crossed the Marquess's face like a shadow over the moon, but a second later, it was gone. He lowered his head to hers, crowding her in. At this angle, he was so large and all-consuming, he blotted out the bare branches above them. All she could do was try to remember how to breathe.

"If you know what is best for you, you will trust me," he

murmured against the line of her jaw. She felt the rush of his breath, felt the proximity of his lips, but he did not touch her. This was no kiss; it was a disguise.

Her head was spinning, caught between *run* and *freeze*.

The footsteps grew even closer.

"Keep your head down," he breathed, the hand by her waist finally landing, just as hot as she had imagined. And larger, too; his thumb pressed against her stomach. "When Helmsley sees me, the last thing he would assume is that I'm here with you, so play along, little bird. Can you be coquettish?"

That was the very last thing she was capable of. Her hands came up to his lapels in a silent plea, and he stiffened. The gesture wasn't designed to bring him closer, but after a moment, it appeared to; his nose nudged her earlobe and her breath stuttered. There was something illicit about the darkness, the way his breath grew heavier, his head dipping lower, his lips *just* grazing the corner of her mouth.

There was a weight in her legs even as her head swam. Their breath mingled in the scant space between them.

"Lady Annabelle?" Lord Helmsley called from close by. "I know you're there somewhere."

She jumped, and the Marquess's hand flexed on her waist. A silent warning.

Then he turned his head, glancing over his shoulder, his voice impatient as he said, "*Must* you be so loud?"

Annabelle fought back the urge to squeak and practically pressed her face into his chest so Lord Helmsley wouldn't see her face. Then she prayed the moonlight could perform magic and turn her dress a different colour.

After a heartbeat, the hand that had been braced behind her on the tree came to cup the back of her neck, holding her against him. He smelt like cotton and amber and something darker that reminded her of a rain-soaked night. Wild, yet oddly comforting.

"God, Barrington," Lord Helmsley said. "At every event?"

"What is the point of accompanying a lady to a house as large as this if one cannot take advantage of the privacy," the Marquess drawled. He pinched the back of her neck, which was presumably her cue to do something 'coquettish'.

She, unsurprisingly, froze.

"I quite agree," Lord Helmsley said. "And on that note, have you seen Lady Annabelle? She came outside, presumably so we can enjoy the privacy of the garden, but I can't find her."

Annabelle's fingers curled more firmly against the Marquess's lapels. If he moved or revealed it was her, she would be ruined forever. Her heart was uncomfortably large in her throat. She closed her eyes.

"If you have not found her despite all that abominable noise, I suspect she doesn't want to be found," the Marquess said, and turned back to Annabelle, crushing her so firmly against the tree, she would have been unable to breathe if she'd tried. The hand cupping her neck tilted her head, and his mouth came within half an inch of hers, his breath hot and steady. She opened her eyes and looked into his face. His eyes were dark holes, shadowed voids, a honey trap.

She was the fly.

"So you have not seen her?" Lord Helmsley asked plaintively.

The Marquess raised his head enough to say, "I have not. If you find her, by all means have your way with her, and in the cold if that pleases you. But stop making a racket. Chances are, she's returned to the house."

"The cold does not pose an obstacle to you."

A muscle in the Marquess's jaw leaped. "*I* am not deflowering a maiden, Helmsley. The difference is subtle, but it is there."

Lord Helmsley made a sound like a curse and thankfully walked away. Annabelle held herself still, trembling, until he had finally strode away. Then she released a breath, relief mixing potently with the concoction of other emotions in her body.

The Marquess stepped away from her and frigid air rushed between them. He brushed a hand down his crumpled lapels. "I suppose this will add to the veracity of my story, although my valet will not be pleased."

Annabelle's mouth opened, then closed. She shivered.

He cut a cool glance at her. "You can thank me, you know. Before you return to the house."

She fully intended to thank him, but what came out of her mouth was, "Could you not have headed him off sooner?"

"I might have if he hadn't come so close. He would have seen you if I had so much as turned." The next look he slanted at her was flat. "You might be surprised to hear this, little bird, but I have no intention of being caught with an unmarried lady."

"Why, because you might be expected to marry her?" she demanded.

"Something like that."

"Well, it's lucky I have no intention of marrying, then." She folded her arms. She still ought to thank him, but there was something about him that made her wary, the way she imagined she might feel when confronted with a panther. Unpredictable.

Hungry.

"How singular," he murmured. "Your pursuer will be disappointed to learn that."

"It's a difficult thing to learn when the Dowager Duchess of Norfolk introduces me to scores of eligible gentlemen and implies I am an object to be bartered away," she snapped, then flushed. She hadn't intended to give so much of herself away, and she took a breath, trying to think about how to retract her statement. But, to her surprise, the Marquess laughed.

"My brother truly was barking up the wrong tree," he said, a note of curling, ironic amusement threaded through his voice. "Alas."

"Your brother?"

"I believe he danced with you once."

"I remember." How could she have forgotten? He was the first gentleman she had met that had shared her interests, and whom she had been marginally less vehemently against marrying.

Then he had died and she had been thrust back into the marriage mart with renewed force, as though the burden of the Marquess's death fell on her shoulders.

She shivered as another chilly gust of wind snaked its way down the garden, and the Marquess looked down at her. "You should return to the house. Helmsley will probably be inside by now."

"What about you?"

"I'll wait out here a few more minutes. The last thing either of us needs is for anyone to see us entering the house together." His gaze found hers in the darkness. "And remember, tell no one of this. Not even your sister."

Annabelle had conveniently forgotten to tell Theo about

that kiss they had shared three months prior; she would certainly not be telling her about this. "Believe me, I have no intention of telling anyone."

"Good." He stepped back, away from her. "Now go. And let us both hope I don't find you alone again, little bird."

The threat in his voice had her picking up her skirts. "For both our sakes," she said over her shoulder. Then he was gone, lost to the shadows of the garden. And Annabelle, no less overwhelmed than she had been when she had fled from Lord Helmsley, spent altogether too long in the powder room before venturing out to find her sister.

Chapter Seven

A shriek rent the air. Annabelle, in the midst of buttering her bread, looked up in alarm. Theo was holding the newspaper to her face, eyes narrowed, her nostrils flared.

Annabelle took a moment to collect herself before responding. A week had passed since Lady Cavendish's recital, and Annabelle had done her best to put it fully from her mind. Just as she had the way Lord Helmsley had touched her, and the way he had assumed she would accept his unwelcome caresses.

The way he had *assumed* she had gone into the garden to be clandestinely with him.

Her blood boiled every time she thought about that.

But he had not called on her since then, and she had every hope that his inability to find her had resulted in him losing interest. She had slipped back inside the house and spent an inordinate amount of time in the washroom, staring at her flushed reflection in the mirror and trying to remember what had happened to the person she had been before the Marquess of Sunderland had put his hands on her.

In the time that had passed, she had thought she had got away with her indiscretion.

Theo looked at her in shock, however, that made Annabelle wonder if news had finally come out. Her hands shook and she closed them around her knife. "What is it?"

"Have you seen this?" Theo thrust the paper at Annabelle, who scanned the announcements. Once, then again.

Lord Shrewsbury, the fourth Earl of Shrewsbury, and his wife, Lady Shrewsbury, announce the engagement of their daughter, Lady Annabelle Beaumont, to Lord Sunderland, the sixth Marquess of Sunderland.

There was no marriage date mentioned.

For five long seconds, she was speechless.

Surely this had to be a mistake of some kind. Someone had printed her name beside his in error. She could not be *engaged*. The Marquess had not so much as asked her—and although she was no expert on the matter, she did think a proposal was a requirement for an engagement.

"No," she said, shaking her head. "No. I am not engaged." With the words came all her memories of *that night*, and she cleared her throat to block them out. "I barely even know him. This has to be a mistake."

"In *The Times*?" Theo clucked her tongue. "Unlikely, I think."

"But how can this be real? I am *not* engaged, Theo!"

"Perhaps he thinks you are?" Theo suggested. "Or perhaps Mama does." Theo paused as though gathering her thoughts, and Annabelle tried to force her shock into a smaller, more manageable ball. "Or, perhaps, Mama hoped to hurry things along and took matters into her own hands?"

Annabelle felt as though she could not take any more blows. Her head pounded. "You mean she may have sent an announcement to the newspaper to encourage the Marquess to propose to me?"

"Well, it *reads* as though it is from the parents of the bride, and that is tradition, you know. And she *is* keen to get you married." Theo made a noise akin to a scream and threw her napkin to the table. "Where *is* Nate? Of all days to be late to breakfast."

Annabelle cast a glance at the clock. It was not yet ten, and Nathanial did not like an early breakfast, especially when they'd been at a function the night before. "What do I do?" she asked faintly. "I won't marry him."

"Barrington?" Theo shuddered. "I should think not. *I* heard he killed a highwayman in cold blood and *left his body on the road.*"

Annabelle thought back to the prowling, roiling energy about the Marquess. Yes, she could believe it, and the thought made her blood ice in her veins. "I won't do it," she repeated.

Velvet darkness, his hand on her waist, his lips grazing her ear. Hot breath and burning skin and that heady, endless sensation of being wanted.

No. She most certainly could not marry him.

Nathanial pushed open the door of the morning room and yawned. "What has happened so early in the morning to cause such a ruckus?" he asked as he took his place at the head of the table. "I could hear you at the other end of the hall."

"*Someone* has put an announcement in *The Times* of the engagement of Annabelle's forthcoming marriage to Lord Sunderland!" Theo said, snatching the paper from Annabelle and shaking it.

Nathanial blinked. "An announcement of their engagement?"

"Were you not listening? Yes. And it's written as though Mama and Papa are announcing it, though I hardly know why they would. Well," Theo amended. "I doubt Papa had anything to do with it."

But why the Marquess of all people? That was the point Annabelle could not move past. Coming a week after their clandestine meeting in the garden, no matter how innocent, it felt as though it must be connected, but she could not see *how*.

"Intriguing," Nathanial murmured, reading the paper. "It is a good thing my mother is indisposed." He looked back up at Theo. "You think your mother did this?"

"Well who else? Think, Nathanial. If Anna married Lord Sunderland, Mama would have one daughter married to a duke and the other to a marquess. That has always been her dream."

"While I'm flattered to have played a role in her machinations," Nathanial said, half distractedly, "I feel I must remind you that I proposed to you unprompted."

"And a terrible proposal it was too, but that's not the *point*, Nate." Theo turned to face Annabelle again. "We need to get to the bottom of this."

He heaved a sigh. "Then I suppose we need to visit your mother."

* * *

Annabelle had not visited her parents' London house many times that Season. Theo had offered to sponsor her, now she was a duchess, and Annabelle had been only too relieved to escape the escalating tension in her parents' home. Her father hadn't stopped his gambling habits, even with the debts pouring in, and only Nathanial's generosity kept them afloat. It was safer, and made more sense, for Annabelle to leave.

As a result, she had a peculiar feeling of foreboding as she followed Theo into the house. Everything was just as she remembered it, although some of the paintings and ornaments had gone; sold, probably, to pay for their household bills.

"Theo," their mother said from the drawing room where she had been writing a letter. "Annabelle. And oh, Nathanial. What an unexpected surprise. I was going to call on you later." She dropped a butterfly-light kiss on Theo and Annabelle's cheeks. "Don't you both look lovely. I was just writing a letter to your Aunt Theresa, girls, if you remember her, to update her on this Season's happenings."

"Mama," Theo said carefully. "Have you read the papers today?"

"Read the papers?" Their mother shuddered. "Why should I do that? If there's anything important there, I'm sure your father will see."

Theo and Annabelle exchanged a look. If her mother *was* playing innocent, she was doing so extremely well.

Annabelle had the overwhelming temptation to throw her head back and scream at the ceiling. It would achieve nothing but perhaps it would ease the overwhelming knot in her chest.

Engaged.

The word stuck in her brain, tripping up every other sentence. And to Lord Sunderland. Jacob Barrington. The Devil of St James. A man who gambled fortunes away at the card table and picked fights wherever he could. Reckless and rash and almost always, in her limited experience, at least a little drunk. Of all the men in London she could have been engaged to, it had to be him.

"There's been a development," Theo said. "About Annabelle. It was in the papers today."

"About Annabelle." Her mother looked up again, eyes sharp and slightly wary. "How so?"

"There was a notice announcing Annabelle's engagement to the Marquess of Sunderland," Nathanial said smoothly. "Written as though her parents had been the ones to insert it."

"The Marquess of Sunderland?" her mother clarified, a line appearing between her brows. "But he hasn't even been courting you. Has he, my dear?"

Annabelle gritted her teeth. "He has not. And—" She bit back the words before she could tell everyone he had told her he had no wish to be married.

"Well I certainly made no announcement," her mother said, looking at them both. "And neither did your father. He has probably forgotten he has one daughter yet unmarried," she added with a trace of bitterness.

"As I thought." Nathanial's voice was a little grim.

Annabelle rubbed her eyes wearily. "But if you didn't, then who did?"

"An excellent question." Theo threw herself down on the sofa and tugged her gloves off. "And one I desire the answer to immediately."

"I'll make enquiries," Nathanial said.

"As shall I." Theo chewed her bottom lip. "We're supposed to be attending Lady Windermere's dinner in Vauxhall tonight. The perfect place to find out any gossip. Do you think someone has done it as a prank, Anna?"

"A prank?" Annabelle tried to think past the roaring in her ears. "Why would someone do this for *fun*?"

"I agree," Nathanial said. "It's unlikely anyone would do this as a joke, and if they did, it's in extremely poor taste. Not to mention risky once word gets out of who was behind it." His expression left Annabelle under no illusions as to what measures he would take. "I suspect whoever was behind this had something to gain."

"Like what?" Theo tossed her hands in the air. "Who could possibly have anything to gain from unifying the biggest rake in London to my sister?"

Nathanial sent Annabelle a long look that made her stomach curl in dread. "A dowry, perhaps? Or a union with the sister of a duchess?"

The Marquess had told her he had no wish of being found with her, implied he had no desire to be married, but perhaps he had lied. And if her mother was not responsible, there could be no other explanation.

"Lord Sunderland," she said.

Nathanial gave a grim nod. "Lord Sunderland."

* * *

Jacob was accustomed to being an object of scandal. He had spent half his life fashioning himself into someone who was frequently associated with depravity and to have whispers follow him wherever he went was hardly unusual.

What was unusual, however, was the fact that the whispers did not seem to involve the fact he had, the night before, challenged a viscount's brother to a duel. Something he would have achieved if the viscount himself hadn't stepped in and towed his unfortunate brother home. Ordinarily, that would have been a cause of gossip, but it appeared as though there was something else going on.

For once, Jacob was at a loss what had inspired this particular set of interest. He prowled through Vauxhall's dimly lit paths, dodging courtesans in too much rouge and young gentlemen in laughing, cocky groups, doing his best to avoid the curious gazes.

When he joined his friends by the orchestra box, Viscount Villiers was staring at him with an expression torn between disgust and hilarity.

"Not you too," he said.

"Unspecific." Jacob selected a glass of champagne from the silver platters being carried around by blank-faced waiters. The orchestra was playing now, Jacob and his friends stood at the back of the crowd. "You will have to try harder."

"Marriage," Villiers said, making a face. "You've finally fallen foul of the last trap left to mankind."

Jacob tossed his champagne back, the bubbles stinging the back of his throat. "Hardly."

"It's in the papers."

"What?"

"Your marriage," Villiers said impatiently. The girl on his arm, a redhead with abundant freckles, stared at him curiously. "This morning. Don't you read the papers?"

"Not if I can get away with it." Attention finally caught, Jacob looked away from the redhead's ample cleavage. "What do you mean, my marriage is in the papers. I'm not married."

"You're engaged."

"I can assure you," Jacob said, suppressing a snort, "I am not."

"That's what it said in the papers, my lord," the redhead said, a broad accent betraying her unfortunate background. An opera dancer, perhaps. Or a singer. Or perhaps just one of the ladies that patrolled these shadowed havens, looking for a gentleman all too willing to part with his purse. Either way, Jacob knew Villiers kept company like this in part to pique his father. "You're to marry Lady Annabelle Beaumont."

Jacob froze, the effects of the champagne dissipating. There was the chill of dread in his chest. Above it all was disbelief.

"Quite," Villiers said when he saw Jacob's dumbstruck face. "I take it you didn't know about this?"

Anger replaced his shock by inches, burning away the ice that had momentarily formed in his chest. That little minx— she had told him she had no intention of marrying and now here she was, trying to trick him into marriage. No doubt she would use the garden incident against him.

Well, if she was hoping she would capture a gentleman that way, she hoped wrong. He was *not* a gentleman, and he had no intention of being caught. If she refused to end the engagement, he would, and to hell with any damage it would do to his reputation—he didn't exactly have much of one to begin with.

"She's a pretty thing," Villiers said dismissively. "A little quiet for my taste."

The Lady Annabelle he had come to know, in the sorts of quiet corners a young lady should never inhabit, had not precisely been quiet. Then again, the fact she frequented places like darkened libraries and gardens should have been a sign that she was as much a lady as he was a gentleman.

He eyed his glass darkly. He was not drunk enough for this. "Then you can have her," he said. "For I, you can be sure, will not."

Chapter Eight

To Annabelle's dismay, news of her engagement had spread like wildfire, rendering it impossible for them to merely quietly break the engagement off. Whatever they did would end in scandal. Her only, brief, reprieve was that Nathanial's mother was bed-bound with a fever, and so Annabelle would not have to endure her shock at the engagement. She was not sure if the Dowager would be relieved Annabelle was finally to be married, or disappointed in her apparent choice of husband.

Regardless, Annabelle endeavoured to put it from her mind. If she thought about the Dowager's disapproval, she would never have the strength to end the engagement; whatever the Dowager's thoughts on the marriage, she would not condone a lady breaking it off once an announcement had been made, and without a severe transgression on the gentleman's behalf.

In that regard, at least, she could still have hope.

As Annabelle and her party entered Vauxhall Gardens and reached Lady Windermere's box, they had been subject to a level of attention Annabelle never wished to be accustomed to. Theo, chatting away as though nothing in the world was wrong, seemed to have no problem keeping a smile on her face. Annabelle, who had never been good at chatting, and was certainly no expert on smiling, kept her eyes fixed to her plate. For something to do, she counted her peas and thought about all the ways she wanted to throttle Lord Sunderland. With her hands would be the most satisfying, but she rather suspected ribbons would be fitting, in a way.

Something light and feminine around his throat, his dark eyes on her as she took hold of the ends and pulled.

There was something somewhat appealing about that image, but not for strictly bloodthirsty reasons, so she abandoned that train of thought before it disturbed her too much.

When she glanced across at Theo again, her face was a little blank, and Nathanial appeared to be nodding off in front of his empty place setting.

"Have you considered chickens?" Lady Windermere asked Theo. "I have found there is something particularly relaxing about all that clucking."

Annabelle gaped then let out a snort she tried to pass as a cough. Theo's foot connected with her ankle.

"No," Theo said, her voice a little strained. "That is—darling, do we keep chickens?"

Nathanial jerked fully awake and looked up in alarm. "Chickens? Where? I hope not."

The terrible, hysterical urge to laugh assailed Annabelle as Theo pushed back from her chair and held out her hand to Annabelle. "I believe there is dancing over there," she said in blind disregard for the fact Annabelle hated dancing. Anything would be better than this and both sisters knew it. "Will you join us, Lady Windermere?"

Lady Windermere, a lady in her early middle age who had been widowed a few years prior, chuckled gently. "No, no.

You young folk enjoy yourself."

Theo gripped Annabelle's arm almost painfully as they made it to other couples swirling around a small quartet. "Heavens, I'd forgotten how boring she was," Theo said, gasping like she hadn't been breathing for their entire conversation. "I'm sorry, Anna, but surely dancing with Nathanial would be preferable to sitting there one moment longer."

Annabelle didn't have the heart to confess she hadn't been paying attention to the conversation at all. "But who will you dance with?"

"Anyone. I hardly mind."

Nathanial raised an eyebrow. "*Anyone*, my love?"

"Well I would dance with Annabelle if I could, but I think Lady Windermere would burst a blood vessel," Theo said. "It's a good thing your mother is ill, Nate, or she'd have had an apoplexy."

"Luckily for us all, even if she were well, my mother would never deign to be seen in Vauxhall Gardens," Nathanial said. "Not even for fireworks."

Considering fireworks were loud, bright, and overpowering, Annabelle wished *she* could have been spared the delight as well. But just as she'd resigned herself to dancing at least one with Nathanial, she spied a tall gentleman approaching, daggers in his eyes aimed straight for her heart.

"Lady Annabelle," he said when he reached them, his voice all soft menace. She felt the danger of it curling around her. "Just the lady I was hoping to see."

Nathanial caught her eye, and she knew if she gave him the signal, he would step in for her. But she shook her head.

This was something she needed to do. And if he thought he was going to take advantage of her, he was going to have another think coming.

"Lord Sunderland," Theo said, not bothering to curtsy. The tension deepened and everyone must be able to sense it. People turned to them.

The Marquess either didn't notice or didn't care. His eyes glittered as he looked at Annabelle again, and she had that same urge to throttle him. Maybe stab him with a hairpin or two. He had *no* right to look at her with that air of night and unspeakable sin as though *she* should have something to apologise for.

I'm ever so sorry for having a dowry you covert, my lord. Evidently you despise it as much as I do.

"Would you do me the honour of this next dance, my lady?" he asked, still looking straight at Annabelle. Her toes curled as she looked back. *I hate you*, her eyes said.

His smouldered. *I know.*

"Actually," Nathanial said, but she cut him off, not looking away from the Marquess.

"Very well," she said, letting her reluctance colour her voice. "One dance."

"Believe me, I would not ask for more."

She doubted that, but said nothing as he brought her into the middle of the floor. Of course, fate was not on her side, and the next dance was a waltz. Naturally it would have been impossible for her to dance with her nemesis to anything else.

He looked down at her, gaze moving from her eyes to her cheekbones to eventually her lips, and back to her eyes. Fury was alive in his face, and it was a dark thing, ravenous. A starving wolf confronted with a rabbit.

She lifted her chin. If he decided to take a bite, he would discover she was no rabbit.

"So," he said, a hard edge to his words. "I hear you have been busy."

"Not as busy as you."

He narrowed his eyes at her and she narrowed hers right back. Two could play at that game. But when his hand gripped hers and his other, rather scandalously, landed on her waist and drew her close, her expression slipped, mortification creeping in. This was not how gentlemen danced the waltz— or at least, not how they danced it in public.

It would have been too much to ask for him not to go out of his way to humiliate her at every given opportunity.

"I thought we agreed not to tell anyone about our little jaunt in the garden," he said, bowing his head to hers. The dance began and she felt his proximity like a flare. Her skin tingled even though he wasn't touching her directly, because she could remember the way he *had*.

Darkness. Warm breath. That heady sense of being *wanted*.

"I said nothing," she hissed back.

"And yet here we are."

"Because of *you*."

He frowned, eyes slits now. "No, little bird. Because of you. My brother died before you could get your hands on his title, so you supposed you could entrap me into marriage. But if you ever thought that would succeed then I'm delighted to disappoint you."

She would have jerked away if he wasn't holding her so tightly. "Entrap *you*?"

"Well, what would you call it? I am a marquess and you are the daughter of a man whose only defining feature is his propensity to lose at the card table."

Annabelle forgot she was in full view; she forgot they were

outside with the darkened sky and flaming torches, and that a quartet played slow, gentle music around them. All she could think about was how much she *hated* Jacob Barrington.

"You do not get to speak about my father like that!"

"Is that not his reputation?"

"Is not yours *worse*?"

He smirked. "Believe me, my lady, when I tell you I know *exactly* what my reputation is."

"Then you should have a very clear idea of why I *don't* want to marry you."

"Is that so?" His voice lowered into a sticky hum that clung to all her senses, soaking her in awareness that felt as flammable as tar. His fingers dug in uncomfortably on her waist, and although there was a smile on his face, it didn't reach his eyes. "You may pretend you dislike me, but I know better, sweetheart." His gaze latched onto the uneven thrum of her pulse and his smile was all cruel amusement. "You want me, Annabelle. And you hate yourself for it."

Her heart thudded, betraying her. Every part of her was aware of him—and he was right, she despised herself for it. "This is entirely untrue," she snapped. "*I don't want to marry you*. Is that so difficult to understand?"

His eyes widened very slightly, and his lips thinned. "Then why," he said, pulling her indecently close so he could breathe in her ear, "is there an announcement in the newspaper claiming we are engaged?"

"I thought you had put it there."

"Me?" He threw his head back and laughed. "Why would I *possibly* want to marry you, little bird?"

The words stung, though she tried not to let them. "I have a large dowry."

"And I have a fortune all of my own to squander."

"Fine." She glowered up at him, contriving to forget the eyes on them and the hot bodies that occasionally brushed against her. Nothing held her attention long except for the Marquess, who looked down at her as though he knew *exactly* what she was thinking.

"So if neither of us did, then that poses the question of who *did* put the announcement there," she said.

"Your sister?"

"Of course not! Theo would never do such a thing. She doesn't even *want* me to marry you. And my mother was as surprised as we all were. Natha—the Duke's theory is that whoever did it had something to gain." She gave him a meaningful look.

"Then you would be better looking elsewhere," he said smoothly. "Marriage is not something I aspire towards."

"What is?" she heard herself say, though she didn't know why. She didn't have interest in this man and his unconventional life choices.

The corner of his mouth kicked up. "Debauchery, mostly, little bird. Why, do you want in?"

"No!" Her cheeks flushed and he chuckled, the sound soft and sinful, making her think of silken sheets and midnight kisses. He would, no doubt, be a better lover than any of the men in *Fanny Hill*. And she had absolutely no interest in learning more about it.

She had already long come to terms with the fact that if she was to remain unmarried, she would also remain chaste.

"So we are agreed," she said, in part to distract herself. "There is no engagement, there never was an engagement, and we will just say it was a prank."

He gave an elegant shrug. "An odd prank, to be sure, but you can tell anyone anything you like. Including that I jilted you, if that's preferable."

"That is *not* preferable." There was nothing she wanted less than for anyone to think that she *wanted* to marry him. "It would be better to tell people I was the one who jilted you."

"I think few would believe you, sweetheart. I'm not known for being jilted." He gave a bright, glittering smile. "At least, not without some prior . . . connection."

"You're despicable."

"But *extremely* fun." He winked and she glowered at him. The sooner they had no more to do with each other, the better.

The dance came to an end and he released her, not bothering to kiss her hand. She gave him a smile she didn't feel and when she turned, Theo was already surging through the crowd towards her.

"Go," the Marquess said, a trace of amusement in his voice at Theo's determined expression. "And let us hope this is the last time we meet."

Chapter Nine

Smoke, lit by the Bengal lights, hung heavy and noxious in the air as above Annabelle, fireworks burst and glittered in a shower of sparks. Directly ahead, a tightrope walker made his precarious way across the rope. So confident was he in his ability, nothing had been placed underneath to catch him if he fell. Annabelle stared at him in mingled horror and wonder.

With every bang, Lady Windermere tittered, and Theo looked into the air with a rapt expression. To her, it was probably deeply romantic, and Annabelle noticed the way Nathanial's arm curved around her waist.

Now she had come to an agreement with the Marquess, it felt as though there was a weight off her chest. She'd explained the situation to Theo, and although it hadn't solved the question of who had attempted to force them into matrimony, it had at least posed an immediate solution.

She was not to be married.

Relief made her giddy, and she found she didn't mind the noise as much as usual. As they walked, their little group becoming somewhat less tightly knit, Annabelle trailed her fingers along the freshly budding leaves of the hedges. May had come fast, and the nights were warming.

She was not to be married. What was more, the Marquess had no *desire* to marry her. A little too vehemently, perhaps, but better be too vehement than harbouring a secret desire to be her husband.

With a sigh, she tipped her head back to the distant stars. The fireworks continued, their bangs and pops combating the orchestra playing in the pit, and she took a deep breath of the smoky air, savouring the unexpected sense of freedom the night had brought her.

Perhaps now she would be seen to turn down the Marquess of Sunderland, no other gentlemen would ask for her hand.

When she looked up again, her party had vanished.

The sense of peace she'd been nurturing faded away on the breeze. All around were the bustling figures of strangers, and when she hurried forwards, all she could see were strangers. Panicked now, she pushed through the crowd, searching for Nathanial's tall frame or Theo's dark hair. All she saw were strangers. The smoke was acrid, cloying in her throat, and she coughed, her eyes watering.

Air, she needed air.

Her heart pounding, her vision blurring, she turned in a full circle, searching blindly for someone she knew. An acquaintance, any acquaintance. Theo would be preferable, but she would have even taken the Dowager Duchess.

A hand clamped on her arm. "Lady Annabelle," Lord Helmsley said with a smile like a shark scenting blood. "Are you lost?"

* * *

Jacob was drunk. Not surprising, given this was his preferred state of being every time he came too close to feeling something. It allowed him to forget.

For Jacob, forgetting was a necessity.

Villiers and his companion for the night—he had already forgotten her name and it wouldn't matter come morning anyway—talked in low voices beside him, probably debating what dark corner they could hide in. He smiled suggestively at a courtesan in a revealing dress, and was contemplating drawing her into a less crowded area when he saw her.

A flash of gold hair. A dress that, in daylight, might have been a pale powder blue, and in this light looked more like white or grey. A pale face with too-large eyes and a nose that was a fraction too small. She looked like a lost fairy, and over her, looking more like a goblin king, loomed Lord Helmsley, one hand at her waist, the other gripping her hair.

Jacob hesitated. Villiers paused and shot him a frown.

"Everything all right, Barrington?"

He was not a knight in shining armour and he certainly did not possess a horse. But the sight of Helmsley pushing the fairy against the hedge was displeasing enough that he shook his head at Villiers.

"You go on."

Villiers shrugged and continued, more interested in the beauty by his side than Jacob's noble-adjacent intentions.

The dark anger in Jacob, the one he usually released in the boxing ring, bubbled up inside him. Not for Annabelle—he didn't care about her in particular. But Helmsley, with his wandering hands and greasy smile, was the kind of man it was Jacob's pleasure to hate.

No, he was definitely not a knight.

But if there was one thing that went against his blackened, blood-stained moral code, it was to force oneself on an unwilling woman.

"Stop struggling," Helmsley spat as he hauled her into a dark, quiet path, away from the lights and the crowds. No one stopped or gave them a second glance. Pickpockets weaved through the crowd, and the later the hour became, the rowdier Vauxhaul was likely to get.

"Let *go* of me!" Annabelle's voice was too quiet, deathly afraid.

"Hide from me, will you?" he sneered. "I know you were out in the garden that night."

Annabelle shook her head, eyes wide, terrified. She locked eyes with Jacob and recognition flooded her gaze. *Please*, she mouthed.

"I had it all planned," Helmsley said, roughly dragging her another few feet. "I spread the rumour that you were in the gardens with the Marquess of Sunderland. That should have ruined you nicely. And then I hear you're engaged to him?"

Tears streamed down her face as she shook her head again.

"You were supposed to be engaged to *me*."

Jacob stepped into the deserted path after them, letting the darkness cloak him. "Do you know," he said conversationally, "I rather suspect she was trying to avoid you in those gardens after all." Then he grabbed a handful of Helmsley's coat, hauled him back, and planted his fist in Helmsley's face.

* * *

Annabelle attempted to scream, but no sound came out. Her hair was half undone, falling from its pins, the soft weight of it brushing her neck. Her hands shook. She wanted to vomit.

Lord Helmsley was on the floor. The Marquess of Sunderland, his breath smelling of wine though his posture was perfectly steady, stood over him.

She was definitely going to vomit.

"A word of advice," the Marquess said, his voice deadly soft. Lord Helmsley spat a tooth onto the grass. "Touch another lady without her express permission again, and I will put a bullet through your worthless heart. Do you understand me?"

Lord Helmsley swallowed, his expression half hidden in the darkness. But there was defiance mingled with the fear in his voice as he said, "You would not dare."

"Wouldn't I?" He leant forward, one foot coming to crush Lord Helmsley's chest. Annabelle let out a squeak. "Do you think yours would be the first body I've left behind me? Do you think I have any qualms about squashing you like an ant?" He pressed and the air visibly left Lord Helmsley's chest. "Believe me when I say you have no comprehension of what I'm capable of."

Annabelle pressed her palms into her eyes. Seconds later, she heard Lord Helmsley climb to his feet and flee.

Then she was alone with the Marquess. Equal parts fear and relief flooded her. Fear because she believed every word he'd said—she had no comprehension of what he was capable of—and relief that at least he wasn't Lord Helmsley, whose capabilities she fully comprehended.

Warm fingers wrapped around her wrists, drawing her hands down from her eyes. "Did he hurt you?" the Marquess asked flatly. She would have thought he hadn't consumed any wine at all except for the smell of it on its breath and the dangerous glitter in his eyes.

"No, but I—"

"Good. Now pull yourself together." He dropped her hands like she had burnt him.

She raised her gaze to his shadowed face. The urge to vomit was replaced by the urge to cry. They were trapped. If Helmsley had spread a rumour they were in the garden together, she *had* to marry him or she truly would be ruined forever.

"This changes everything." She pressed a hand to her eyes. "We can't just end the engagement as though it never happened."

"On the contrary."

"But I will be ruined," she said helplessly. "And I wouldn't care so much for myself, but my family—they don't deserve this. Theo is a duchess and my mother—my *father.*"

"Will he disown you?" the Marquess asked, and there was something in his voice—unarticulated hurt, the kind of deep pain that punctured through to the marrow.

"I–I don't think so." Hopefully. She wasn't entirely sure what her father would do if she was ruined. Certainly, it would mean she was unlikely to ever marry, which would displease him, but would he care enough to take action?

Theo, at least, would protect her. But at what cost? A woman with a ruined reputation could not mingle in Society, and her family would be tainted by association. Yes, she would finally see her dream to remain unmarried, but she had wanted that decision to be her own, not forced on her by the actions of others.

"Can you not tell everyone that we were never in the

garden?" she asked desperately. "Or perhaps something else to avoid scandal?"

He gave a short, hard laugh that dispelled the last of her hope. "Do I strike you as the sort of man who avoids scandal, little bird?"

"*Please.*"

"Please what? Marry you?" He shook his head. "I'm afraid I'm not the marrying sort."

"There has to be some way to convince everyone nothing happened."

"I'm all ears."

She desperately cast around for a way out of this mess. Lord Helmsley had been the one to spread the rumour, and if it was known that she had slighted him, perhaps some people would believe he had done it out of spite, but the engagement notice only confirmed the situation.

"I would have thought you were an expert on avoiding marriage."

"Oh I am," he said, the glitter turning to a gleam. "But I achieve that by not involving myself with unmarried ladies. You were a mistake."

The words punched the air from her lungs. "Then you have nothing? No solution?"

"Scandal doesn't last forever. Ride it out, and once it's over, people will have forgotten."

"Hardly reassuring given the way they will treat me in the meantime," she said, hating the way her voice broke. "And what about my family?"

"So long as they will not turn you out, that is all that matters."

"That is *not* all that matters!" She touched a hand to her tangled hair. Everyone was going to see her and make an assumption about what she had been doing. The moment she stepped back into the light, she would be even more ruined. They would assume the worst because that was what people loved to do—they loved to make the worst of every given situation.

They would stare at her. Whisper. Already, the prospective weight of their attention made her want to sink into the ground. And they would assume, again, that she had been with the Marquess of Sunderland, who was well known for having a different woman for breakfast, lunch and dinner.

Her lip quivered. And the Marquess, damn him, was just staring at her, his face impassive, nothing moving but those eyes as they travelled across her face.

She sniffed, valiantly holding in her tears. When she was home and it was all over, then she would cry.

"You look dishevelled," he said as she turned, steeling herself to enter the fray once more.

"No, I—" Her protest cut off as he took hold of her shoulders and turned her to face the hedge. He gathered the hair that had fallen loose across her shoulders and repinned it with fingers that had no right being so nimble. "My lord," she said, her voice uncertain. "What are you doing?"

"Rendering you slightly *less* dishevelled, my lady," he said. "Fear not—I have some experience in this area."

"Dishevelment?"

"And the aftermath." His fingers trailed along her neck and she had to bite back the urge to shiver. It made no sense how Lord Helmsley's touch made her want to gag, and the Marquess's made her skin prickle with sensitivity.

"I wasn't aware debauchery had this sort of aftermath," she said.

"Of course you weren't." He stepped back and when she turned, he offered her his arm. "Allow me to assist you in finding your party."

She gaped at him, and he tucked her hand in his arm, flashing her a brilliant smile.

"I don't understand," she said weakly.

"I'm escorting you."

"Why?"

"Because much as your reputation may suffer from being with me, I didn't punch that man merely so another could assault you." His tone was very slightly bored, and she peeked into his face to get an idea of his expression. Blank.

So, he wouldn't consent to marrying her—which was both a relief and a travesty—but he was insisting on escorting her. She couldn't quite work him out. It seemed he had a trace of conscience, after all.

A thought that seemed to plague him as much as it did her, by the brief flash of irritation across his face as he led her back into the crowd.

"Never mind a knight," he muttered, more to himself, it seemed, than her. "I'm an upstanding bloody saint."

Chapter Ten

Jacob didn't like Annabelle.

That was what he told himself after he delivered her to her party, disappearing into the crowd before any of said party could see him. He didn't like her and he had absolutely no intention of being married to her. Not even to save her reputation.

She was bookish. She had been Cecil's first choice, and he had become involved with Cecil's choice before—and look how well that had turned out. All excellent reasons he had made the right choice in refusing to honour this ridiculous engagement. Who had done this, anyway?

Maybe it was her mother after all. Someone with a stake in matters surely had to be responsible.

Regardless, it was better for them all if he remained uninvolved. Madeline would have been better off if she had stayed away from him, and Annabelle was no different.

He reminded himself of this—apparently it transpired he still had a kernel of conscience left, and it was exclusively directed at young, unmarried women in danger of ruination—as he left his lodgings in Albany shortly before noon the next day.

And there, opposite him, was Annabelle, emerging from Hatchards with packages in her hands. There was a footman, similarly loaded down, just behind her, and her face was pale and pinched, a line between her brows.

The rush of anger and desire hit him like a boot to the gut.

She glanced up, seeing him, and the colour fled from her cheeks. One of her books tumbled from her arms onto the pavement, and she bent to pick it up, scarlet replacing the unnatural white.

"Lord Sunderland," she said breathlessly, retrieving her book. He briefly entertained the idea of walking away. "I was hoping we would see each other today."

"You were?" He raised an eyebrow. The first time he'd seen her, in Cecil's arms, she hadn't struck him as being especially pretty. Too small and pale for his liking. But that had been before he had kissed her, and before he had been tempted to kiss her again on multiple occasions.

Lust was an emotion easily overcome, in his experience, but only if one stopped encountering the object of their lust in dark, private spaces.

The thought irritated him still more, so he gave her a sensual smile. "I can only imagine for what, seeing as I expressly told you I would not be marrying you."

The irritation in her sigh matched his. "How many times must I tell you, I have no desire to be married?"

"Then we are done here."

"No, my lord, we are not."

This was bold for a lady who could not look at a gentleman without blushing. "Ah, so you *are* intrigued by what I can do for you?"

"It must be trialling, I know, but I do ask that you at least

95

try not to be obnoxious."

He raised his eyebrows. "But I'm so good at it?"

Annabelle clicked her tongue, her little mouth pursing as she looked at him. There didn't seem to be any admiration in her gaze, which was frankly unusual for a woman who looked him up and down. Perhaps she really did hate him, after all.

Well, it would make throwing her to the wolves more palatable.

Until he remembered Madeline. Echoes of grief, mindless in its intensity, pounded in his head.

He had been the reason she had died. Because of him, she had been ruined, and she lost everything. If he abandoned this lady to her fate, would it be the same? Would the rumours spread in the same way they had with Madeline?

Would he ruin her as thoroughly?

He cursed under his breath as those last dregs of conscience came to life.

"Let us walk," he said, taking the books from her arms. Damn his conscience, and damn the girl for reminding him of Madeline.

Damn Madeline for ever allowing him to seduce her. She should have known better. Even then, before his course had been set, he was the vilified younger brother of a marquess who despised him.

"Do you know who put the engagement in the paper?" he asked.

"No, not yet." She bit her lip, and he decided it would be better for his sanity if he didn't look at her mouth. "Nathanial— that is to say, the Duke, is going to make enquiries."

"Not that it really matters now," he muttered. If Helmsley had been spreading rumours about them in order to ruin her, the damage was already done to her reputation.

"No," she agreed. "I suppose it does not."

"What outcome are you hoping for?" he asked her abruptly. "You've already said you don't want to marry me, but if people believe you were in the gardens with me, marriage *is* your only solution to avoid scandal. And I have already told *you* I am not the marrying sort."

"At least give us more *time*." She cast him a pleading glance. "Say nothing to contradict the engagement so we have longer to discover a way out."

The way out for him was simple: he would not marry her and to hell with the consequences.

"A way out?" He gestured impatiently. "You say you do not want to marry, but marriage is your only solution."

Her jaw set, but to his surprise, she said nothing to argue with him.

"What, precisely, are your objections to marriage?" he asked. "Do you dislike the institution, dislike men, or merely find yourself unable to form meaningful attachments?"

Her mouth fell open with a pop. "I am not incapable of forming meaningful attachments."

"Then why?"

"My *objection* is that I have yet to find a gentleman who might offer me the life I want."

"And what is that?" he pressed.

She sent him a dour look. "I doubt you are that gentleman."

He flashed her a sharp smile. "I never claimed to be a gentleman. Now, the question?"

He could see her reluctance in the way she looked at the ground. They strolled slowly along the road, looking for all the world like a promenading couple. Given their engagement, and the presence of her footman walking just behind, no one would think anything amiss.

The idea came to him in a flash: a ludicrous, preposterous idea. One that, though he tried to shake it off, followed him with the tenacity of a shadow.

It would both ensure history did not play out again *and* that he would not end up having to marry this girl.

"How about another question," he said when she didn't answer. "What if I were able to find you a gentleman you preferred? That would hardly be a difficult task, I think. Would you marry him then?"

* * *

Annabelle gaped at the Marquess. When she had asked for his help finding a solution, she had hoped said solution would involve *no* husbands.

"Another gentleman?" she repeated.

"Well, *I* have no intention of marrying you."

The very thing she had been trying to avoid all Season. But if the Marquess, whose hobbies included ruination, gambling and quite possibly murder, could think of no other alternative, it struck her there probably was none.

"Here's my suggestion," he said as though coming to a decision. "I will not say anything against the engagement. In fact, I will actively court you. If nothing else, that will pique Helmsley. No doubt he never thought I would actually marry you."

Annabelle gave a wry smile, though the thought of Helmsley

brought back the nausea. "If someone had not written to *The Times*, you would not have done."

"Nuance." He had the gall to wave a dismissive hand. "So, I will allow the engagement to proceed. At the same time, I will teach you how to flirt, and deliver you into the waiting arms of a gentleman who would better suit you."

There was a lot to digest in that sentence, but one word alone jumped out at her. "You will teach me to *flirt?*"

"It strikes me you are singularly poor at it."

She wasn't sure if she was more offended or amused. "Why would I be good at it?"

"Why, to attract gentlemen, of course." He waggled his eyebrows at her. "And because it's fun."

Fun for him, perhaps. Fun for anyone who didn't feel cripplingly anxious whenever they were in public. The only time she didn't, for a reason she couldn't articulate, was when she was with the Marquess. Probably because, as far as bad opinion went, he soaked it all up.

He, like her, was an outsider.

"You will have to learn how to be coquettish," he went on. "I know you have no experience in *that*."

"That is because I have no interest in it."

"Plenty other girls your age do." There was a wry expression in his eyes, as though he knew something she didn't—or had been on the receiving end of that coquettishness. Considering he was the rakish Devil of St James, she suspected he had. "It's a useful skill to have in your arsenal, believe me."

She blinked at him. Then, when his expression didn't change, she blinked again. "How long do you suppose it will take for you to find me another husband?" she asked doubtfully. "My sister will want me to marry by the end of the month."

He only paused for a second. "Then I suppose it is lucky my brother died not three months ago," he said. "It would not be seemly to marry too soon after his death. Six months would be more appropriate. Three months from now."

The Marquess did not appear to be overly concerned with what was seemly. He had barely taken any time to grieve his brother at all, wearing only the minimal amount of black and almost immediately kicking up such hell around London, it was a surprise he was ever invited anywhere.

Then again, he had plenty of older ladies who enjoyed his company. Annabelle wasn't privy to *those* conversations, but it seemed as though he had become somewhat of a trophy to be won. A prize to be flouted on the arm of one lady or another, a claim that they had tamed the devil. Annabelle wondered what he felt about it. Then she reminded herself she didn't care.

"Three months," she said, tasting the words. Three months did not seem very long. "Very well. You have until the end of the summer to find me another husband. Then I will officially break our engagement. But only if I am assured the other gentleman will propose."

The Marquess's eyes glittered dangerously. "Or what, little bird? Do you think you will succeed in dragging me to the altar? I assure you, you are mistaken."

Panic flared across her senses and she forced it back. Although she did not like the Marquess, she would need a husband if everything went wrong. There was no guarantee that he could find another gentleman prepared to offer for her in that time-frame, and she needed to know her reputation would be safe.

Or rather, for her family's sake she needed to do this.

But she could not persuade the Marquess the ordinary way; he would not marry her from duty alone. Already she knew that. He had killed a man and left him lifeless on the road behind him.

She would have to appeal to the one thing that could control him now: his ego.

"Why," she asked, tilting her head to look at him assessingly, "do you believe it's impossible?"

He smirked. "I could render even you desirable, little bird, and your dowry is an added boon."

"Then you will have no issue making a deal with me," she said, heart racing. "If you believe there is no chance of you succeeding."

His eyes gleamed before he could shut down the expression, and she knew she had chosen well. Perhaps the only thing that could inspire him to make a deal with her was a challenge. She had learnt how much he liked *that* when she had informed him that she did not like kissing—or kissing him.

"You are very bold, little bird," he murmured, leaning in closer. "Why should I agree?"

"I'll do what is necessary. Learn to flirt, be coquettish, whatever it is you need from me." Her words were too fast, a torrent tumbling from her but she could not have stopped them if she had desired. This was a deal she *needed*. Theo needed her to make it. "And you guarantee that if, by some miracle, you do not find me a husband I am willing to marry in three months . . ." She held her breath. "You must marry me yourself."

Chapter Eleven

Jacob knew better than to agree to such a foolhardy arrangement. His plans for the future—disgracing the family name and ensuring it could not continue, which had been his purpose since Cecil had so thoughtlessly burdened him with the title—did not involve a wife.

But the way she had issued the challenge, as though she knew he would have no choice but to indulge her, intrigued him. And it was not as though it was an impossible task: she was pretty, when she remembered to smile, and most importantly, she was rich.

"If I were to agree," he said, holding up one finger, "you would have to also swear that you will accept the offer of an eligible gentleman."

"I would rather marry most men than you," she said with enough scorn that he believed her. Good. It was better they were on the same page. "But the gentleman *must* be eligible. And to my liking, at least a bit."

What she meant, no doubt, was not a man like Helmsley, and at the thought, his blood heated. He had not seen the man since their altercation in Vauxhall, and it was a good thing, or he might not have waited to issue a challenge before throwing the first punch.

His fists itched. Scum like that did not belong on the earth.

"Of course he would be . . . respectable," he said through gritted teeth. "And for you, I shall even be a rake reformed. The *ton* will be shocked to see how well you have won me over." Doing so would draw attention to her and her charms, which would be no bad thing, especially if she flirted with others. It would be a small sting to be seen as losing out to another, but he did not mind overmuch. "I have but one final request, little bird."

"What is it?"

He flashed her his most charming smile. "You must not fall in love with me."

She arched a single brow. "I hardly think that will be an issue."

"Then you have yourself a deal." He extended a hand, but she eyed it suspiciously, making no move to shake it. "What is it?"

"Are you sober?"

"As the grave."

"I believe this is the first time I have seen you so."

He nodded. "That is likely."

"If we are to do this, I think you should be sober more often. Around me, I mean," she added hurriedly. "As part of your reformed rake act."

He frowned. This was one of the many reasons he had never seriously courted anyone since Madeline—and even then, the way he had behaved had hardly consisted of *courting*. Having ladies come to him, keen to win him over, was far more satisfying, and required very little effort on his behalf.

But in order to make other gentlemen jealous, he would

need to flaunt her and show them precisely what they were missing. And for that, he would have to pretend to be smitten with her.

"Very well," he said. "I shall remain sober while escorting you, and you may have all the flowers and trinkets your heart desires. And before the time is out, I will have a veritable line of gentlemen queueing for your hand in marriage."

Her brows drew together and one corner of her mouth curved into a smile that looked a little too cynical for her fresh, innocent face. "We shall see," she said.

* * *

With the agreement, no matter how foolishly made, in hand, Jacob paid a visit to Lady Louisa Bolton. They had met shortly after Madeline's death, when she was married to a much older gentleman she despised. In a fit of pique and heartbreak, they had briefly become lovers, but quickly came to the conclusion they were better as friends. And considering Villiers was all too happy to see the world burn as long as he made a bet on who held the torch, she was perhaps his only true friend.

He did not stop to examine how painfully tragic that was.

He found her painting in her drawing room, one brush behind her ear and her apron splattered with paint. When she saw him, she raised her eyebrows, putting her brushes down—all except the one behind her ear.

"Goodness, Jacob," she said, wiping her hands on a rag as she rose. "It's barely past noon."

"An achievement I agree," he said dryly, plucking the

paintbrush from her head. "Is your mind disturbed, Louisa? You only paint when you're in a foul mood."

She gave him a dirty look. "It's none of your business."

"I'll take that as a yes."

She rang for tea. "I hear I have to offer you congratulations. Tell me, Jacob, what charms does she have that she enticed *you* into matrimony?"

He took a seat and stretched his legs out in front of him. "It is not real."

"Excuse me?"

"The engagement is merely a front to protect her reputation while I find her a more suitable husband."

Louisa stared at him for a few moments. "I think you should start from the beginning."

In as few words as possible, he explained the predicament they had found themselves in. At the mention of Helmsley's involvement, her face darkened with angry colour, and she squeezed the rag between her fingers as though it was his neck.

"Someone ought to put the man out of his misery," she said viciously.

He raised an eyebrow. "How bloodthirsty. Are you *quite* sure you're well?"

"Enough about me. Explain to me how you anticipate finding a more suitable husband than a marquess for the daughter of an earl."

"I presume you haven't forgotten my reputation."

She waved a dismissive hand. "All that can be forgiven. But tell me—was this your idea?"

He gave her a disparaging look. "Obviously."

"And she agreed?"

105

"Would I be here if she hadn't?"

She rocked back, eyes wide and a little glassy. "My God. She reminds you of Madeline."

He scowled, all the more irritated because she was right. "She does not. And *if* she did—only if, mind you—that would not change the fact she dislikes me. And I do not like her. This is a business arrangement."

Louisa, who had always been able to read him better than a book, raised an elegant brow. "A business arrangement you allowed yourself to be caught up in because she reminds you of Madeline. What is your plan?"

"The fact of the matter is, Louisa," he confided, leaning forward and resting his elbows on his knees, "I was hoping you might help me."

"Help you," she repeated. "With finding her a husband?"

"Naturally."

Louisa leant back in her seat and looked at him contemplatively. It was not a look he particularly enjoyed; it usually meant a conclusion he disliked was just around the corner.

"You have met her a total of four times," she said. "One of which you kissed her—"

"I did not know who she was then," he said, although that was only true for the first kiss. The second had been done in full knowledge of her identity, and while he occasionally felt a flare of shame, he could not bring himself to regret it.

"You do now. Tell me, Jacob, why do you not just marry her yourself?"

He stared at her. She stared back. Asking her for help had evidently been a mistake. "Because neither of us wants to be married," he said. "And particularly not to one another."

"That is all the reason you possess?"

"I hardly need more."

She threw up her paint-splattered hands. "Why do you need my help? You told Lady Annabelle that you could manage to find her a husband on your own."

He flashed her a grin. "On my own but with your help. You have more mobility than I, and you can introduce her to a selection of gentlemen who have a chance of being tempted into wanting her for their own. I'll be there to make them jealous, and you can spread the rumour that Annabelle would be open to another match with a more suitable gentleman. *Et voila*, the bargain is complete."

"And if we don't achieve this momentous task?"

"Well . . ." He paused over his words, contemplating. "She believes that after three months are up, if I haven't found her a husband, I'll marry her myself."

Louisa's grey eyes widened and she placed a hand over her heart. Then the same eyes narrowed. "You said *believe*."

"I won't, of course. But there's no need for her to know that. It won't come to pass."

"Jacob, you cannot be serious."

"Have you ever met her?" he asked, hooking his ankle on his knee and accepting the tea she now offered him. "It should be easy enough to pair her off. She probably has the largest dowry in the country."

Louisa's face twisted as she drank. "I know *of* her," she said after a moment. "Do you want me to befriend her?"

"She shares your opinion of me, so I expect you'll get on delightfully. And frankly she needs a friend. I hardly count."

"No," Louisa muttered. "You do not." She glanced at the painting in the corner of the room, which Jacob had almost immediately forgotten about in his preoccupation with his own news.

She sighed. "Annabelle Beaumont is Henry's sister."

It took a few moments for the words to penetrate and for Jacob to parse their meaning. Henry's name had been mentioned between them once before, shortly after their one and only moment of intimacy. And even then the mention of him had been brief—Henry Beaumont, the Viscount Eynsham, the future Earl of Shrewsbury, had been Louisa's first love.

It had ended badly and Henry had gone off to war. Everything Louisa had done in those early years, Jacob knew, was a form of revenge. She was older now, and more poised, but the hurt was still there, lingering in her heart like a bruise that had been pressed.

"You told me you never think about him," he said. He had never known any of the details, and now he itched to learn.

She directed a glare at him, her eyes sharp enough to cut glass. "That was before I heard he was coming back to London."

* * *

The announcement that Henry was returning from the war greeted Annabelle when she rose for breakfast. Her mother was already there, having made the walk to Norfolk House that morning, and she was full of the news.

"He writes that he's sorry he's been gone so long and he hopes to see us soon," she read from the letter clutched in her hands. Annabelle poured herself some tea and tried to recall everything she knew about Henry.

Seven years ago, when she'd been just thirteen, he had left to fight the French, and since then he had returned home rarely. When he *had* been here, he had argued with their father almost constantly, which made her stomach curl with worry.

As for what she remembered of him . . . he was so much older than her—by eleven years—that they had never played much together as children. She was closer with Oliver, her second brother who was currently at Cambridge; they were of a similar age.

Theo poured herself some coffee "Does he say when, Mama?"

"He gives no date, but I expect we can see him before the month is out."

Annabelle's stomach gave a little lurch. Once Henry was back, he might do things like force the marriage, or disapprove of her marrying one man after she was engaged to another.

"Will he be coming to London, do you think?" she asked cautiously.

Her mother frowned at her. "Well of course. This is where his family is, after all." She hugged the paper to her chest again. She was the kind of mother who, despite her attempts to hide it, rather obviously preferred one child over all others. Henry was her darling and had been since he was born, especially since she had lost many children after. Theo had been born a full ten years after Henry.

There was no doubt that their mother loved them all. But she unequivocally loved Henry the best.

Theo grinned at Annabelle from across the table, mouthing *Mama's favourite*. Annabelle did her best to smile back. She glanced at the clock. Jacob had promised to call on her that morning with a gift, and she was already, absurdly, nervous.

109

Their mother stayed a little longer, reading Henry's letter to them a total of three disjointed times, and exclaiming how good things would be once he was there, before finally leaving to spread the news elsewhere.

They ate the rest of their breakfast in near silence, Annabelle reading a book on her lap and Theo staring into the distance. After breakfast, Annabelle carried the same book into the drawing room and continued reading as Theo practised some scales on the pianoforte. Nathanial joined them, bringing in some of the work he usually did in his study and spreading it across the table. It was the picture of domestic bliss.

That was, of course, until the butler escorted a familiar face and a rather obnoxiously large bouquet of flowers into the room.

"Your Graces," the Marquess said with a devilish smile directed at Annabelle as he bowed. He offered the flowers to her, and Annabelle was aware of Theo's pursed lips and Nathanial's frown. She had told them of her intention to maintain the engagement, though she had not revealed her intention of marrying another, but neither had been pleased at the idea.

Only her mother had been happy at the news. But Annabelle could be marrying an octogenarian and if he was a duke, her mother would have been happy.

The Marquess's gaze was warm with false affection, but his smile was all wickedness, and her stomach flipped uncomfortably. She had thought when she was making the deal that she was doing the right thing, but seeing him here, now, with these flowers, sober and with every intention of appearing to woo her, she could not help thinking she had made a mistake.

Chapter Twelve

Jacob watched the way Annabelle swallowed back whatever retort was in her mouth before attempting a smile.

"Sunderland," Norfolk said, rising and giving a stiff nod. His wife laid a hand on his arm, presumably to stop him from saying anything more.

So, Jacob wasn't a favourite in the family. No matter. He didn't intend to be part of it for long.

"I'll ring for the flowers to be put in water," the Duchess said, hurrying for the bellpull. Jacob didn't spare her a single glance, putting all his predatory focus on Annabelle. Today, they were going to make strides towards his goal: teach her to flirt. And, if he had his way, he would test her out on some of his acquaintances, too, in preparation for when Louisa would introduce her to gentlemen who may actually be inclined to marry.

"Lord Sunderland," she said, flushing a delicious colour all the way down her neck when she finally tore her gaze away from his, her eyes alive with annoyance. Oh yes, she wanted him, and she truly did despise herself for it.

All he had to do was make sure that continued as long as they were 'engaged'. That wouldn't be too challenging. He had a particular knack for making people hate him. She would be no different. After all, he had done an admirable job so far.

"I hope you like your flowers, Lady Annabelle," he said in a low, intimate voice.

"Oh." Now the attention of the room was on her, she looked slightly strained. "They're lovely, thank you."

She did not sound as though they were lovely. He suppressed a smile. Her sister took the flowers from her and she sagged in relief.

Tomorrow, he would bring her an outrageous necklace and expect her to wear it. Something with rubies and diamonds in, perhaps. Something ostentatious she would hate and have to pretend to love. What better thing to spend his newly acquired wealth on?

He smiled at her, and her brows pinched together like she knew precisely what he was thinking.

"How about a walk?" she suggested, sending a less-than-subtle glance at the Duke and Duchess.

"We can promenade," he said smoothly. "In Hyde Park."

What followed was a bustle of activity, but eventually they were on their way. It was a colder day, so she wore a woollen shawl over her shoulders, and her hand was warm in the crook of his arm.

"The flowers were excessive," she told him. They were a few steps behind the Duke and Duchess, who were lively in their own conversation, so he wasn't concerned they would be overheard.

"I thought you asked me to court you?"

"Yes, but be *reasonable*."

"I'm being perfectly reasonable." He grinned down at her, enjoying the way she shifted awkwardly. Really, this was too easy. "Admittedly, I don't have a lot of experience courting ladies, but I am positive flowers are involved. And expensive jewellery. How else will the world know that I want to marry you?"

"You could be nice to me."

"Ah, but that's no fun."

She made a tiny noise that might have been a snort of amusement, and after glancing at her sister, she leant in and asked, "What about your connection with Mrs Bentley?"

"Clarissa?" He blinked, surprised that she knew about Clarissa, and reminded somewhat abruptly of her existence. "I haven't seen her in a while."

"Did you not court her?"

"Ah, little bird." Her innocence was too adorable for her own good. "No. That's not how it works. There was no need for courting. We both knew what we wanted from the other and we took it. That was all."

"Oh," she said, and more quietly, "I thought it was a little more romantic than that."

"Not at all. There is no romance in any aspect of my life, sweetheart." They reached the gates and finally began to promenade. The purpose of the exercise was, of course, so the *ton* could see him escorting her, but as the attention began to settle on them, her body language changed. She stiffened, imperceptibly at first, then more as time went by. Her conversation slowed to monosyllables, and she stared at her feet more often than not.

Odd. The last time they had been this public together, they had been dancing at Vauxhall Gardens, and—

She had been angry at him.

"Don't stare at the ground," he said when she avoided yet

113

another person's curious gaze. "No one is going to eat you."

"Easy for you to say," she muttered. "If they ate you, they would spit you back out."

"Insult me louder; perhaps that might give you more confidence."

She glared up at him, shyness forgotten in her irritation, and he almost laughed out loud. "You are odious," she informed him.

"Do continue. My ego hasn't yet been dented."

"I despise you."

"As we have already ascertained."

"You are obnoxious and difficult and I wish I had never met you."

"Better," he said, taking note of the way her chin rose. "Now look at me, little bird. Hate me all you will, but look at me."

She did, raising her gaze to his face with those blue eyes spitting fire. When she forgot to be shy, she really was lovely, and he shut away the thought before it could take root, smirking at her instead. If he could just keep her hating him, these three months would go past quickly enough.

"Good. Always remember to look at the gentlemen you're talking with. Now pretend I am a respectable gentleman approaching you," he said. "I will bow, like this. What do you do?"

"Freeze, usually," she said candidly, her irritation fading into frustration. "And I can hardly pretend you are one of them when you don't scare me the way they do."

"Scare you?" Of all the gentlemen she had spent time with of late, he would have thought he was the *most* likely to scare a girl. "Why do they scare you?"

"Because they have *expectations*. Because no matter where I go, there are eyes on me. Watching. Which is bad enough, but when they speak to me, it's like this crushing weight and I can't *breathe* past it. And then I stammer or stumble or worse, stand mute, and I know, I just know, they think I'm an idiot." The colour had risen in her cheeks again and her breathing was erratic. "But they're interested in my dowry, so they converse with me anyway and I want to sink through the floor every time they do."

"But you attend balls."

"Not of my own volition, I assure you. I can think of nothing worse."

"No," he said with a flash of amusement. "Me neither. So, in sum, you dislike conversing, especially with gentlemen?"

"Especially with strangers." She sighed, her shoulders slumping. "I wish I wasn't like this sometimes, but I am, and I can't change it."

"But you're not with me," he said thoughtfully. "I wonder if that has something to do with the manner by which we met."

She sent him a dark look. "If you are suggesting I kiss all acquaintances in darkened rooms, you will find yourself greatly disappointed."

"While I am certain that would do excellent things for your confidence, I am *not* suggesting that." The thought made something dark and jealous erupt in his chest, and he ignored the feeling. It would do her a world of good to learn how to give in to someone, and that sort of confidence would sit well on her.

As it was, he would just have to teach her that she was desirable.

"Then what are you suggesting?" she asked.

"Flirtation." He gave her the kind of lazy, wicked smile

he knew people never looked past—and that he knew from experience would make her blush. "Think of it as a shield. People see only what you want them to see."

"That is all very well," she said, folding her arms across her chest, "but I do not *know* how to flirt."

He remembered, somewhat against his will, the way she'd grasped his lapels in a mixture of desperation and fright while they were hiding from Helmsley. She hadn't known then—how could she—how much he had liked the action.

But there was no room for lapel-holding while in ballrooms.

"Pretend I am a gentleman approaching you," he told her now in a low voice. "Smile at me. Wider. Good. Now look up at me through your eyelashes." She gave him an unintentionally scorching glance that had heat prickling down his spine. "Excellent. Now, I will say something inane about the weather. What do you do?"

She looked at him helplessly. "Flutter my eyelashes?"

"Not a bad idea. Try it."

The way she looked as she squeezed her eyes shut and opened them in quick succession forced him to reconsider. "Softer," he said, pulling them to a halt and looking down at her. "It's a small movement."

More of that delectable blush heated her cheeks. "I've never done it before."

"Then let us move on. Bite your lip instead, like you're thinking of the answer." He demonstrated, and the way her gaze landed on his mouth sent another hot pulse of desire through him. It would be better if he didn't know how she tasted, or how innocently clumsy her mouth had been as it returned his kiss.

"Like this?" she asked, taking her bottom lip delicately

between her teeth and holding it there, the skin turning white.

"Yes," he said, sparing it only the briefest glance. "Just like that."

"And flirting is as simple as biting my lips when a gentleman speaks to me?" she asked doubtfully.

"Lip," he corrected. "And despite your scepticism, yes. Men are simple creatures."

"And yet I never know what you want."

Telling her exactly *what* most men wanted was not the best of ideas, so he settled for, "What men—what most people— want is to feel special. So smile, look interested, look at them as though they are the only thing in your world."

"How?"

He lowered his gaze to hers and focused on the gold threading through her blue eyes. The lashes that framed them faded to invisible tips, and the expression in them was at first curiously searching. Then he smiled, razoring his attention on her, and touched her arm. "Like this," he said, lowering his voice and stepping closer. She visibly swallowed. "Try it."

A flush broke out across her skin, and he really, really should not be trying to make her flush, but it was irresistible. "Stop looking at me like that," she said, her expression flitting between confused and worried.

"Peace, little bird," he said, letting amusement enter his tone. "I'm not going to eat you."

"You *look* as though you might."

The idea wasn't exactly unpleasant. "That's another business deal entirely. Unless you would like to try?" He gave her a seductive smile, and her confusion dissolved into a deeper, hotter flush.

"Beast."

"Concentrate, Beaumont. We are discussing flirtation." He paused to think of an explanation that might make sense to her, pushing all other thoughts to one side. "Think of yourself as the lure."

"The lure?"

"Fishing, sweetheart. Are you not familiar? The fisherman casts the lure and the fish, attracted to its false promises, bites the hook."

She frowned. "I am a false promise?"

"Every woman is." He took hold of her chin and her eyes widened. "Every smile you send, every time you look up through your eyelashes, every time you put your hand on their arm, you are sending out a lure. See if they bite."

"That doesn't sound very . . ." She wrinkled her nose. "Romantic."

"You may find your romance once you have the gentleman's attention." He assessed her face. Still slightly flushed, eyes sparkling. Even this would be charming enough without any overt attempt at flirtation, if only he could get her to look this way around strangers.

"My lord?" she asked cautiously as he assessed her, still pinching her chin between his fingers. Finally, he released her and looked around, finding Villiers strolling along the path in the height of good fashion.

He looked down at Annabelle. "Remember everything I've told you. It's time to practise."

"What?" She clutched at his arm. "With an actual gentleman?"

"Villiers is the perfect target," he assured her. "He's my friend and not in the market for a wife, but he is *always* in the market for a flirtation."

"I can't!"

"Of course you can. It's easy, and he'll make it especially so. Just remember all the things I've told you."

"Regular gentlemen scare me," she muttered.

Regular gentlemen. Jacob almost laughed. "I'm flattered. Now smile. He's coming over. And *relax*, little bird. There's nothing to be afraid of. If you're at a loss, remember how much you hate me."

She dug her nails into his arm and he almost laughed. But Villiers was upon them, a lazy smile on his face and his eyes alight with interest.

"Barrington," he said with casual grace. "I see you're taking your beloved for a walk. How delightful."

Jacob toyed idly with Annabelle's fingers in an attempt to ease the vise-like grip on his arm. "Just doing my duty," he said. "As you know, I take it extremely seriously."

Villiers offered Annabelle a sweeping bow. "Lady Annabelle. I'm delighted to make your acquaintance."

Jacob nudged her and she glanced up at him, eyes wide. If she were any other girl, she would have giggled, maybe blushed. Villiers was a handsome devil, that was for sure. But after he nodded at Villiers, she just plastered a mechanical smile on her face and nodded back.

"The pleasure is mine," she said, and immediately blushed to her hair.

At least her blush was pretty. If she was going to do it to everyone regardless, it was better she looked well doing it.

"It's a beautiful day," Villiers said. "Made all the more beautiful when one makes new acquaintances."

Annabelle drew in a deep breath, her body stiff and radiating tension. Her gaze dropped to the ground, and when he nudged her, she looked back up with a frightened expression, similar to the one a doe might wear when it was caught off-guard.

Petrified.

Good Lord, he was going to have to do some rethinking if this was how she responded to every gentleman except for him.

Making the snap decision to end the conversation, he nodded to his friend. "We should rejoin the Duke and Duchess."

Villiers touched his hat and Annabelle's fingers dug into his arm with what he could only assume was approval. They walked slowly away, Annabelle's face reddening still further until it looked as though she was deeply in shame.

"Well," he said with forced bravado. This deal he'd taken felt a great sight harder if she couldn't so much as *talk* to anyone else. "What happened to the flirting?"

"I *couldn't*." She closed her eyes as though in repentance. "I'm sorry, I know you tried, and I'm sure Lord Villiers is excessively agreeable, but as soon as I'm faced with gentlemen, it's as though my tongue is twisted and I feel so *stupid*. Which, of course, makes it worse, because once I feel stupid, I don't even dare look at them in case I see it on their face."

"Why should you care what they think?" As her shocked gaze met his, he shrugged. "I don't."

"Yes, but you're . . ."

"Commonly despised?" he supplied with a sardonic smile. "Deplorable? Despicable? What other epithets have you used to describe me?"

"It's different," she said, though her gaze was back on her feet.

"Only because you care for others' opinions."

120

"No," she said, glancing up at him seriously. "It's because I'm a woman. You are a man and a marquess to boot. You can get away with doing almost anything you choose. I, however, must watch my reputation. For my family's sake, if not my own."

Her damned family. And *Henry Beaumont*, Lord Eynsham, coming to disturb their peace in the next few weeks. No doubt he would find a way to disrupt things. At least, Jacob reflected grimly, no man could force him down the aisle before the summer was out.

Their three months had well and truly begun.

Chapter Thirteen

"An engagement ball?" Jacob drawled from where he was sprawled across Annabelle's sofa. While she sat primly to one side, as she'd been taught, he took up an inordinate amount of space. Although perhaps that was something to do with his sheer size.

"My sister seems to think it's necessary to announce the engagement officially." Annabelle glanced at Theo, who was writing a letter quietly in the corner, and lowered her voice. "I was hoping you would have an excuse."

"To get out of it? Aside from the rather obvious fact that all of London knows we are engaged already?"

"Precisely. And we even promenaded yesterday," she said, although she had been attempting to forget her utter failure at flirting with Viscount Villiers.

"Promenading does not an engagement make. A ball, however . . ."

She shot him a dirty look. "Much you would know on the subject."

"It appears I know more than you," he said idly. "I even brought you jewels."

The jewels in question, which were just as much of a

statement as the enormous bouquet of flowers currently displayed on a side table, belonged to an enormous ruby necklace. Annabelle had tried and failed to refuse it.

"I don't want your jewels."

He flashed her a smug smile. "I know."

"Pig."

"You are always so eloquent, little bird."

She scowled at him and he grinned back, utterly at ease in Nathanial's drawing room. She often envied the way he seemed to be at ease anywhere he went, while she struggled to fit herself in the shapes expected of the younger sister of a duchess.

Elegant, refined, charming. And now, if Jacob had his way, flirtatious.

Privately, she could not see that happening any time soon. For that, she would have to find a way of conversing with strangers *and* playing a part. It was hard enough to play the part of Annabelle Beaumont, heiress, never mind adding flirtation into the mix. Plus, the way he had reacted when she had attempted to flutter her eyelashes made her want to curl into a ball and never look at a gentleman again. Attempting to flirt made her look ridiculous.

"I think a ball is a good idea," he said slowly. "In fact, balls in general are a good idea for this to work. You will have ample opportunity to dance."

"I don't like dancing," she said flatly.

"Ah yes, of course. Just as you don't enjoy conversing. Tell me, little bird, what *do* you like?"

She looked longingly at the book she had been reading before he arrived. With everything in her life seeming to conspire against her, she was finding particular solace in books these days.

"Aside from reading," he added dryly.

"I . . . like walking. And riding. And not *all* conversing is bad."

He placed a hand to his heart in feigned shock. "Do you mean to tell me you don't hate conversing with me?"

She glared at him even as she felt her blush rising. "Of course not, and there is no need to be so obnoxious, Lord Sunderland."

"Jacob," he said lazily.

"Excuse me?"

"I don't like the title and it doesn't suit me. Call me Jacob."

"I can't!"

"Are we not engaged?"

Even engaged couples rarely called each other by their first names. In fact, Annabelle knew some married couples who still referred to each other by their titles. She could not imagine anything worse, although frankly she still hadn't come to terms with the idea of marriage at all.

"In name only," she muttered. "And besides, it's not proper."

"Dear me, Annabelle." Jacob's eyes took on a devilish twinkle, and his lips curved seductively as his gaze trailed from her lips down her neck. "I hardly think you are always proper."

She flushed and resisted the urge to fling a cushion at him and his stupid, smug face. "Do you have to say such things?"

"I recall a certain young lady in a library—this library, in fact—who took a great deal of delight in—"

"Hush," she hissed, glancing back at Theo. "Stop it!"

"Very well." He heaved a sigh and took a sip of his tea. "Tell me about this engagement ball. Is everyone to be there, or have the most elite of the *ton* made their excuses, considering it's being held in my honour?"

"It's not arranged yet. Theo suggested it to me with the understanding that I could refuse if it made me truly uncomfortable. I said I would speak to you about it."

"And hope I would refuse so you didn't have to," he finished, reading her with uncanny accuracy. "Well, unfortunately for you, little bird, I think it's an excellent opportunity for you."

"To flirt with other gentlemen? At my own engagement ball?"

"They will be delighted to get to know you."

Stubbornly, she folded her arms. He had an excellent point, because she would need to meet some other gentlemen at some point, but she had really hoped he would have found an excuse. "You will have to be sober," she said, her tone accusatory. "At the ball."

He gave her a wicked smile that made her pulse, for absolutely no reason, race. "I remember the terms of our deal, sweetheart."

"And don't call me that. We are not lovers."

"No." He left an odd pause as though he was considering it, and the fact she thought *he* was thinking about it made her recall the way he had kissed her. No doubt he was an excellent lover.

How distressing. She would rather he was terrible at it and she would never have to feel as though she was missing out on some crucial act.

Perhaps her future husband would be a wonderful lover. Somehow, though, she doubted it. From what she understood of gentlemen's tastes, they preferred to indulge *outside* the bedchamber.

125

That was not the marriage she wanted. If she were to marry, she would want a faithful husband who indulged only in her.

Perhaps she was a romantic after all.

"Do you think my future husband will allow me to retire from London?" she asked.

"If you persuaded him to," he said, casting her a low glance through his eyelashes. The sunlight streaming in through the windows added notes of gold to those dark irises. "Charm him well enough and you can become the recluse your little heart desires."

"After yesterday's performance, I'm amazed you think that still an option."

"Practise makes perfect." The look in his eyes suggested he was not only talking about flirtation. He gestured to her primrose morning dress, which was patterned with daisies. "Pretty, I grant you, but you have an excellent figure. Make more of it."

Her colour rose, again. "This is—"

"Smile at me," he commanded, and although she could not believe she was doing it, she obeyed, the authority in his voice compelling her. He nodded in approval. "There. Good. Now lower your eyelashes a little, look at me through them." She did as he asked and he gave her a charming smile in response. "Very good. You see? My confidence is never misplaced."

"Is this what the ladies who charm *you* do?" she asked, giving her book another wistful glance and pouring herself some more tea.

Darkness crossed his face, too fast for her to see the details or identify the emotion. "There are no such ladies," he said, stretching languidly, the darkness so thoroughly banished it might never have been there at all. He was, in this, the epitome of the Devil of St James. "I am immune to all charm."

"I doubt that," Annabelle said, picking up her teacup. "Do you not have a reputation for being an excellent lover?"

"What do you know about that, little bird?"

"Who *doesn't* know about it?"

He leant back in his chair, unaffected. "An excellent rejoiner. Yes, I do have quite the reputation, and I would not say it is entirely unfounded." His smile was positively sinful, making her think of silken sheets and clutching hands. Her face burned again. "But that is not because a lady charmed me into bed."

"Why do you do it, then?" she asked before she could help herself.

"For the thrill of it? For the pleasure?" His eyelids lowered, his dark eyes magnetic, and she fumbled for her tea for something to do. He may be immune to charm, but she, it transpired, was not.

"Tell me," he said, his voice indecently low. "What are your preferences in a husband?"

"My preferences?"

"A list of attributes, if you will." He leant back and smiled "So I may ensure you are introduced to the right gentlemen."

Of course. Other gentlemen. Marriage. Annabelle cleared her throat, trying to banish all improper thoughts. It was harder than it should have been. "I see," she said, the prospect making her feel vaguely ill. "How kind of you."

"Yes, that *is* one of the things I'm known for." He looked at her, waiting, and she was forced to consider what things were important to her in a life partner. Someone who would leave her alone hardly seemed like an attribute.

"Well, he must be . . . nice."

Jacob smirked. "Obviously."

"And he must read."

"Like my dear brother." There was a sardonic note to his voice, a mockery that Annabelle tried not to listen to. "Go on."

"Not too old, if possible."

"And what constitutes as too old?"

She was nineteen, nearly twenty; what was too old? "Not above forty, I think."

"A generous range."

"Are you going to mock me all morning?" she snapped.

"It's delightfully entertaining," he drawled. "But in summary, you require a bookish man under forty who will be kind and allow you to rusticate year-round at his estate."

She blinked in surprise. "Well, perhaps not year-round. I would like to continue seeing my family."

"Noted. Already I can think of several gentlemen who might appeal."

Annabelle raised her eyebrows. "You mean to say you are acquainted with men who can read?"

His bark of laughter disturbed Theo. "Vixen," he said, and she thought she even heard a trace of affection in his voice.

She might have answered in kind had the Dowager Duchess not swept into the room unannounced.

During the Dowager's illness, Annabelle had been given a reprieve from her judgemental eye and intense matchmaking. Something, of course, that was entirely unnecessary now she was so-called engaged. But what would the Dowager think of her shock engagement to Jacob?

She wanted to vomit.

"Duchess," Theo said in surprise, rising immediately to her feet. Annabelle did the same, curtsying with her face turned to the floor. Jacob frowned in her direction, but she could do no more than listen to the rushing in her ears.

Most of her acquaintances thought she was stupid, but it was far worse to know the former Duchess of Norfolk shared their opinion.

"Are you well?" Theo asked, hurrying across. "You did not say you were well enough for a visit or we should have come sooner. I thought the physician said—"

"The physician! Bah!" The Dowager lowered herself into the nearest chair, gnarled hands gripping her cane tightly. "Seemed to think a bit of pneumonia would be enough to carry me off. But I'm not done yet."

Annabelle sank back into her seat, staring at her hands. Jacob sat beside her, rather closer than before, his legs spread until his thigh almost touched her knee. She stared at the almost contact, her anxiety spiking. The Dowager had always managed to make her feel smaller than an ant. One look from her, and Annabelle was struggling to remember where her tongue was, never mind how to use it.

"I'll call for Nate," Theo said. "He won't want to miss you."

"Never mind my son," the Dowager said, and although Annabelle wasn't looking up, her heart was pounding, and she could almost feel the scratchy weight of the Dowager's attention landing on her. "I've come to speak with Annabelle here. And you, young man, I presume are Lord Sunderland."

"I am, ma'am." His tone was crisp.

"Then I am glad you have finally seen sense."

Jacob tensed beside her. "In what way, ma'am?"

"Marrying Lady Annabelle, of course," she said, and Annabelle looked up to see the Dowager looking straight at her. "You may thank me, Annabelle, for being the one to prompt this lump into action. His mother would have been disappointed in him."

The words penetrated, but it took a moment for them to lodge and make sense in her head. The *Dowager* had been the one to prompt the matter?

Annabelle's mouth fell open as the full weight of meaning crashed into her.

"You?" Theo asked in hushed, disbelieving shock. "You were the one to put the announcement in the paper?"

"Well of course." The Dowager sounded impatient, as though their shock was entirely unwarranted, but Annabelle couldn't think past the fact her own family member had manipulated her into an engagement neither of them had wanted. "When Lady Ingram said something to me about Lady Annabelle and Lord Sunderland meeting clandestinely in Lady Cavendish's garden, what else was I to say except they were engaged?" Her grey eyes were like a hawk's, piercing and not necessarily friendly. "I expected the boy to do the right thing and offer, but when he didn't, I made sure of it myself."

Jacob stood, his back ramrod straight and his eyes blazing. "You," was all he said, but his voice was like splitting ice, and Annabelle had the terrible premonition he was going to do something awful. Would he end the engagement over this? Blame her? The Dowager's choices were nothing to do with her, but if he didn't know that, or if he didn't believe her—

"Oh, sit down," the Dowager said impatiently. "I don't have the time for theatrics at my age. Yes, it was I; and yes, no doubt you think me presumptuous, given you had no intention of doing the honourable thing."

"You had no idea of my intentions, seeing as you at no point stopped to ask."

Annabelle rose too, putting her hand on Jacob's arm, and Theo stepped between them before it could turn into a confrontation. She'd never seen Jacob so angry; even when he had been furious at her, it was different.

"You should have told someone, ma'am," Theo said as Annabelle pleaded silently with Jacob not to cause a fuss. He glanced down at her like he had forgotten she was there, rage a roiling storm on his face. For one dreadful moment, she thought he would lose himself to his anger, but his expression softened a shade as he looked at her, and she was able to guide him down.

"Perhaps I would have done," the Dowager said, "if it weren't for that dreadful illness. It was all I could do to write to *The Times* and ask for an announcement to be placed."

"And you could not, in that moment, have written to us too?" Jacob enquired coldly. "Instead of forcing us to wonder."

"I had intended to call and deliver the news and my intention personally," she said, eyes narrowed at him. "I had not thought you would find yourself quite so put out at the prospect of marrying the richest heiress in London."

Annabelle wanted to close her eyes. Once again, her value was attached to her money. The only thing she had to offer a prospective husband, even according to a member of her extended family, was her dowry.

"It is not the lady I object to," Jacob said, his voice flat. "It was the manner by which I discovered I was engaged to her without so much as approaching her father."

"Then *that* fault lies in you."

"I was not aware such a rumour existed."

"Would anyone like some tea?" Theo asked desperately. "I believe the cook has made some fruitcake."

Jacob's narrowed gaze never left the Dowager's face. "If you had concerns about my honour, you should have expressed them to my face."

She tutted. "I am aware of your reputation, boy. I needed to ensure you would not ruin my granddaughter by any means necessary. She *must* have a husband, and as *you* were the one to ruin her, it must be you."

"Your Grace!" Theo said forcefully, looking at Annabelle, who knew she was flushing. Her face burned and she had every desire to sink between the sofa cushions and never emerge. "There's no need to use such language around my sister."

"Then she should know better than to consort with rakes in darkened gardens," the Dowager said dismissively. "It seems nothing we tried to teach her about decorum has stuck. And thus even Lord Sunderland is better than no husband at all, which is what would happen if they were not engaged."

Jacob's thigh shifted closer to Annabelle's. "If you had taken the time to enquire what had happened, you might have discovered that the situation was not as you thought."

"It does not matter what the situation was." The Dowager waved a dismissive hand. "All that matters is what people *think* it is." She directed her beady gaze at Annabelle, who shrank back. "I hope you have an engagement ball planned. If not, I will be happy to organise one." She made an impatient noise. "Don't look so terrified, Annabelle. An engagement ball will be good practise for when you're a marchioness. You will need to learn how to conduct yourself in Society without looking as though you're about to faint."

"I beg you will not speak to my future wife in that manner," Jacob said, still with that awful ice in his voice.

Theo motioned with her hands behind her back, clearly indicating that they should leave.

Annabelle had never wanted to leave a place so badly in her life.

"Excuse me," Jacob said, and stood. "I have just recalled an urgent engagement that requires my immediate attention." He bowed and strode from the room. Annabelle mumbled something about escorting him out and followed. As soon as the door closed behind them, he caught her hand and tugged her into the first room they came across: a small closet used for storing cleaning supplies. A mop tumbled across his shoulder as he closed the door on them, casting them into darkness.

Annabelle's heartbeat shook her entire body. She looked up at where she knew his face to be, so far above her own that he would have to lean down to kiss her.

No, she should not be thinking about kissing. Except his body was dangerously close to hers, sending her alight and forcing her to remember what had happened the last time they had been like this, lined up, his heat soaking into her like a warm bath, and his breath fanning over her face.

"Jacob?" she whispered, and he jolted. His hand found her waist, spanning it almost entirely, fingers tightening until they dug in. He didn't draw her closer, but he didn't push her away, either.

"Did you know?" he asked in a low, angry voice.

"Of course not! She has been trying to marry me off for months, but I never suspected . . ." Her voice trailed away. "I know you're angry, but—"

"Angry? I'm furious." He leant closer, and although she couldn't see him, she could sense his proximity. Every muscle in her body tightened in wild, helpless anticipation.

"Jacob," she whispered again.

"I take it back. I don't want you saying my name."

"Why?"

"Because it makes me want to do this."

The moment his mouth crushed against hers, Annabelle knew she had been lying to herself. All those times she had told herself she didn't want the Marquess to kiss her again had been a delusion. Every moment she had convinced herself that because she disliked him, she didn't want him, had been a fabrication.

There was no denying she wanted this.

He pushed her until her back collided with the wall. Something clattered to the ground beside her, but with his mouth hot on hers, his tongue sliding inside her mouth with practised sensuality, there was nothing else that existed in Annabelle's world. Of their own accord, her hands reached up and gripped his lapels, holding him closer, drinking him in like fine wine. He nipped at her lip, and foreign heat spread through her. She had never felt so alive.

She had never felt so much like she was falling.

If she had been in her right mind, she might have been petrified of the landing. The Marquess wasn't gentleman enough to catch her, and reality was sure to be a sharp, unpleasant shock. As it was, she bowed her back, pressing her body against his every way it could. Her skirts rustled as he stepped into them, one thigh between her legs, pressing up against her core, the friction sending a rush of molten pleasure through her. Unable to help herself, she moaned as he pushed his leg more firmly against her. His breath was ragged against her neck as she tipped her head back, staring into darkness.

"Do you like that?" he murmured.

"Yes, but—"

His knee rubbed more insistently against her, and his hand found her hip, gripping it in a way that made her feel as though he had reached the very edge of his control. "I need you to be quiet for me, little bird. Can you do that?"

She let out a shuddering breath, and he cupped her breast with his other hand, squeezing until her nipples pinched. She felt the touch as though it had been against her bare skin, and he let out a rough laugh, the sound barely audible in the darkness.

"Your husband will be a lucky man, Annabelle."

Her husband. Her *husband*.

Annabelle was no expert in the matter, but she rather suspected her future husband would not look kindly on her having frolicked in a darkened closet with a man whose reputation was one of ruination.

The Devil of St James. And she had almost let him ruin her, too.

He felt her hesitation and pulled away, one hand at her throat, fingers lightly pressing, the sheer possessiveness of the gesture making her head spin and her core throb with need.

"We can't," she said, shifting away from his fingers and catching something rigid at his groin with her hip. He grunted, angling himself away from her.

"Your mouth is saying one thing." With his thumb, he traced her bottom lip, and she felt the breath rush out of her on a shaky exhale. "And your body is saying another. What do you want, sweetheart?"

The flagrant rush of desire made her want to throw her

caution to the wind.

But this was not a marriage; it was an engagement. A *fake* engagement.

"We can't," she whispered. "Not here, not like this."

His hands dropped from around her, leaving her feeling bare, almost desolate in the rush of cold air. Through the darkness, she sensed his mood change, the fervour that had gripped him fading.

"Well I suppose that took the edge off," he said, voice laconic, no hint of the rasping need that had suffused him just seconds before.

Before she could formulate an answer, he opened the door and slipped out, closing it behind him and leaving her in relative darkness. A slit of light illuminated her rumpled dress. She could still feel the clasp of his fingers around her throat, the way he had sounded, cutting and cold, when he had informed her their kiss had taken the edge off.

Quietly, she pushed open the door and exited, running upstairs and to her room, which she locked behind her.

Her body still ached, still wanted him, even though she could have screamed in his face, thrown something at him, broken off their faux engagement there and then.

Two months of this. She couldn't bear it.

The sooner she found another gentleman to marry, the better.

Chapter Fourteen

The engagement ball was arranged for two weeks' time, and although Jacob sent Annabelle several gifts to keep up the pretence, he made excuses not to see her. She probably thought the worst of him, but the truth was, he was ashamed. For five years, he had kept his heart and his cock entirely separate; he never lost control.

Never.

Until he had pushed Annabelle Beaumont into a closet and attempted to ravish her. *Would* have ravished her if she had not put a stop to it. It was beneath him and he should have known better.

It exposed a weakness in him that he hadn't thought he still possessed. Despite his every intention, it transpired a pair of big blue eyes and pretty lips could make him forget himself, and when he was furious at the Dowager Duchess, unable to do anything about it without hurting Annabelle or her family, his control had slipped.

And it had been the most intoxicating kiss of his life. Little Annabelle Beaumont, the lady he had every intention of marrying to someone else, had kissed him with all the passion of a lady well practised in the art of kissing. But unless something had changed, she had just become practised at kissing *him*. A fast learner.

He still wanted her. And *that* was his main reason for staying away. If he could not rely on his restraint to hold himself in check, he could not trust himself being around her. Neither of them could afford for him to be carried away. He attended two boxing matches and took to training at Gentleman Jackson's club just to work off the excess energy.

On the day of the ball, he arrived early to dine with the family, and he saw Annabelle for the first time in two weeks. She was pale, eyes dark like the dusk sky, and any attempt he'd made to convince himself he was unaffected by what had taken place between them was immediately dashed. The moment he saw her face, he felt the soft, gasping way she had moaned in his ear when he had pressed his knee between her legs.

He wondered if she could climax that way, and the thought was so immediately erotic, he felt himself harden.

This was not what he'd had in mind for the evening.

Then he noticed the Dowager Duchess of Norfolk and all thoughts of seduction left his head. Anger swept in its place, and Annabelle's face, which had been distant and resolute, melted into a look of pleading.

Damn it, he could have borne anything but that.

"Lord Sunderland," the Dowager Duchess said without preamble when she saw him. "I do hope you're past that terrible temper outburst you showed the last time we met."

Annabelle stiffened, and he knew precisely what she was thinking: no, he was not past it. The Devil of St James, the man who had pulled her into a closet and kissed her senseless, did not have it within himself to bite his tongue.

138

His temper grated against his restraint, and he gritted his teeth behind his smile as he bowed. "If you're asking if I have forgiven you, ma'am, then you surely know the answer as well as I."

She tutted and tapped her fan against his hand in admonishment as the Duchess of Norfolk, to his surprise, took his other hand as she curtsied. Her face was almost as pale as Annbaelle's, and there were unusual dark circles under her eyes, but she sent him an apologetic glance.

At least the Dowager Duchess's actions had resulted in another ally. Although, of course, if she knew his true purpose in coming here and attending the ball, she would revoke that soon enough.

Strange. He had never wanted anyone's approval before. His entire reputation, in fact, had been based on the assumption that he craved no one's approbation, and especially not by anyone close to him.

Annabelle took his proffered arm without a smile, her eyes remote, and he led her into the dining room behind the Duke and Duchess. Dinner passed quickly without so much as a word directed to him from Annabelle, the Dowager Duchess dominating much of the conversation. The anger he had repressed rose with every word, making it difficult to eat, and it was a relief to collect Annabelle and wait for the guests to arrive.

"I presume your intention this evening is to say nothing to me," he murmured after the first few guests arrived.

She stiffened. "What could I possibly have to say to you?"

His gaze fell to the large ruby necklace she wore—the one he had gifted her. "It looks well on you."

"Theo insisted I wear it."

139

"Then she has excellent taste."

"I beg to differ." Her tone was frosty, and he glanced down at the top of her head. Her golden hair was in pretty ringlets, but he was transfixed by the tendrils of soft curls at the back of her tender neck. She was heartbreakingly lovely in the cream silk, and her clear dismissal of him stung, his insides twisting oddly.

"I see you are still on speaking terms with the Dowager Duchess even after she manipulated the both of us."

Annabelle let out a tiny hissing breath before being forced to smile at yet another guest. Jacob greeted them absently, far more interested by the soft, angry flush that rose on Annabelle's neck. He should not feel so victorious at provoking this sort of response from her, but anger sat on her like a crown, and anything was better than the cool distance she had greeted him with at the beginning.

"Is there anything else I can do?" she demanded in a low voice. "She is Nathanial's mother and she thinks I am a disappointment. He has spoken with her, but the thing is done now."

"It should not have been."

"If you think you will gain anything by pointing that out to her, then by all means, go ahead."

He clenched his jaw. "Don't push me, little bird. I could just as easily end this arrangement. I only entered it for your sake."

"Your reputation would be destroyed if you pulled out of an engagement of honour."

"Do you really think that would change anything?" He gave a bitter little laugh. "Destroying my reputation has been my goal since I was old enough to understand the name I carried."

She frowned as she glanced at him. "Why?"

"Is it not obvious? Because I despise my family and everything they stand for." He smiled at another set of guests. There were plenty—he supposed this was what happened when a duchess sent the invitations.

"You despise your family? Why?"

"This is hardly a conversation for the present time."

"If you would rather not tell me, you may just say so." She exchanged her glower for a smile as yet more guests entered the house.

"Very well: I would rather not tell you. Satisfied?"

"Not at all," she said icily.

They said nothing more as they finally finished greeting the endless line of guests and entered the ballroom together.

"Smile," he reminded her. "If you can remember how."

She stiffened under the hand on her back. A dangerous place for his hand to be—it made him think of all the other places he'd touched her.

"Perhaps you should leave," she said, her voice equally low but her eyes flashing a little too brightly when she looked up at him.

Good, this was good. He needed her anger, not her desire. He had more than enough desire for the both of them.

"And here I was thinking you delighted in my company," he murmured.

"I have no idea what gave you that impression."

"Oh, I do." He leant in closer, the warm press of her arm against his chest his own personal lure. "If you recall, when we were in the closet, you—"

"Enough!" She pushed him back with a hand on his chest and seemed to realise it a second after he did, curling her fingers into a fist and snatching it back. Her colour was high and she looked abominably pretty. "Seeing as you never wanted to marry me in the first place, maybe I should be the one to call off the engagement."

"I don't think you would." He smirked at her. "You enjoy kissing me too much to—"

She did not slap him, but he saw the temptation written across her face, and he knew he had crossed a line. Taunted her too far. Hurt and anger crossed her face and she yanked her arm free.

"Annabelle," he said, reaching for her, "wait."

With a dexterity he had not expected, she dodged him and weaved through the crush, ignoring several people who called to her.

Damn. He curled his hand into a fist, trying to ignore the urge to find the nearest drink. That was yet another promise he had made to her.

What was it about her that made him want to do this? To hurt her?

Louisa raised her glass from where she stood nearby. "That went well," she said dryly. "You truly are talented at pushing people away."

"Usually that is not an issue." He ground his teeth together. This evening had been a disaster already, and he could feel the Dowager's eyes on him. The temptation to confront her conflicted with the need to chase after Annabelle and erase the hurt on her face.

She had no right inspiring a protective instinct in him when he had spent five years pretending he had none.

"She isn't usual." Louisa flicked her fingers after Annabelle. "Go after her and use some of that charm to repair the damage before it's too late. Then, unless you've changed your mind about marrying her yourself, introduce her to me. I'll look after her—and a deal sight better than you will, judging by your performance."

At the thought of introducing her to other gentlemen, every muscle in Jacob's body tensed. But, of course, Louisa was right, and he didn't want to marry Annabelle. She deserved someone better than him. Someone who could love her instead of just wanting her; someone who wasn't despised by the vast majority of Society. Even his title didn't make up for that, and she wasn't someone who cared about position or wealth. She wanted respect and peace.

Two things he did not command.

"Go," Louisa said, shooing him away. "Grovel. There is nothing more a young woman likes than to see the man she hates on his knees before her."

"I'm not adept at grovelling."

"Then learn. Surely you can at least do it for her."

There was no *at least* for Annabelle; she was not the exception to his rules. He wouldn't let her be. But he did need to find her.

"I'll bring her to you," he said, and turned on his heel, striding through the crowd. Annabelle was nowhere he could see inside the ballroom, and although she could have been outside, he doubted she would risk it after the last time.

There was only one other place she could be.

He almost laughed at the inevitability of it as he walked the now somewhat familiar halls of Norfolk House until he came to the library.

This time, there was a lamp casting golden light across the floor and the window, and Annabelle was curled on the window seat, her dress falling beside her, utterly absorbed in a book. There was an uneven stack of novels on the table beside her, he noted, and as she read, the pad of her thumb brushed the soft edges of her page. The faint rasp, imperceptible except in the break in music and laughter that drifted towards them, was almost enough to send him mad.

For a moment, he merely watched her. The anxious line between her brows was absent here; she looked at peace.

He was going to disturb that.

With an odd fierceness, he found he didn't *want* to disrupt her. This odd picture of domesticity sent an uncomfortable coiling sensation into his stomach, and he rolled his shoulders, trying to dispel the feeling.

This was a deal and it had always been. The only reason he had entered this sham engagement was to save her reputation by finding her another, and neither of them were going to find one in the library.

"You know, you should really lock the door," he said conversationally as he strolled towards her. "Anyone could get in."

She jolted and looked up, and he saw with a lurch that she had been crying.

All other thoughts left his head. She had been crying . . . because of him.

"Leave me alone," she said, turning back to her book. "I don't want you here."

He dropped to his knees in front of her. "Annabelle, I—"

"It's Lady Annabelle to you."

"Annabelle." He gave her a grin he didn't feel. "Don't shut me out. Be angry at me. What happened to the temper you cannot help when you are around me?"

"I have nothing to say to you."

"Not even to abuse me to my face?" He reached for her hand but she drew hers away, and he cursed himself. This was not the sort of situation he was accustomed to. "I apologise," he said abruptly, holding her gaze. "What I said was out of order."

"Yes. It was."

"I never intended to hurt you." He almost said that he hadn't thought her capable of being hurt, but that was unfair. He had known, of course he had, that she was sensitive, and he was someone who had seen some of her most unguarded moments.

He had taken advantage of her most unguarded moments.

She looked down again, but before she did, he caught the glisten in her eyes, and it was like a punch to his gut. Normally, no one cared enough about him one way or the other to cry when he disappointed them. But Annabelle had, and watching it made him ache.

"I'm your servant," he said, taking her hand and retaining it when she tried to pull away. "At your mercy. What would you have me do?"

"Go away."

He attempted another smile. "Anything but that. You see, little bird, there is a ballroom filled with guests hoping to see us, and I am honour-bound to take you back, much as I know you would rather remain here."

"Without you," she said, although she was no longer trying to remove her hand from his.

"Without me," he repeated, the words carrying an odd little sting.

"And you are not honour-bound." Her gaze cut back to his, tears gone and her eyes blazing. Looking into them was a little like looking into the sun, and much as he had done when he was a boy, braving the damage, he held his gaze.

"Very well, I am a rogue. But for tonight, I am your rogue, and I have made a promise I intend to keep."

She sighed, looking tired and so sad, he had the irrational urge to gather her into his arms.

This was not the behaviour of the Devil. But when he was with her, he was nothing like the man he had driven himself to become, and the thought held a vague fear with it.

"I don't want to fight with you again," she said eventually, and the rush of relief made him exhale sharply. "I'm too tired."

"Then I shall be on my best behaviour." His knees ached so he rose and sat beside her. "What book are you reading?" He tilted the cover towards him so he could read the embossed cover. "*Belinda?*"

"It's one of my favourites," she said defensively.

"Then I'm certain it's excellent. What's it about?"

A tiny line appeared between her brows. "Do you really want to know?"

"Of course I do," he said, and found he meant it. Reading as an activity had never held any draw, but that was largely because it was *Cecil's* chosen activity, and if it was Cecil's, it could not be his. With Annabelle, though, the appeal of books was different. He found himself interested in anything that could make her eyes light like twin stars. The sadness melted from her face as she looked back at the book.

"I suppose it's about people," she said thoughtfully. "And the misconceptions we can have when we judge with incomplete information. And it's about love, of course."

"Of course," he echoed. "Tell me, Annabelle, are books like these why you never wanted to marry? Because you thought no gentleman could match up to the ones you have read about?"

"Well . . ." Her cheeks flushed, just as delectable when the underlying emotion was self-consciousness as when it had been anger. Perhaps even more so. "Not precisely, although no man *has* lived up to the ones in books. I merely . . . Theo had her great love—that's enough for me. I'm content to read."

"And you never thought that perhaps someone could love you as much as the Duke loves your sister?"

A pale brow rose as she glanced at him. "Why would he?"

Because you are captivating.

Crushing that rogue, alarming thought, he stood and held out his hand. "Because, sweetheart, you are going to be the belle of the ball. Come, I have a friend I would like to introduce you to. She has promised to help find you a husband."

Annabelle eyed him dubiously, but she accepted his hand. He tucked it in his arm and led her back to the ballroom. The door was cracked, and they slipped in discreetly. Her chin trembled as they stepped into the overpowering swirl of heat and sweat, and he wanted to lead her right back out to the library.

But he had made her a promise.

"My friend's name is Lady Bolton," he said, leading her confidently through the fray. "She's a little older, a widow, and—don't give me that look, little bird. She is nothing but a friend. We met after another gentleman broke her heart, and she's been pining away for him ever since, though she would never admit it." And that gentleman was Lord Eyresham, Annabelle's brother.

"That sounds sad," Annabelle said with a frown.

"Oh, she won't make you feel like she's sad. And she

would never forgive you for pitying her, so make sure you don't. She lives a charmed life now, with all the freedom and independence a lady could want. She'll make you an excellent friend."

"What if she doesn't want to be my friend?" Annabelle asked, sounding as though she was genuinely concerned about the prospect.

"Impossible." He steered her to where Louisa was standing, an expression of distinct amusement on her face as she watched them approach. "Lady Bolton, may I present the delightful Lady Annabelle Beaumont?"

Chapter Fifteen

Annabelle waited for the inevitable moment where she wanted to shrink back into obscurity as Lady Bolton looked at her. Curiously, it didn't come. Lady Bolton had the same air of unshakable confidence as Jacob, but when she smiled, the confidence was replaced by gentle understanding that put Annabelle immediately at ease.

"It's all so overwhelming, isn't it?" she asked, nodding at the crowd and the lights and the flowers and the *noise*. It scraped at Annabelle's senses, rubbing them raw. "I remember when I was first out, I hated it."

"What did you do?" Annabelle asked, unable to help herself.

"I fell in love. Nasty business; I don't recommend it." She gave a lively smile that made her hazel eyes twinkle. Closer to thirty than she was twenty, she was someone Annabelle's mother would have referred to as 'on the shelf' if she had been unmarried. Yet despite the very fine lines around her eyes, and the sense of weary disillusionment that cloaked her, she was rather devastatingly beautiful. It was to do with the way she held herself, wearing a shimmering green gown that caught the light and sent it sparkling back in every direction.

Annabelle wanted to learn how to be like her.

"But," Lady Bolton continued, "I then married an older gentleman, retired to the country for a few years to further refine myself and establish myself as a lady, and when I returned to London I discovered it wasn't as terrifying as I'd believed it to be."

"It was never terrifying, you just hadn't found your place in it," Jacob said, gazing out across the crowd. "There's Mr Comerford. Son of a viscount, I believe, and fond of a more gentle life." He flashed a brilliant smile that Annabelle was coming to suspect hid something. "As you can imagine, I can count on one hand the number of times we've attended the same events. Louisa, you should introduce her."

Annabelle's heart rate accelerated. Mr Comerford was with a large group of young men, and as she had learnt from experience, groups of gentlemen were far worse than ones on their own. And ones on their own were bad enough. Her palms began to sweat. Would they laugh at her once they realised she was incapable of stringing more than two words together?

"Jacob," Lady Bolton ordered. "Look at her."

With a raised eyebrow, he did so, and Annabelle tried not to notice the flash of heat that split his dark eyes like lightning when he glanced at her mouth, so quickly if she hadn't been looking, she would have missed it.

"Now," she continued. "Tell her what they will see."

He sent Lady Bolton an impatient look. "What is this achieving?"

"Just do it."

"Very well." He turned back to Annabelle and took her hand, lowering his voice until it felt as though there was no one else in the room. She still didn't know how he could do that, make

150

her forget the world whenever he fixed his full attention on her.

She licked her lips and his eyes darkened into pitch.

"They will see a beautiful young lady approaching them," he said, his voice mesmerising. "Shy, but prettier because of it, and utterly oblivious to her own charms. The way she blushes ought to be criminal."

Heat swept over her, head to toe, and he gave an appreciative, sensual smile that sent heat flooding through her.

"They know that you are engaged to me, and they will be curious that you, of all the young ladies I could have married, are my choice. They will be thinking the kind of thoughts that should never be uttered aloud in a ballroom. And they'll be wondering if they can convince you to change your mind. Both for the money, and so they have an opportunity to know what those sweet lips taste like."

"That's enough," Lady Bolton said, her voice alive with merriment. "One would think you're preparing her for you, not other gentlemen."

He gave her a dirty look Annabelle could barely process through her reeling senses. "You asked me to describe what they would see."

"And you did an admirable job." She patted his shoulder in the kind of dismissal Annabelle had often longed to give him. "Now go and brood somewhere visible."

"No doubt you think this is hilarious," he muttered, dropping Annabelle's hand as though it burned him and striding through the crowd. Several young ladies hailed him, but he barely paused, giving them a brief nod before reaching the refreshments.

"Now," Lady Bolton said, tucking Annabelle's hand under

her arm. "Shall we find an eligible gentleman?"

Annabelle's knees were weak, certainly not structurally sound enough for walking through the crowd, but Lady Bolton didn't seem to notice, practically dragging Annabelle along after her.

"Now, remember," Lady Bolton said, "Jacob Barrington is a connoisseur of beauty, and he doesn't give compliments lightly. You may be sure he told the truth."

"But those ridiculous things—"

"If you keep your head up, they will think you beautiful." Lady Bolton gave a small, derisive snort. "And if you say nothing, they will think you all the more so."

"So I should *not* say anything?"

"If you're feeling tongue-tied, merely smile. It'll take some time to get used to, but once you've mastered it, it will be your defence for all things. Remember." She turned back with an oddly twisted expression. "You, the core of you, is sheltering within the armour of your body. Close yourself off to the arrows of their derision, and I promise they will not land."

Annabelle blinked. She had not thought of her skin as armour before, had not thought she might be able to crawl up inside herself and hide from the barrage of words and sensations around her, all while keeping a smile on her face.

"You see, surviving Society is merely about having the tools to do so," Lady Bolton said. "Now remember what Jacob told you. Here we go."

They approached a small group of gentlemen, and she broke on them like a crashing wave, splitting them with an air of cultured pleasure, and isolating a young blonde man.

"Mr Comerford," she said, cooing with practised delight. "How delightful to see you."

With effort, Annabelle kept her head up and the smile on her lips. Her heart pounded and her palms were sweaty, but every time she considered bolting, she remembered the way Jacob had looked at her, and the way he had said every gentleman would be wondering how her sweet lips would taste.

Did that mean he thought her lips were sweet? Did *he* want to taste them again?

Mr Comerford bowed to her and she hitched her smile back into place, forcing her thoughts away from Jacob and to the gentleman in front of her. "Lady Annabelle," he said. "I have not yet had the pleasure of meeting you this Season."

Her skin felt clammy and her tongue was in knots. But when she looked up into his face, she realised his warmth was genuine, and he had kind brown eyes. Not the intense dark of Jacob's but a softer shade that made her think of spring days.

"Indeed," she said, her voice managing to sound relatively normal rather than her usual breathy fare. "It's a pleasure."

"The pleasure is mine." He took her hand and pressed his lips to her knuckles in a pointed gesture. "A shame it came a little too late, I suppose. Still, I don't suppose you would honour me with a dance?"

Annabelle glanced at Lady Bolton, who gave an imperceptible nod. In the distance, standing at the edge of the ballroom with a glass of punch in his hands, was Lord Sunderland. Jacob. Her Marquess. He was watching her from across the room, just as brooding as Lady Bolton had instructed.

Maybe he was in love with Lady Bolton. That would explain why he had obeyed her every command.

The thought sank like a stone to the bottom of her stomach, and she sucked in a deep breath.

"I would be delighted," she said to Mr Comerford, accepting

his hand and allowing him to lead her into the centre of the room.

* * *

Jacob sipped his drink, feeling again the ridiculousness of the situation as he watched Annabelle smile up at her partner. It was a hesitant smile, not like the occasional wide smile she'd given when she knew no one was looking, but it was something. More than he had expected.

And while she was there enjoying herself and charming another gentleman into wanting her, he was condemned to bore himself by watching. Usually, by this time in the proceedings, he would have already made his way into the card room, letting people believe he could think of nothing but whist and pharaoh. Given the alternative, it was hardly a poor choice.

Instead, he was here. He ground his teeth, placing his half-full glass on a table. He'd made Annabelle a promise that he wouldn't drink while they were together, but the urge to dull the sensations in his chest wouldn't leave him.

He was becoming precisely the man his father and Cecil had thought him to be; it was no longer a pretence. The thought should have comforted him, but it felt a little as though he had swallowed jagged glass.

The Duke of Norfolk came to stand beside him, leaning against the wall with deceptive idleness. "She's lovely, isn't she?" he said, nodding towards Annabelle. "We're both very fond of her."

Jacob sent Norfolk a sidelong glance. They were only a few years apart in age, but they ran in very different circles. "I have no doubt."

"I know you never wanted to marry her," the Duke said. "And I know she doesn't want to be married. In another world, I'd indulge her. But we don't always have a choice. And I should warn you now, Barrington—if you ever, ever hurt her, you will feel the consequences."

"A trifle overdone, don't you think?" Jacob drawled, knowing it would irritate, needing it to. He wanted to dig his claws into something and make it hurt. The urge was primal and he wasn't sure from where it originated. "I think Lady Annabelle and I have come to an understanding."

"Oh?"

Jacob had no intention of explaining the terms. "Suffice to say she's satisfied."

"She looks it," Norfolk said dryly, watching her smile at her partner. The urge to rip things to shreds increased. "If she asked it, would you let her retire from society?"

Considering they were not intending to marry, it hardly mattered what he said. He gave Norfolk a cool smile. "If she asked, she could have the moon on a platter."

"I see."

"If you wanted to allow her not to marry, you should not have placed the burden of a large dowry on her head."

"Is that your way of saying you're marrying her for her money?"

"We're engaged to save her reputation." He gave the Duke a long look. "I hardly care for mine."

Across the room, Annabelle was dancing with another gentleman. Now she was making her interest known, the gentlemen were lining up for her attention and the soft, shy smiles she passed around like delicate treasures. His plan was working and no doubt soon, with enough prompting that she would be receptive, she would have at least *someone* prepared to marry her.

He cast a disgusted look at the punch beside him, wishing it was wine, and snatched it up. It shouldn't have stung, seeing her prefer others the way everyone else did, but somehow it did.

The Duke of Norfolk was still watching him, so he made his way to the refreshment table, taking a glass of wine with him, and continued to the open doors leading to the patio. The curtains fluttered behind him and the moon scowled coldly on the garden.

He stared at the world beyond, but although the wine was held loosely in his hands, he made no move to drink it.

Chapter Sixteen

Annabelle lost track of the hours. Jacob's words still lingered in her head, and she was learning to read the expression on gentlemen's faces when they looked at her. The want, half concealed, the way their gazes lingered on her mouth. If there was one thing she was concluding from this ball, it was that men liked mouths. Lips were something they paid special attention to.

Smiling was easier than talking, and she discovered that if she gave an encouraging smile to a gentleman, he needed nothing more from her. Strange how she had never unlocked the power before, though that was probably because she had never looked into the gentleman's face as often until now. So while her brain worked overtime and she dissected every comment delivered to her with a physician's precision, she found she was able to uphold a conversation by doing little more than maintaining her expression. Occasionally, she found, a word here or there was necessary, but often the smile would do.

It was a trick she wished she had learnt years ago.

Still, after her third dance in which she did nothing but smile until her cheeks hurt, stuck on the outside of a discourse which she really had no part in, she was exhausted. All she wanted was the comfort of a friend with whom she could *talk*. Express her opinions. The gentlemen she had been dancing with would have been surprised to know she had opinions.

The thought of doing this every year for the rest of her life filled her with a peculiar sense of dread. As a single woman, after a few Seasons she would have been able to largely retire from Society; as a married woman, she would not have that luxury.

The prospect was horrifying.

After her fifth partner bid her farewell, she cast a look around for Jacob, who had abandoned his brooding for something else. Theo was talking with their mother, her fan working overtime, and Annabelle would have joined them except she didn't want to face their questions.

There was nothing for it—she took refuge behind her potted plants. There was no book this time, but at least she had the luxury of some space to pull herself together. She released a long, slow breath. The music still continued, a lively jig that sent her thoughts flurrying about her head, and the overbearing noise of the ball ground her down until she felt like a husk. Like dust, blown about in the wind, reduced to nothing. If she could have had her way, she would have sent everyone home at midnight. As it was, the ball would likely continue until daybreak unless something drastic happened.

What if she faked an illness? Theo would whisk her away from the ball immediately.

But then she'd worry her sister unnecessarily, and that seemed cruel.

Maybe she would just stay here. At least for a few more minutes until her heart rate slowed. Until she would be able to put the smile back on her face without snapping.

"There she is!" A hand reached down and pulled her up, and the unwelcomely familiar face of Lady Tabitha came into view. "Don't tell me you were resting on a night like tonight." She was accompanied by a gaggle of other debutantes, looking at Annabelle with mingled curiosity, envy and pity. "You have to tell us how you did it."

"We already know how she did it," another girl said. Her aquiline nose was a little upturned. "She lured Lord Sunderland into the garden and as soon as rumour spread, he had no choice but to marry her."

Annabelle gaped, her face flushing, her tongue doing its usual job of sticking to the roof of her mouth. Under their beady eyes and not-so-silent judgement, she felt as small as a caterpillar under their feet: easily squashed.

"That's not fair, Lucy," another voice said. This girl looked kinder and a little older; not a debutante in her first Season, then. "I've seen the way he looks at her."

"Ruination," the first girl snorted. "That's all it amounts to."

"How did you manage it?" Lady Tabitha pressed. "I mean, to entice him out into the gardens with you alone."

Annabelle wanted to close her eyes and disappear. "I-I didn't."

"You must have done *something*," the first girl said impatiently. "Why else would he be hanging around you like this? Everyone knows the Devil of St James had no plans of marriage."

"That's why it's so ingenious," Lady Tabitha said. "How else could she ensure a marriage with him? And after his brother died and he inherited. I wish I had your foresight!"

"No," Annabelle tried. "I didn't."

But the girls kept pushing around her, crushing her, making her hot and uncomfortable and pressed to answer questions she had no answer to. Like "what is he like?" and "is he as devastating as I heard?"

He was devastating, in his own way. Criminally long eyelashes around eyes so dark they could have held the night sky, wicked amusement gleaming in them like the cold moon. His mouth was a sensual slash, caught halfway between mockery and an odd grimness that sat unsettlingly on a man so young. Perhaps that was how he had become a rake in the first place, because he had a masculine beauty no lady could deny.

"Excuse me," came the voice she was looking for. When she glanced up, it was to find that dark gaze pinning her to the floor. Within it, she was utterly caught. "I have come to collect my bride-to-be."

At once the girls parted, and Jacob strode up to her. His eyes were hard, glittering with anger, but his fingers were gentle as they took hold of hers. "My lady," he said, his voice low and intimate. Slowly, achingly slowly, he brought her knuckles to his lips and kissed them.

Annabelle felt that kiss all over, in places she should adamantly not. Under her gloves, her skin burned.

Lady Tabitha's titter was loud enough to disturb nesting birds, but Annabelle hardly noticed. Her embarrassment faded as he took her hand and led her away. Past the musicians sawing at their strings, past Theo and her mother, who watched her with a cautious look in their eyes, and out onto the patio.

"There," Jacob said briefly, releasing her hand. "Take a breath."

160

"Thank you, I—"

"Don't thank me. Just breathe and stop your fretting over their opinion. They're not worth your time or energy."

"Easy for you to say."

"Is it?" His gaze rested on her for a moment, and she knew now that in the light, they were brown threaded with gold. Compelling enough for her to fall into; deep enough she might drown.

He reached for a glass he had rested on the windowsill, breaking her gaze, and she noticed it was filled with wine. "You're drinking," she accused.

"On the contrary; I have yet to have a sip. But I thought you might like some." At her start, he gave a half-smile. Not cocky or arrogant or pointedly sensual, like so many of his smiles had been, but an expression of genuine amusement. "Don't look at me like that, little bird. There comes a point when there's nothing else for it. Sometimes you need a little liquid courage."

"You appear to need liquid courage often."

"Live a day in my shoes and you might understand why." He offered her the glass and this time she took it. The burgundy was rich and almost sour against her tongue, strong enough she made a face. At home, she only ever had ratafia or lemonade. But under his curious gaze, she took another, then another, until she'd finished the last of it.

"It's not bad," she said eventually.

"You'll get used to it."

"I'm not sure I want to." She looked at him. "I've seen what it can do."

His expression flickered, just for a moment, then he took the glass and put it carefully to one side. "If you are just going

161

to lecture me, feel free to leave."

Even a few hours ago, she might have done, if he had not apologised to her. But something had changed between them—or perhaps she was the one who had changed. Out here, in full view of the ballroom, he didn't look like a rake capable of eating women's hearts for breakfast. He just looked tired, the sharpness in his expression worn away, lines appearing that she hadn't seen before.

Perhaps his reputation was as exhausting to maintain as her facade. Having people hate him had to be draining, just as trying to convince people to like her made her feel as though her energy was being sucked dry.

Earlier that evening, she had thought she could not hate him more, but now she thought perhaps she didn't hate him at all. He was the same as her, just angrier. Maybe hurting more.

They stood in silence for a while, the soft air of early summer refreshing after the stifling heat of the ballroom, and she thought about how easy it was to be with him. No pointless conversation to fill the silence; he was as comfortable in it as she was. He had no expectations of her other than she should be herself, and that was remarkably freeing.

"So," he drawled, dragging his attention back to her. "How did you enjoy yourself?"

"I didn't meet anyone I wanted to marry."

He tensed. "Is that so? It's early days yet."

"You know, not one of them asked me about my opinion on any matter we discussed. Or should I say, *they* discussed."

A reluctant laugh broke from him, husky and low. Too intimate for the bright candlelight behind them. "Am I supposed to be surprised?"

"But why? Even the kind ones were . . ." She struggled to find a word. "Dismissive. Why is that?"

"Probably because they have greater respect for their opinions than yours."

"Do you?"

He contemplated that for a moment, a crease appearing between his brows. "No," he said eventually.

"Why is that?"

"Probably because I was never taught to respect my opinions." Bitterness coated his words like the bite of November snow. "And despite all appearances to the contrary, you do have a brain."

"A good thing you're trying not to charm me," she said, and he gave a snort.

"I rather suspect that ship has long since sailed."

"And sunk."

"In full view of the harbour."

It was her turn to laugh—not a delicate thing, either. It came straight from her belly and erupted into the night air. He half turned, a line appearing between his brows.

"That's the first time I've heard you laugh," he said. "Genuinely, I mean."

"I could say the same about you."

"What a pair we are," he mused, the amusement turning wry. "Are you so very unhappy, Annabelle?"

"Not *so* very most of the time. I enjoy reading." Instinctively, she thought back to Jacob's brother and the way he had discussed books with her. At the time, she had not wanted to marry anyone at all, but if any one of her partners this evening had entered a discussion, not a one-sided monologue, she would have considered him as a potential marriage partner.

How short-sighted she had been to dismiss him so easily.

She sighed and he glanced at her. "What are you thinking, little bird?"

"Your brother enjoyed reading, too," she said, leaning against the wall as she looked across the garden.

"I'm aware."

"He offered to bring me some books he thought I would enjoy."

Something shuttered in Jacob, and although he gave her a smile, it was a little too mocking. "If it were anyone other than my brother, I might have suspected him of trying to seduce you." He picked up the glass, running his finger along the rim in a way that was downright sensual. "Then again, given the way you seem to adore books, perhaps it would have worked."

"He *listened* to me."

Jacob's eyes were very dark. "Did he now?"

"We debated the merits of female authors and how easy it is, or isn't, to become one."

"Riveting." There was a hard edge to his voice, but Annabelle was looking into the distance, away from him, lost in the past.

"If he were alive now, he would be the man I would choose."

Silence followed her words, but this was not like the silence they had shared before. This was sharp, slicing into her, and she looked back at him, frowning. His fingers had stilled on the glass, and he looked oddly distant, as though he was carved from marble.

"I assure you," he said, giving her a bow that felt vaguely contemptuous, "you would not be the first."

Then she was alone on the patio.

Chapter Seventeen

It was with great reluctance that Jacob moved into his brother's house. Long ago, it had been his father's, too, and as he walked through the empty rooms, furniture swathed in white sheets, the ghosts of memory tickled his senses. The library was large and spacious, filled with books that had been collected over generations.

The scars across his back throbbed with memory. In front of the fireplace, his father had beaten him with a poker.

The drawing room was a little dated now, last decorated at the turn of the century. Here, on the sofa, Cecil had stabbed him with his quill so hard the injury bled for three hours. He rubbed the scar on his arm unconsciously.

Of course, Cecil had apologised, penitent yet somehow still righteous. He had only behaved that way because of Jacob; if Jacob hadn't been so *difficult*, Cecil would never have hurt him.

The wound had hurt, but not as much as the memory did.

As an adult, Cecil would never have done such a thing—but as an adult, Cecil's crimes had been different and far worse. Jacob would have endured any amount of physical injury if Cecil had just done the right thing by Madeline. Maybe then, she would still have been alive.

If Jacob had his way, he would burn this place to the ground, memories and all. That would best match his intentions of destroying his family's reputation once and for all. What better revenge than burning down the very house his father had so adored? Generations of Barringtons up in smoke.

But the idea no longer held the appeal it once had. If he destroyed all his inheritance, he would be penniless, forced to endure on the fringes of Society, left with no money to his name. Or worse, he would be arrested, though he wasn't sure it counted as a crime if it were his own property.

Perhaps he should consult his lawyer.

Then again, he could take a look at what would need to be done to maintain the estate. Perhaps he could sell this house and purchase another. Far less destructive. And would a quiet life really be so bad? Once, he had thought it would be the worst kind of hell, but recently . . .

Like clockwork, he thought of Annabelle. The wistful look in her eyes when she said she would have preferred Cecil.

Her and everyone else.

Even dead, his brother was preferable.

He should not have yielded to the ridiculous urge to match up to his brother this morning. Annabelle's opinion of him would not be swayed by one small gift, and nor should it be. Once the summer ended, they would go their different ways and this part of his life would be over. And good riddance.

Gritting his teeth, he squashed the lingering hurt and strode into the study. Cecil's study; his father's study. The room smelt faintly of cigar smoke, and even though Cecil had sat here for the past ten years, Jacob could still imagine his father behind the desk, examining the results of his profligacy. Even now, bills awaited him, piling high on the desk. Bills and letters from his man of business, letters from his steward, invitations for Cecil that had continued to pour in the week or two after his death before news of it reached every household in London. Those were the first to go; Jacob did not even glance at them as he tossed them into the empty hearth. Then he rang the bellpull.

"My lord?" The butler, Smythe, was as austere and disapproving as always. No doubt Jacob would receive his letter of resignation soon enough now he had officially moved into the house.

"I want all this moved," Jacob said, nodding to the stack of papers. He considered asking for a scotch, but something stopped him. "Take it to the small parlour."

"Sir?"

"I'll have it converted into a new study. I will work in there."

Smythe's grey eyebrows rose in surprise. "You're intending to see to the post, my lord?"

"Yes, Smythe." Jacob fixed his butler with an icy glare. "Do you have a problem with that?"

Smythe gave a stiff, unwilling bow. "Not at all, sir."

"Then arrange to have this moved and have done with it."

"Very good, sir." With one last disapproving sweep of the room, Smythe took his leave, no doubt to fetch the footmen. Jacob left immediately, preferring to escape the cigar smoke and the residual panic that *still* flared at the scent.

Twenty-six and haunted by a smell. It was pathetic.

While all the paperwork was moved, he took a short lunch and did not once allow his thoughts to stray towards Annabelle.

* * *

Norfolk House was a flurry of activity. Annabelle's mother had sent a note that Henry had finally returned from France, and Theo immediately arranged for them to visit, intending to summon the carriage. Ordinarily, they would have walked, but she was feeling a trifle under the weather.

After ensuring her sister was well enough for the journey, Annabelle lapsed into silence as they waited in the hall for Nathanial. Her morning dress was a shade of pale blue that brought out the colour of her eyes, and she had worn it in the vague, unarticulated hope she would see Jacob that morning.

Instead, she was due to see her brother. Nerves twisted at the thought.

"A delivery for you, my lady," the butler said, cutting into her confusion.

"More jewellery?" she asked tiredly. Of all the gifts she could receive, jewels were her least favourite. She didn't care to wear them and they were usually ostentatious; a demonstration to the world of his affection, not a demonstration to her.

Which, of course, was the purpose of the gifts. But every time she opened another box to reveal rubies, sapphires, diamond-studded bracelets or huge, teardrop earrings, she felt her heart sink a little further.

The butler smiled at her. "Not this time, my lady," he said, handing her a small, rectangular package. There was a note attached, and she opened it with eager fingers.

Little bird,

I have never been an avid reader, but this was always a favourite of mine.

Yours,

Jacob

Her eyes stung as she ripped open the brown paper to reveal a bound collection of Shakespeare's sonnets. Not new—she suspected it had been read a number of times, and if his note was to be believed, by Jacob himself.

She opened the little book, letting it fall naturally to the page that had been read most.

Sonnet 116

Let me not to the marriage of true minds
  Admit impediments; love is not love
  Which alters when it alteration finds,
  Or bends with the remover to remove.
  O no, it is an ever-fixed mark
  That looks on tempests and is never shaken;
  It is the star to every wandering bark,
  Whose worth's unknown, although his height be taken.
  Love's not Time's fool, though rosy lips and cheeks
  Within his bending sickle's compass come;
  Love alters not with his brief hours and weeks,
  But bears it out even to the edge of doom.
  If this be error and upon me proved,
  I never writ, nor no man ever loved.

"He sent you a book?" Theo asked, rousing herself as Annabelle read the sonnet again and again, drinking in the words like sweet, addictive punch. "Well, I suppose he must like you after all."

He had been reading sonnets about love. *Jacob* had read

about love. Irreverent, careless, mocking Jacob had read poetry.

Then she remembered what he had said about his family at the ball. *Because I despise my family and everything they stand for.*

Suddenly, these words of love took on a different context. She pictured him now as a young boy, reading about love being an ever-fixed mark, that looks on tempests and is never shaken. If he had a loveless upbringing . . .

This gift felt like the most precious thing she owned.

"Are you all right?" Theo asked, squinting at her.

Annabelle cleared her throat, handing the book back to the butler. "Jarvis, can you have this taken to my bedchamber, please?"

"Of course, my lady." Jarvis left, as stiff-backed as always, and Annabelle brushed her hair back from her face, trying to push back the emotions swarming her. For an odd reason, Jacob's gift made her want to cry.

"Who would have thought the Devil of St James enjoyed poetry," Theo mused with a grin that almost matched her usual aplomb.

To Annabelle's relief, Nathanial finally descended the stairs, providing a much-needed distraction, and Annabelle was free to dwell on Jacob's gift in relative peace.

What did it mean? Was it a peace offering of sorts? They had not argued, but he had certainly left her looking . . . angry. Hurt, perhaps, although the possibility that *she* could ever have said anything to hurt him seemed ludicrous in the extreme. The Devil of St James was not capable of being hurt.

But he had sent her *poetry*. And not only that, but Shake-speare. *Sonnets*. How was this the same man who had cornered her in a library and kissed her so thoroughly, or after kissing her in a closet, told her she had *taken the edge off*? No matter how she tried to explain the reason behind the sonnets, she could not stop the flutter in her stomach at the thought.

After she had thought she had hurt him, he had sent her sonnets.

The carriage pulled up at her parents' house and there was abruptly no more time for reflection. Servants scurried past them with bags and paintings and everything needed to settle the heir back in his own room, and the sense of urgency sent her anxiety spiking once again.

Henry was here. And he was going to learn, if he did not already know, of her engagement to Jacob—and the circumstances *behind* that engagement, which felt more shameful. She knew nothing had occurred in the garden, but something had occurred in the library.

Something *more* had occurred in the closet. It was a memory she did her best not to dwell on, because it made her think about *other* things he could do for her. Perhaps the act she had read about.

Never had the prospect of ruining herself felt so appealing.

But he had shown no signs of wanting to continue what they had started, and that was for the best. At least, that was what she continued to tell herself. If she was going to marry another man, she could not afford to involve herself with the Marquess, no matter how much she thought she might want to.

"The Duke and Duchess of Norfolk," the butler announced as they reached the drawing room. "And Lady Annabelle Beaumont."

The moment they entered, Annabelle saw her brother, sitting with his mother as though no time had passed. He looked older and grimmer than she could remember. The seven years he had been absent had not been kind to him.

Her mother jumped to her feet and held out her hands. "My dears, you're here! Finally! Look who it is."

"Told you she had a favourite," Theo muttered in Annabelle's ear, and Annabelle stifled a laugh as Henry also rose, the worn expression on his face smoothing into a genuine smile.

"Theo," he said "Anna. You've both grown so much since I last saw you."

"Well I *am* married now," Theo said, and Nathanial grinned, holding out his hand.

"You'll probably thank me for taking her off your hands."

"I can't tell you how relieved I am," Henry said, winking at Theo, who stuck her tongue out at them both.

As always in large gatherings, Annabelle was sidelined. Her personality wasn't large enough to compete with the others', and she found she didn't particularly want to. Overt displays of emotion and affection weren't something she was especially comfortable with either receiving or expressing, and having everyone fawn over her was something she had never liked.

Henry broke past Theo and stood before Annabelle. "Anna," he said, his voice warm. She raised her gaze hesitantly to his face. The war had changed him. The young man she remembered had turned into a grim-faced man of thirty, with crow's feet spreading from the corners of his blue eyes that held shadows she had not noticed in the past.

"How you've grown," he said, still in that affectionate voice.

"I'm almost twenty now," she reminded him.

"Yes, I haven't forgotten."

"And she's engaged," their mother said, hurrying to take part in the conversation. She placed a hand on Henry's arm, looking up at him adoringly. Annabelle's father had been such a disappointment to the whole family, it was hardly surprising that their mother now looked to her eldest son to save them.

Henry blinked at Annabelle in surprise. "Engaged?"

Annabelle wished everyone had kept her business a secret. With Henry back in Town, it would be even harder to extricate herself from this faux engagement when the time came.

"To Lord Sunderland," Theo supplied. "Or Lord Jacob Barrington as you would have known him then."

Henry's jaw snapped shut, muscles flexing, and his eyes darkened. "Jacob Barrington?"

"He's the Marquess now," their mother said, giving Annabelle a rare approving look, as though *she* had been responsible for the prior Marquess's death. As though that was a *good* thing.

Annabelle felt vaguely ill.

"What in the seven hells do you think you're doing marrying Barrington?" Henry demanded. All the joviality that had been on his face previously had dissolved into anger Annabelle didn't understand. There was something hard there, cultivated by the war no doubt, that was as sharp as a diamond-edged blade.

"With all due respect," Annabelle said calmly, her heart pounding in her chest, "it's not your business who I marry and who I don't."

Henry turned to their mother. "Does Father know about this?"

"Of course he does," she said, confusion blooming. "And he has given his permission."

"Of all the men in the world, Anna," Henry snapped, "you had to choose a man who would mistake honour for licentiousness?"

Annabelle thought of the book of sonnets he had gifted her with that very morning. "With all due respect," she repeated, her fingers clenching with impotent anger, "you don't know him."

"Oh, I know him well enough," he said darkly. "And I know the kinds of things he's done."

"Well—"

"Did you know he ruined his brother's betrothed?" Henry demanded. "They were all set to marry before Barrington seduced her so thoroughly, her own father cast her out."

Annabelle went cold. No, she did not know that—all she knew was that the two brothers had not got along, but she had assumed that was because of brotherly bad blood, not because Jacob had . . .

Had he?

Yes, she could well believe it. Her lips parted, ready to defend him, but she had no voice. There was no defence for a crime like that.

"Beaumont," Nathanial said, his tone cutting. "A word outside, if you please."

Henry gave her a disgusted look and left the room with Nathanial, and Annabelle tried to control her racing thoughts as she sank down onto the sofa. Theo took her hand, squeezing it.

"Whatever mistakes he made in the past, he is not making them now. Unless you *were* in the garden being seduced," she added dryly. "And even then, he is marrying you."

"He never mentioned anything about this," she said, her lips numb. "And no, Theo, he did not seduce me in the garden." In fact, he had gone out of his way to *prevent* her seduction, even though there had been a moment when she had thought she would not have minded.

And she had thought *he* would not have minded, either.

But to seduce his own brother's betrothed and ruin her utterly?

"Henry should have known better than to spring this on you like this," Theo said, rubbing her hand. "It's an old scandal. Before either of our times. Do you really care for him so much, Anna?"

Annabelle shook her head, though she was not entirely sure it was the truth. At their engagement ball, she had told Jacob she would have married his brother.

I assure you, you would not be the first.

How much had she hurt him? What would he do to assuage that hurt?

Surely Henry could not have been correct.

She felt positively ill.

"Let's return home," Theo said bracingly, squeezing her hand. "Nate can find his own way home after he's finished berating Henry." Her expression darkened, but Annabelle couldn't help but notice her lips looked a little too pale. "I don't know *what* he was thinking."

Her mother sat on Annabelle's other side. "He was just trying to look out for you, dear," she said placatingly. "I'm sure he'll come around and see sense."

"Mama," Theo said sharply. "Henry was out of line. You can't defend him."

Their mother fell silent, and Annabelle rose on shaky legs. "Yes," she said, formulating a plan as she spoke. She needed to see Jacob—now. "Let's return home."

Chapter Eighteen

As Annabelle had hoped, Theo took to her bed for a nap, and Annabelle lingered only long enough to leave a note for Nathanial informing him that she had gone to Hatchards. Ever since discovering that Jacob lived opposite, she had avoided it in favour of smaller bookshops and circulating libraries, but for her purposes, Hatchards was necessary—she needed no one to doubt the veracity of her story.

She sneaked out of the side door, closing it softly behind her, and started down the road. She had never been on her own before, and especially not like this, but no one could know where she was going, or what her intentions were. After some deliberation, she'd decided to visit Lady Bolton; as one of Jacob's oldest friends, she no doubt knew all about this young lady Jacob had ruined, and she would even perhaps be able to take Annabelle to see him.

She needed to see him.

Henry had been so angry, as though he had known a thousand things she didn't. And perhaps he did. Perhaps this girl was only the beginning. After knowing Jacob better, she had dismissed most of the stories about him as being rumour, but perhaps she'd been wrong. All this time, even when she had hated him, she had assumed he was, in his heart, a good person. He had agreed to this engagement for her sake—if there was one thing she believed, it was that he did not care for his own reputation.

Ergo, he cared for hers.

But was that possible when he had done so much to hurt others?

His own *brother's* betrothed?

She dashed a hand across her eyes and tried to focus on what she knew for certain. He had stopped drinking for her sake, although he said something about needing to drink for 'liquid courage'. At the time, she hadn't thought too deeply into it, but now she stopped to analyse every moment, turning it over and examining it from all sides. Unspoken implications, the way he had touched her, the things he had said to her. The longer she had known him, the more she felt as though she had been peeling back the layers defending himself—the armour he wore to defend against the arrows of Society's derision, as Lady Bolton had said. But what if she had been deceiving herself?

Perhaps he truly was as bad as everyone thought him to be, and she had seen what she had *wanted* to see, because the attention had been pleasant.

If so, then she was a fool.

By the time she arrived at Lady Bolton's house, she was in a state, sweaty hair sticking to the nape of her neck. It was a particularly warm May day, and her thoughts had made her increasingly heated. Her nerves were frayed, and when the butler led her into the drawing room where Lady Bolton was having her footmen place a new painting on the wall, she found herself alarmingly close to tears.

"A little to the left," Lady Bolton said, cocking her head as she examined the angles. "Higher. Higher—there. Perfect."

"A Lady Annabelle here to see you, ma'am," the butler said.

"Lady Annabelle?" Lady Bolton whirled so fast her skirts tangled around her legs, and Annabelle had a glimpse of wide hazel eyes before her expression settled into a smile.

"Goodness, my dear," she said, advancing with her hand outstretched. "I wasn't expecting to see you today."

"I need to speak with you," Annabelle burst out.

Lady Bolton took one look at Annabelle's face and took charge of the situation. "That positioning is excellent," she informed her footmen. "Ralph, have some tea sent up to my dressing room. I have a few dresses I would like to show Lady Annabelle."

The butler bowed. "Of course, my lady."

"Come," Lady Bolton said to Annabelle, leading the way through the house and up the stairs until they reached her large and extensive dressing room. The moment the door closed behind them, she sank onto the couch and motioned for Annabelle to do the same.

"Well?" she asked. "What is so urgent that you have come here at this time?" Her eyebrows rose. "And alone?"

"Is it true Jacob seduced his brother's betrothed and her father disowned her?"

Lady Bolton stiffened. "Who told you that?"

"Then it's true?" Annabelle wrung her hands together. "I hadn't thought him capable of that."

Lady Bolton's eyes softened as she looked at her. "That's not entirely the full story. But I'm not the one to tell you the particulars. Let us just say, it does not have a happy ending, and Jacob cut himself off from the world ever since. I met him eye."

and resentful. It's hardly surprising the two never saw eye to

taught to be proud and cosseted. Jacob was taught to be wild

believe Cecil would have been a decent man if he were not

enough misunderstandings between them to fill a book. I

can imagine how he was treated in comparison. There were

was sorrow at the corners of his mouth. "As for Cecil—you

and Jacob has never been." She shook her head, and there

recall how Cecil was fair? The rest of the family were fair,

"The black sheep in more than one sense. You perhaps

wasn't his?"

Annabelle's eyes widened. "You mean he thought Jacob

there were some questions surrounding Jacob's legitimacy."

to him. Well, I believe he was a cruel man to begin with, and

rest of them were dead. "His father in particular was . . . cruel

so terrible that Jacob hated his family name even when the

distant look, and Annabelle wondered what could have been

childhood was not precisely . . . happy." Her face took on a

I don't know the full story. From what I understand, his

"I suppose that is the long and short of it, although even

not sure what to make of it.

and everything they stand for." Annoyingly vague—she was

Annabelle shook her head. "Only that he despises his family

to you about his upbringing or family?"

wondering. He and Cecil . . ." She sighed. "Has he ever spoken

decision on his part. I believe it began precisely how you're

"That was unfortunate," Lady Bolton agreed. "And a poor

being together. "His brother's betrothed?"

together in the presence of a lady who struck her as always

"But—" Annabelle bit her lip, doing her best to hold herself

shortly after, and I had never encountered a man so broken."

"But that doesn't explain why Jacob set out to seduce his brother's betrothed," Annabelle whispered, even as she felt a pang of sympathy. Her upbringing had never been precisely easy as the younger, shyer, *lesser* sister, but she'd always had Theo in her corner. When she didn't have a voice, Theo spoke for her.

Probably because I've never been taught to respect my opinions. The sound of Jacob's voice pounded around her head. The odd way he had spoken, free from his usual smirk or lazy, wicked smile, had seemed almost surprising at the time, but now she understood it.

"I know it must seem strange to you," Lady Bolton said. "But there was no love lost between them, especially then, and Cecil wasn't marrying for love. He had recently inherited the title and Jacob was left with nothing, of course, and Jacob . . ." Lady Bolton lifted an elegant shoulder in a shrug, and they were interrupted by the tea. "Thank you, Maria. That will be all."

The maid bobbed a curtsy and left the room again.

Annabelle stared at the tea set blindly, trying to put the events of Jacob's life into an order that made sense. He had intended to hurt his brother by taking something that was his, but by the sounds of it, he had been the one hurt.

"You must ask him the rest of the story," Lady Bolton said, pouring the tea. "Believe me when I say it is not my story to tell. Nor, I suppose, do I know all the details."

"The *ton* discovered it, presumably."

"There were rumours, although no one knew the details, as I say. But Jacob's reputation was set then, and he decided that was how he was content to be known."

Annabelle shook her head, hands trembling as she took a

sip of her tea. "This girl," she said quietly, "did he love her?"

Lady Bolton gave her a long look for a moment, her brows pulling together as she considered. "What do you think?"

If he were alive now, he would be the man I would choose. I assure you, you would not be the first.

"I think he did," she whispered. "You said he was broken. You can't hurt without loving something first."

And she, mindless of the hurt *she* was causing, had told Jacob she would have preferred to marry his brother. What a foolish, ridiculous statement. But he needed to know she had said it without considering him as a potential candidate for her hand.

She looked at Lady Bolton pleadingly. "I need to go to him. Please help me."

* * *

Jacob wiped the sweat from his brow as he faced his opponent, a large man with fists like hams. His bottle man handed him some water, and he took a swig, not caring as the cold rivulets dribbled down his throat. All morning, he'd been trying to decipher Cecil's papers until his head hurt, and he needed this opportunity to be someone else.

The scars on his back meant nothing. His reputation meant nothing. The men in the crowd were betting on Jacob, not Lord Sunderland. They believed he was one of them. Even the few gentlemen milling around seemed oblivious. There were few today, considering the match was being held in the lower rooms of a tavern, and the doors were being well guarded to ensure no magistrates found their way inside.

His entire body burned with excess energy that he had not been able to shake, and he rolled his shoulders a few times before approaching the line in the middle of the ring. This man was large enough to feel like a challenge, although truthfully Jacob hardly cared if he won or lost, so long as he could lose himself in the fight.

Jacob exhaled, finally finding the peace he had been searching for, and the match began.

* * *

The tavern was dark and smoky. Annabelle had never been inside such an establishment before, and she was unprepared for the dirty straw on the floor, the scent of cigar smoke that seemed to cling to everything, and the tang of unwashed bodies mingling with alcohol. Somewhere underneath the floorboards, a roar rose that shook the entire building.

"It's not seemly for ladies to enter," a man was telling Lady Bolton. Annabelle watched, half in amusement and half in awe as Lady Bolton narrowed her eyes at him.

"It is convenient, then, that I am a lady only in name," she said, and stepped forward. Surprised, the man stepped back.

"Do you think I fear a little blood? This is not the first boxing match I have attended, and I doubt it will be the last. Now, unless you wish to have every magistrate in the air discovering this little illegal match, allow me downstairs at once."

The man faltered, evidently not accustomed to being spoken to in such a manner, and Lady Bolton brushed past him.

Annabelle followed, staying close enough so she would not get lost.

They were akin to parrots among pigeons. The brightness of Lady Bolton's maroon dress and Annabelle's blue morning dress stood in stark contrast to the greys and browns of the working men's suits. There were a few other gentlemen present, but even they were wearing more muted waistcoats. A far cry from the flamboyant colours she often saw while promenading or at social events. This was not a social event. The floor was sticky with spilt beer and men were jeering at the figures in the ring.

Ring was perhaps an optimistic term for the boxed rectangle in the centre of the room, featuring the two fighting men.

Annabelle paused to stare at the men in shock and horror. They fought with bare knuckles, shirtless, bruises already blooming on their ribs and stomachs. One man, a veritable giant, had his back to her, which meant she could see portions of the other man's torso and the way his ridged muscles tensed and moved as he struck.

Blood splattered the ground as the large man's nose crunched. The other man seemed to have got off lightly in comparison, although he was breathing hard and his bronzed skin was gleaming with sweat.

He looked up, and Annabelle's stomach bottomed out. His eyes looked so much darker than she could ever remember them being, and his lip was bleeding, but his face was painfully familiar. For a moment, their eyes locked, and his opponent sank a fist into his stomach.

Annabelle gasped in shock at the raw violence of the blow. Jacob doubled over, and she stumbled forward a few steps as though she could personally shield him from attack. But

CHAPTER EIGHTEEN

already he was moving, not giving himself time to recover, dodging the other man's next blow.

"Come," Lady Bolton said, reappearing, "We're not here to distract him."

"When you said he would be boxing, I didn't know you meant *boxing*." Annabelle tried to get the shock of his dark eyes and the way the other man had struck him. "I thought you meant he would be attending the boxing."

"He's boxed as long as I've known him," Lady Bolton said. "There's always been a bit of darkness in him, and this is his favourite way of expressing it. Here, there are some chairs."

The current occupants moved out of the way for them to sit, and Annabelle sank into the rickety wooden chair, her head spinning. In the ring before her, Jacob knocked the larger man to the ground. A small bell rang.

How long would this last? Her stomach churned, but she forced herself to keep watching as the larger man picked himself up. A referee to one side had his gaze glued to his pocket watch. Jacob turned to look at her, something furious in his expression. There was no sign of the suave, charming man she had encountered in Society.

"He's angry," Lady Bolton noted cheerfully from beside her. "No doubt he will channel that into his fighting. He's very good, you know."

"Do you think he'll be hurt?"

Lady Bolton shrugged. "Not unduly. Fear not—he has been doing this for years, and he's never come to serious harm. A few bruises are nothing. I have a feeling he craves the pain."

"I can't bear to see him fight." As the two men took their places again, Annabelle squeezed her eyes half shut, peering at them through her eyelashes.

"Watch," Lady Bolton said, her tone gentle even as she tapped Annabelle's arm with her fan. "You should know all the sides to the man you're going to marry."

Annabelle linked her hands too tightly in her lap. "I thought you knew—Jacob and I are not intending to marry. Our engagement is a sham."

"Piddle." Lady Bolton's gaze never left Jacob, but there was something assessing in it. The next round began, just as terrifyingly, aggressively violent as before. "I have only seen him fight like this once before, and that was when I first met him. Shortly after Madeline."

"What does that mean?"

"It means," Lady Bolton said with a grim satisfaction, "you are the first person he has cared about in five years, whether he admits it or not."

Chapter Nineteen

Jacob won the next round with a burst of aggression Annabelle had never seen from him—or anyone—before. The violence grated, but something else stood out in vivid relief. When he fought, there was something quiet about him. Even when the room erupted into cheers, he was still and quiet, as though he had found some inner peace she could not access.

Lady Bolton rose, brushing down her skirts. "Just as disagreeably noisy as I remember these events being," she said. "And he will be disagreeable too, so we should head him off before he attempts to escape without us."

Annabelle nodded and followed Lady Bolton as she made her way to the edge of the ring just as Jacob, a towel around his neck and his shirt in his hands, emerged. She did her best not to stare at his exposed torso close up, but it was a battle quickly lost; her gaze traced over the curves and dips of his stomach and hipbones. She hadn't known there could be so much power and elegance in a male body. Sculptures, for all they were lifelike, did not capture the way they shifted as he moved, or the tantalising gleam of sweat in the candlelight.

She felt a little lightheaded.

Jacob glowered at them both, taking hold of the towel and

running it through his hair. "You shouldn't be here. This is no place for a lady."

"Oh tosh," Lady Bolton said dismissively. Jacob pulled his shirt over his head and Annabelle told herself it was a good thing he was covering up. Just as it was a bad thing the material clung to his damp skin, the bronzed colour visible through the white cotton.

"Excellent game," a man said to Jacob, and he winked—*winked*—at Annabelle. "You've got some swell supporters. My wife never comes to see me fight."

Jacob grunted and took Annabelle's elbow. "Go," he said tersely.

"She knows about Madeline," Lady Bolton said, and Jacob froze. Emotions flitted across his face, too fast and too many to note, before he settled into a blank expression that hurt to look at.

"My brother told me," Annabelle said quickly. Behind them, a bunch of men began singing a loud and rather bawdy song.

"About . . . the gist of it."

Beside her, Lady Bolton also froze. "Your brother was the one to tell you?"

"He returned home today and discovered the engagement and was . . ." Annabelle winced. "Displeased."

"Is that so," Lady Bolton said with a hard note to her voice. "Just as high-handed as ever, then?"

Annabelle frowned. "You know him?"

"She knew him before he went to war," Jacob said, his hand still on Annabelle's elbow. She felt his fingers flex. Someone stumbled into them and he scowled, pulling her closer. "For God's sake, Louisa, you should have known better than to bring her here. Leave and I'll follow as soon as I've concluded my business."

"You need to explain," Lady Bolton said. "She deserves to know."

Jacob ran a hand through his damp hair. "Very well, I will explain, but you should *go* before one or both of you get trampled. These men have been drinking for hours."

But it's only mid-afternoon, Annabelle wanted to protest. It would have been futile; there was no denying the crowd was increasingly boisterous, and they were the only two ladies she could see.

"Never mind," Jacob muttered, striding through the laughing men and pulling Annabelle in his wake. "I'll escort you out. What were you thinking, sneaking off to see me today of all days?"

"I hardly knew you were going to be *here,*" Annabelle said, fisting her hand in the loose shirt on his back to steady herself.

"And what does it matter? We can look after ourselves."

"Not in a place like this," he said grimly. "You're a walking target."

"It was an excellent way to ensure you paid us heed," Lady Bolton said from behind them.

"It was an excellent way of putting yourselves in danger. I have enough on my plate without worrying about the two of you."

"Heavens, Jacob," Lady Bolton said in mock surprise. "Are you telling me our wellbeing is of your concern?"

They climbed a set of rickety stairs and Annabelle corrected herself, because here there were other ladies, but they wore provocative dresses and too much rouge, holding themselves as though they knew they were a prize to be won.

"Congratulations on your victory," one said to Jacob, run-

ning her tongue along her top lip. She was sultriness personi-
fied, and Annabelle disliked her immediately. "Visit me later
if you want to celebrate in style."

Annabelle was aware of a violent, and hitherto unknown,
desire to do harm to a fellow woman.

"Try targeting a man who doesn't have two ladies in his
company," Lady Bolton told the girl coolly.

Jacob said nothing, and Annabelle had the awful thought
that perhaps Jacob would have taken her up on her offer, or
perhaps still would, once they were out of the way.

The idea of it made her want to cry.

They stepped out onto the street into misting rain, and
she turned her hot face into the soft moisture, welcoming its
coolness.

"Did you really do it?" she asked, not looking at him. "Did
you really seduce your brother's betrothed?"

Jacob was silent long enough that she looked at him, the
rain catching on her eyelashes. His shirt was rapidly growing
damper, clinging to his body in a positively indecent fashion.
He should not be seen without his waistcoat, at the very least,
but he didn't seem to notice as he watched her, his eyes very
dark. Lady Bolton wandered away to peer in a nearby shop
window, giving them at least the illusion of privacy.

"We shouldn't have this conversation now," he said at last.
"It is not an easy one to have."

"Then that's a yes." She'd known, but somehow hearing
it from his lips was different. "I know you didn't like your
brother, but what about the girl?"

"Madeline?" he scoffed. "Do you think I could have seduced
her if she wasn't willing? Everyone looks to blame the man,
and you're right, I was fully in the wrong for ever approaching

her, but she never loved my brother, and he never loved her. She welcomed my attentions because she was lonely and because I offered her what she wanted. And I, who thought myself immune to love, came to love her. Do you think it was merely for fun? That I ruined her out of spite?"

The rain came down harder now, soaking into her shoulders and through to her skin, and all Annabelle could do was look at him. His hair was black as coal in the rain, slicked against his forehead, and there was almost a desperate, pleading look in his eyes.

He had loved her. This Madeline. Regardless of anything else, Annabelle believed that—she had known the moment she had asked Louisa, and the raw agony that flitted across his face was confirmation. But although she had told herself this was what she had hoped for, the reality hit her like a brick to the heart. He, Jacob Barrington, the Devil of St James, had loved a girl named Madeline, and she had broken his heart.

He had loved her.

"You should return home," he said after a long moment. "Tell no one you were here with me."

"Wait." She reached out a hand, finding his wet cuff and holding it. "When will I next see you again?"

"We are engaged, little bird," he said wryly, reaching out to disentangle her. "I hardly think you could avoid me if you wanted to."

She didn't want to. There was more to this story that had put such bleakness in his eyes, and she wanted to hear it and understand it, she wanted to know what it meant to have hated his brother so much he would have betrayed him in this way.

She wanted to know what about Madeline had made him

191

love her so.

But all she said was, "You sent me the sonnets this morning." He stiffened on his way back to the tavern entrance. "What of it?"

"Why?"

He glanced back then, bitter, mocking amusement in his voice as he said, "I suppose I wanted to be a little more like my brother."

* * *

Jacob strode back into the basement. The ring had already been dismantled should any magistrates come knocking. Bettors congratulated him on his victory, and he collected his winnings with a smile he didn't feel.

Madeline. Annabelle. In his head, they had merged to the point when if he thought of Madeline's green eyes, he could only think of Annabelle's blue ones. He should have explained the entire situation, but in the rain with her looking at him as though he had just kicked her favourite puppy, he hadn't had the words. How did one explain that he had been the reason for her death?

Everyone close to him met their end. Even Cecil had died because of him. Their argument had been the reason for his heart giving out. The strain of being his brother had been too much, and although Jacob did his best to never think about it, sometimes the thought crept up to him at night.

All you will know is misery. That is your curse, Jacob.

If he allowed himself to care about Annabelle the way he

CHAPTER NINETEEN

had cared for Madeline, he would find a way of cursing her, too. Her brother was already kicking up a fuss about their engagement; if he persisted in getting closer to her, things would only get worse.

Sending her the book of sonnets had been a mistake. He'd been angry at Cecil, angry at her, angry at himself, and that was something he could not risk again. She deserved better than anything he had to offer.

"Barrington!" one of his friends clapped him on the back. "Great fight. Coming for a drink?" He leaned in. "I've organised for a few girls to join us."

A few months ago, he would never have hesitated, but when he closed his eyes, all he could see was Annabelle's expression when she said she wished she could have married Cecil.

He gritted his teeth, angry at himself for caring. "Thank you, no," he said, leaving the tavern before anyone else could tempt him in with a drink. One drink would turn into five, which would turn into many more, and the rest of the day would be lost. He'd stumble home drunk at dawn and face a headache the next day.

Once, he would have welcomed it, but he had some idea in his head of being—well, he didn't fully know. The person his father had never thought he could be. Taking revenge on people who were dead and would never see the fruits of his work seemed shortsighted and a distinct waste of effort. Thus, when he was home, he would wipe off whatever blood was on his person, and he would channel his remaining frustration into taking charge of the estate. The fight had taken the edge off, though he still itched with restless energy. Seeing Annabelle had disturbed him more than he wanted to admit. After sending her the book of sonnets, he hadn't expected to see her for a few days, so he would have time to come to terms with just how foolish that impulse had been.

He was not Cecil. No matter how many books he sent her, he would *never* be good enough to suit her. And he didn't want to be. What he wanted was for the engagement to be over so he could go back to his life without thinking about the ways in which his decisions would affect her. He wanted to be able to go to sleep without wanting her.

He wanted to not see the wistful expression on her face when she thought about his brother and what he had to offer.

History was playing out again and Cecil wasn't even *here* to control the narrative.

Jacob rolled his shoulders, wishing he knew a better, more effective way of burning off the energy that still roiled inside him.

Although it was still raining mistily, he opted to walk, strolling past all London had to offer as he moved west into the more salubrious areas the *ton* chose to inhabit. Hopefully Louisa had taken Annabelle home in a hackney at the very least.

No, he needed to stop thinking about her.

By the time he arrived home, he was wet to the bone, and he had just divested himself of his sodden coat when Smythe said, "You have a visitor, my lord." His tone implied the visitor was not at all to his taste. Jacob ran through who it could be. A debtor come to collect? Unlikely; he hadn't even, to his knowledge, received any threatening notes.

Villiers? No doubt Smythe would disapprove. But he would have given the gentleman's name immediately.

"Well?" he asked, unbuttoning his waistcoat as he moved to the stairs. His visitor could wait until he had changed at least.

CHAPTER NINETEEN

"Who is it?"

"I'm not entirely sure, sir," Smythe said stiffly. "She wouldn't give her name."

She? That stopped Jacob in his tracks. "Is she alone?"

"Yes, sir."

"Where is she?"

"In the receiving room, my lord."

The receiving room was a small room beside the door tradespeople usually waited in if they wished to speak directly to the family. Not a place for a well-bred lady, but if a lady had come here alone, no doubt she wasn't well-bred.

He had no outstanding debts with brothels. Truth be told, he hadn't visited for months.

Annabelle. Her face flashed in his mind and he went cold all over. If she had risked coming here, something dreadful must have happened. It was one thing to follow Louisa after him, but entirely another to come to his house alone.

"Take me to her," he said.

Chapter Twenty

Annabelle paced around the small, plain room, wishing she had never come. Several times, she eyed the door, wondering if she ought to make a break for it. Coming here had been risky, both for her reputation and her reception. Jacob hadn't been pleased to see her at the tavern and his boxing ring, and she doubted he would be happy to see her here, either. At his house.

Maybe she should just go home and save the apology for another time. Lady Bolton had promised to cover for her; she could leave and tell Theo she'd been with Lady Bolton and no one would be any the wiser.

Before she could bolt, the door opened and Jacob walked in, his waistcoat half open and his shirt damp. He closed the door behind him and came to stand in front of her in two strides. "What is it?" he asked, his dark eyes searching her face. "Is someone hurt? Did someone see you at the tavern?"

Unable to speak, she shook her head. Her face flamed.

"Annabelle." Jacob's hands cupped her face, bringing her gaze back to his. His hands were shockingly warm, though still wet from the rain, and he was frowning. "Tell me. What is it? I thought after learning about Madeline you—" He broke off, throat working, and she reached up to brush her fingertips against the hand that was still against her cheek. So gentle, he could be so gentle with these same hands she had seen break a man's ribs.

Her breath caught.

"What you told me about Madeline wasn't the full story," she whispered. "I want to know—everything."

"That's the reason you came here? To hear me talk about a woman long dead?"

"Dead?" Annabelle jerked back out of his hands and his shoulders went stiff. "She's *dead*?"

Jacob ran a hand through his hair, slicking it back. "It's not what you think, little bird." All of a sudden, he looked exhausted, the lines on his face deepening. Although he was still only in his twenties—a young man by anyone's standard—he looked as though he had seen the dawn of time and everything that came after.

"Then tell me," she urged. "I want to know everything. The truth."

"The truth?" His lip curled. "No one wants that."

"It's part of you. I want to know."

For a long moment, he just looked at her. Then he raked another hand through his hair, his shoulders sagging with the weight of his decision. "Very well. You may sit if you like. It's not a pretty story."

Annabelle perched on the edge of the low couch that had been placed there, and Jacob sat on the other side. He played with his cuffs, eyes cast down as he visibly gathered himself.

"I have no excuse for how the affair began. I hated my brother and everything he stood for, and I hated that he had everything he wanted. So I took the one thing from him I

197

could—the woman he was going to marry. I'll admit, it was an act of spite, at first, and I had enough experience in the bedchamber to think myself capable of it. But the more I got to know her, the more I understood she never wanted the match and her heart was not engaged. We fell in love." There was a mocking edge to his voice. "Or so I thought in my youth and naivety. I offered her everything I had. I said we could elope, I told her I would take a position in politics or the law to support her the best I could. It wouldn't have been the life she was accustomed to, but we would be together and I thought that would be enough."

Annabelle's nose stung. Jacob's voice was flat but she could hear the echoes of hurt behind it. An empty room that had once held screams of pain.

"Of course, what she had truly wanted from my brother was his position, his wealth, his title. I had none of that. So she turned me down, but like a fool I kept coming back to her for more. The affair went on for months, and by the end of it, I'd forgotten why it had ever begun." He shook his head, a humourless smile curling the corner of his mouth. "To this day, I don't know how her father discovered we were together. A rumour, I suppose. Mindless gossip that reached his ears. He believed it enough to throw his daughter onto the street. I offered her marriage, a home, anything she wanted, but she ran to my brother instead."

Annabelle bit her lip in sympathy. "But he no longer wanted her as his bride?"

"He broke the engagement. One of the few times gentlemen can without social repercussions. Everyone thought her a whore and me a low-born bastard." He shrugged, but his eyes were opaque, no emotion seeping through. "My

CHAPTER TWENTY

understanding is, after he rejected her, she came to me again. But she never made it. Her body was discovered a few days later, and . . . I never saw the body, but I understand she was strangled after . . ." He broke off, shaking his head.

Annabelle leant forward and placed her hand on his leg. "That wasn't your fault," she said forcefully. "You can hardly hold yourself accountable."

He looked down at the contact, and she curled her fingers, pulling her hand away again, but he caught her wrist. "Annabelle," he said, his voice low. His thumb swept over her pulse-point.

Annabelle was not prone to disliking other women where she could help it, but she detested this Madeline. For existing, for making Jacob love her, and for breaking his heart so thoroughly he had never been able to put the pieces back together.

"She should have loved you," she said. Jacob's eyes were dark, so dark, when he looked at her. "I fear that would have been impossible."

"Why? Because you didn't have a title?"

"Because in all my life, no one has ever loved me, and why should a girl hoping for a rich husband be any different?" His smile twisted, bitter enough to impale her heart. "What did I have to offer her, little bird? I was the younger brother of a marquess, and considering I was hardly suited for the church, I would have had to find some other occupation. Not the life she had envisaged for herself."

"Then she should have considered what would matter more—a husband who adored her or a man who was marrying her for convenience only."

"My love would not have made us rich," he said, toying with

her fingers absently in a way that made heat steal through her body. "A noblewoman learning to darn socks and make do? Imagine, Annabelle."

"It doesn't sound so terrible to me."

"I hadn't thought you were so much of a romantic," he said, a gleam of *something* in his eye. Unfathomable and dark—there was such darkness in him, but it called to her, begged her to soothe its edges. "But if you recall, she is not the only one to prefer my brother."

"That's why I came here," she said, looking up and meeting his gaze with all the seriousness she could muster. "I wanted to apologise for saying I would marry Cecil over you. When I said it, I was thinking about the books, but—" But he had sent her the sonnets and she had felt seen and heard, and even his tale of Madeline hadn't taken that from him. "If it came down to it, I would far rather marry you than your brother. Even if you were not a marquess and I had to darn my own socks."

His sumptuous mouth pressed into a hard line. "That is not the life you would want."

Better to live with a man who touched her like she was something precious, and kissed her breathless, than a man who married her for her money and convenience. Cecil had wanted her because of her reading, she knew, but he didn't like her. He didn't *know* her.

There was no point arguing with him, but she wanted to offer him something he might accept. They had gone into their agreement as reluctant allies, but things had changed now.

They may never be husband and wife, but at least they could have this.

"I want to start anew," she said, holding out her hand. "As

. . . friends." On the patio at the ball, they had been friends, and she had liked it. Friends enjoyed each other's company and looked out for one another, did they not? And if she sometimes got distracted by the way his shirt indecently hugged his body, then that was not *so* bad.

He eyed her hand. "Friends?"

"Do you dislike me so much?"

An unidentifiable expression flickered across his face, but a heartbeat later, he gave a wry smile and clasped her hand, fingers wrapping almost to her wrist. "Very well. Friends it is."

A more unusual pairing had not been seen. Annabelle shook his hand and rose, taking a deep breath. "Good day, my lord," she said, hoping he would play along. "My name is Lady Annabelle Beaumont."

A surprised laugh lit his eyes, turning them from ebony to honey and chocolate, and he stood to join her. "Lord Sunderland at your service."

She curtsied, letting him keep her hand. With his eyes on her, too much like the ball, he kissed her knuckles. "It's a pleasure to finally meet you," she said. "I've heard so many things."

"All bad, no doubt." He tucked her hand into the crook of her arm. "Would you like a tour of my home? I have an expansive library."

A smile spread across her face. So many people heard but they didn't listen. With Jacob, she felt *seen*. "You do?"

"Do you like libraries, my lady?"

"Very much." She grinned up at him and he glanced down at her with an indulgent smile. As they passed through the hall and receiving rooms, he played the part of host, regaling her with stories—some true and some not, she fancied. His clothes were still wet, but he made no move to change them, and there was a softness to him she hadn't seen before. This was the man who had sent her the sonnets, not the man who had glared at her from a boxing ring with bloodied knuckles.

This was the gentleman, not the fighter.

She found herself intrigued by both. The juxtaposition of one against the other. Soft and hard; rough and gentle. Sophisticated and brutal.

"When I was thirteen, I came with my mother to London and while she was entertaining, I added tiny additions to the paintings." He pointed to a small, obscene drawing in one corner. "No one noticed for a few years, and by the time my father did notice, I was too old for him to punish."

Annabelle remembered what Lady Bolton had told her about Jacob and his childhood—specifically that there was some question as to his heritage. "Did your father often punish you?"

Acting as though he didn't hear, Jacob opened a large door and ushered her through. "And this is the library," he said. Annabelle had wanted to pursue the subject of his family, but with the library in front of her, all other thoughts left her head.

Nathanial had an excellent library, well-stocked and spacious. He often spent time there doing his accounts and sitting by the fire. Theo sometimes joined him with a book. It was a space for relaxation more than for reading, despite the books that lined the shelves.

This was a space directly designed for reading.

Large windows eliminated any gloom, and ladders were placed against the tall bookcases so one could reach any books they wished. Small, cosy chairs were tucked away in corners, and although there was a table, it was stacked high with books. Silk bookmarks were tangled in a pile, and half-burned candles lined shelves that had been designed especially for them, burn-marks marring the wood above.

Unlike in Nathanial's library, the fireplace was not the focal point of the room.

Annabelle's breath rushed out of her as she turned, taking in every detail. The thick velvet curtains could be drawn as necessary to ward away the cold, and the chairs looked worn. Comfortable and cosy.

Jacob, she noticed, didn't look at the space as she did. There was a muscle ticking in his jaw and a dark light in his eyes that reminded her of how she felt when she viewed a ballroom being prepared for a ball. Instantly put in mind of the torture she would have to endure.

"Is this not a room that holds happy memories for you?" she whispered, forgetting her joy in the wake of his grim endurance.

He frowned as he glanced down at her. "Nothing in this house holds happy memories for me, little bird."

"Annabelle."

"Annabelle," he repeated, tongue curling around her name in a way that sounded almost obscene. Their eyes locked and the air was sucked from the room, nothing in the space between them but desire that sizzled like a flame. She was old enough, aware enough, to know what it was, to put a name to it, to acknowledge she felt it when she looked at him.

After they'd kissed in the closet and he had dismissed her, she had told herself she would never let something like that happen again. Now, she wasn't so sure she would be able to stop it. There was a feeling of creeping inevitability here—they had been resisting it for so long, but now they were alone.

He had loved Madeline. He had loved her enough to marry her. The thought made her simultaneously warm and cold.

"You said kissing me took the edge off," she whispered, forgetting the role she'd given herself. Friend. Stranger. "What did you mean?"

His jaw tensed. "I just said that to hurt you." Hesitation cracked across his expression. "Forgive me."

She already had. When he'd come to Nathanial's library and knelt before her, when he had apologised, she had forgiven him then, though she had not meant to.

"We've started afresh," she reminded him. "No more apologies."

"Just friendship?" he asked, eyes burning into hers.

This was no closet. Weak sunlight streamed in through the windows. The tension between them crackled with intensity and purpose.

"If you only came here for friendship, Annabelle, you should leave."

"Why?"

"Because you asked me not to touch you again, and I'm a man of my word." His gaze dropped to her mouth before he wrenched it back to her eyes with a vehemence that shocked her. "So I suggest you leave before I do something one of us might regret."

In the closet, he had kissed her as though she was his last breath. So urgently, she had known nothing but him. At the memory, she grew hot all over.

Annabelle had always been the sensible daughter. The good daughter, the *reliable* daughter. But this man, the Devil of St

James, made her want to forget what it felt like to be good. Weeks ago, before she had ever known him, she would have left now. She would not have come.

She was not the girl she had been weeks ago.

"And if I said I would not mind if you touched me?" she whispered.

He groaned like a man tortured, and through the wild pounding of her heart, an answering thrill ran through her. "I told myself I would not, Annabelle."

"Why?"

"Madeline."

The name sliced through her and she had to take an unsteady breath. "I'm not Madeline."

His throat bobbed as he swallowed. "I know."

"I would not choose your brother over you." She pressed still closer, tilting her head back in invitation. *Kiss me.* "We agreed that by the end of the summer, our arrangement would be over. But for now, we are engaged." She pushed any anticipatory hurt away; later, she would deal with it later. "And I want to know what it's like."

His fingers dug into her hips, drawing her closer, and she let out a long breath. "Then I'll show you, Annabelle, if you are sure this is what you want."

"It is."

With a shudder, he gave in.

Chapter Twenty-One

If Jacob were a better man, he would have refused her. Insisted she leave. They had an agreement in place, and that agreement did not involve him taking her innocence. She was going to marry another; he should have no claim on her.

But she had asked, and he was undone. When she asked, he could refuse her nothing.

Her mouth was warm, parting under his, yielding to him in the most delicious of ways, and he took full advantage, pushing her against a bookcase and kissing her until both their breaths were ragged. He was hard, of course he was hard—he had been hard right from the moment she had looked up at him, games forgotten, nothing but want in her eyes.

Now, she kissed him as though she would die if he stopped, and it fuelled him to nip her bottom lip, to press himself against her, to grind his aching length against her stomach, frustrated by the restriction of his breeches and thankful for them all the same.

It could not go any further than this. He *would* remain in control. Regardless of what happened here today, their agreement had not changed: she was going to be married to another man who would, presumably, want her intact.

Thinking about another man touching her did nothing good to him, so he focused on the practicalities of the situation. The limitations. He would not take her virginity. No matter how much he wanted her. More than Madeline, more than anything he had ever wanted in his life. His existence had been made up of want, of desire, of denial, but nothing had felt as difficult as the knowledge he would come this close to having Annabelle and could not. *Would* not.

He was not a scoundrel.

Well, he *was* a scoundrel, but he had learnt his lesson with Madeline, and he would not ruin Annabelle any more than her presence here had already ruined her.

He did not let himself think about what might happen if she was ruined. Instead, he stroked his knuckles under her breasts, feeling the way her nipples pebbled and her breaths turned heavy and languorous.

"Jacob," she said, shifting against him. It was a plea, and in answer, he took her hand and led her to the large table in the centre of the room. It was covered in books, but he swiped them aside, clearing a space for her. When she hesitated, he took hold of her waist and set her on it. Her chest heaved as she stared at him.

"I want to touch you," he said, giving her time to change her mind. Her breath hitched. "Will you let me?"

Her eyes were a storm-tossed sea, and her mouth was red and swollen. She looked thoroughly debauched as she nodded, and he liked her like that, like this, giving him permission to do what he pleased with her. As she watched him, he drew her skirts up her thighs until he reached her hips. Legs. Bare. Stockings then tantalising pale skin and between her legs, damp curls. His mouth was dry and his cock strained against his breeches, achingly hard, demanding he relieve it. With one hand, he cupped himself, squeezing almost viciously, while with the other, he spread her legs.

"You'll like this." His voice was low. The way she looked at him was a torment.

"What about you?"

"What about me?"

"Do . . ." She swallowed, a red blush creeping up her neck to her cheeks. "Should *I*—"

He leant over and kissed her chastely, softly. "I will enjoy this almost as much as you," he said. "Believe me."

Uncertainly, she nodded, and he placed himself between her legs. He wanted to taste her, but she had never been with a man before. First, he needed to accustom her to being touched intimately. Then—

No. He shut down the thought before it could take root. Touching her was all he would allow himself. But she could not touch him, not if he were to retain what little restraint he had left.

She shifted restlessly and he slid his palm along the soft skin of her inner thigh. As if in invitation, she spread her legs still wider, baring herself to him, and all thoughts left his head.

She was perfection. Even without touching her, he could see how wet she was, her folds slick with desire. When she shifted again, rolling her hips in impatience, he touched her where she needed. A gasping low moan escaped her, and he gripped himself still more tightly as he traced small circles around her sensitive nub. Already, she was ready for him, and that knowledge in itself was an agony.

He slid a finger inside her, kissing her inner thigh at her moan.

"What's this?" she gasped, hips bucking. He added a second finger to the first, revelling in the delicious way she clenched around him. Hot, wet, and utterly inviting.

But he mustn't.

"Quiet, sweetheart."

Her head fell back as she bit her lip, stifling the cries he was drawing from her, and damn him to hell, if this wasn't the most arousing sight he'd ever witnessed. None of the ladies he usually lay with, the experienced widows or the practised mistresses, had ever given themselves to him the way Annabelle did. Innocently, without guile.

To distract himself from the desperate, almost mindless urge to sink inside her, he kissed his way up her thigh to her damp curls.

"Jacob!" Annabelle half sat up again, eyes wide, her legs clamping around his head. "What are you—"

He looked up as he continued to work her with his fingers. "I want to use my mouth on you."

"*There?*"

"Don't look so scandalised, little bird. It's not as uncommon as you might think."

"And you'll like it?" she asked doubtfully.

"There's nothing I want more."

Slowly, she nodded, an expression of mingled anticipation and suspicion and fear on her face, and he took that as an invitation to proceed.

If he had planned a seduction route for her, he would have gone about it differently. He would have made sure everything happened at its proper pace, possibly over several sessions. And he would categorically *not* have put his mouth on her the very first time they came together.

But there might not be another time. There was a slight uneasiness in his stomach at the thought and he pushed it to one side, letting himself focus exclusively on this. Messy, open licks and kisses. There was no finesse here; his reputation as an experienced lover was in tatters at his schoolboy enthusiasm, but the taste of her on his tongue was driving him wild. He would be remembering this for months to come, every time he took himself in hand. The smell of her, the taste, the way she tightened around his fingers as her climax drew closer, and the helpless, pitiful cries she gave past clenched teeth as she strove to be quiet.

He wasn't entirely sure he would ever be able to stop.

He slowed as she reached the edge of climax, holding her there, teasing at the brink but never quite pushing her over.

"Jacob." Her voice was breathy impatience, and the sound of it almost undid him.

He should never have kissed her; then he would never have known how addictive it was. Sweeter than wine, stronger than whisky.

"This is the sweetest moment," he said, pulling back and meeting her gaze. "Savour it."

She wiggled again. "What about you?"

"It's better I . . . don't."

"Why?"

Instead of answering, he kissed her again, drawing her into his mouth and sucking as he crooked his fingers one last time. She shattered, shuddering on the table, the picture of wanton beauty, a hectic flush on her cheeks. He could imagine it extended down her chest to her breasts, too, which even through her clothes he could see were heavy, the nipples peaked.

CHAPTER TWENTY-ONE

She would be his every undoing.

Watching her climax, he didn't care.

If things were different—if he could love her, if she could love him—he would have offered for her there and then, just so he could keep her with him. So he could know the heaven that would be sinking inside her.

But he was cursed to be unlovable, and she was too good for someone like him. Too pure, too sweet, too loving. She deserved a gentleman who could give her the world.

They had an agreement.

Annabelle sat up, her hair slipping loose from its pins the way it had once before, and she smiled at him. Widely, openly, without restraint. And he knew he was totally lost.

She was not Madeline; she was better in every way. Honest, genuine, sincere. When she had thought she'd offended— no, *hurt*—him, she'd come to his house with the intention of apologising. Madeline had wielded her beauty like a well-honed weapon, but Annabelle was oblivious to her charms, and he had no doubt she meant everything she said.

He could not ruin her.

His hand curled into a fist at the urge to brush her hair back from her face.

"Jacob," she said, her smile slipping into confusion at his expression. "What's wrong?"

He tugged her skirts back into place, searching for his usual brusqueness. Why now, of all times, had it failed him? She wrought tenderness from him he had thought died along with Madeline. "Annabelle," he said, then sighed. "I think it's time for you to leave."

Her lips parted, shock crossing her features. "Now?"

"Now."

"Did I do something wrong? I know I did not—"

Unable to help himself, he leaned in to kiss her again, swallowing those words before they could pierce him. "You did nothing wrong," he said when he pulled away. "*Nothing*. But you can't stay here. What if your brother finds out?"

Henry Beaumont. Another obstacle to handle.

"He thinks I'm with Lady Bolton," she said confidently.

"Then return and be with her." He helped her to her feet, supporting her when her legs crumpled a little under her. "I appreciate you coming here today, but what just happened . . ." This was the hardest thing he had ever done. "It can never happen again."

Hurt crossed her features. "Because you don't want it to?"

"Do not talk to me about what I do and do not want." His voice was rough, but she did not flinch away. "You will be happier when you find another man. Better Cecil had lived and you had married him."

"But I don't want—" she started.

"He wanted you." It was a peculiar kind of pain in his chest as he reached out and stroked down her cheek. She looked at him with large, trusting eyes. "And he could have given you what you were looking for."

"I never wanted to marry," she said, although she sounded unsure. "I never thought marriage was—that one person could ever . . ."

He needed to look away from her fragile beauty, like the wings of a butterfly. So easily crushed. "You should go home, love."

"What if I want to stay?"

There were so many rules he had broken already—both his own and societal—that the thought was painfully tempting.

He could keep her here in this house, turning all those ugly memories into something wonderful.

Then he thought of Cecil, and the idea soured. This was history repeating itself, and he was allowing himself to get caught in its allure the way he had before.

Never again. How many times had he sworn that to himself?

"Little bird," he said, and half laughed, shaking his head. "You don't understand. I break everything I touch. Get too close and—" He shook his head, blocking out the thought. "Come. Let me do your hair."

"Is that a rule you have?" she asked in a quiet voice as he repinned her hair, unable to stop his fingers from lingering against the soft skin of her neck. "You only see a lady once?"

"No." He stepped back, his work passable at first inspection. "Just you, Annabelle."

She nodded, still staring at the wall. "I see."

"In time, you will thank me." Even if *he* would always look back on this day and wonder what would have happened if he hadn't adhered to the one rule he had left.

Even if he would always, always regret not being her first.

"I'll send for a cab," he said, reaching for the bellpull. "And I will call in a few days, if your brother allows it."

Her smile didn't touch her eyes, and he wondered what else he had broken by, for the first time in his life, trying to be a better man.

Chapter Twenty-Two

Hatchards was crowded as Annabelle and Henry walked through the door together. He had called earlier, suggesting he take her out, and she knew this was his idea of a peace offering. Not that he had directly apologised for the way he had responded to the news she was engaged—but he had offered to buy her a book. Under any other circumstance, she would have been delighted.

Now, she was barely able to concentrate on her brother as he made aimless conversation. Her thoughts were taken up with Jacob. What had happened the last time they had met. What he had *said*.

You will be happier when you find another man. Better Cecil had lived and you had married him.

No doubt he hadn't intended to hurt her, but after he had touched her so intimately—with his *mouth*—his words had sunk into her skin. Painful. Barbed. Visiting him had been reckless, a necessity of sorts after seeing him at the tavern boxing, and to have him use her so summarily and insist she leave before, she was sure, he had received any pleasure, had stung. If it hadn't been for the darkness in his eyes, and the way he had kissed her after, with a touch of desperation he hadn't given voice to, she would have felt used and discarded.

As it was, she could not help thinking he had some strange notion in his head that either she would regret going further, or that he would contrive to destroy her the way he had ruined Madeline.

Henry looked down at her in mingled exasperation and amusement. "Are you listening to me?"

She blinked, coming back into her body, aware once more of her surroundings—shelves of books, the smell of ink and paper. Young ladies clustered in giggling groups; a young boy being dragged sullenly around by his mother.

"Yes?" she hazarded.

He sighed and pinched his nose. "I understand if you're still angry with me, but we should discuss this."

"Discuss . . . what, exactly?"

"Your betrothed," he said, levelling her a long look.

Well, that *was* a departure from life on the Continent, which was the last thing she'd registered him saying.

"Oh," she said.

"Firstly, as you clearly didn't hear me the first time, I wanted to apologise for my response to the news of your engagement." He said the words a little unwillingly, and Annabelle wondered if Theo had prodded him into it. Or perhaps it was his sense of duty. He always had been a stickler for duty—right until he had argued with his father and taken off to war.

She glanced up, noting the dark circles under his eyes. Was he sleeping at all? He did not look like it.

"I was displeased," he continued. An understatement. "His reputation is . . . unsavoury." Also an understatement. "I was concerned you would be hurt."

Annabelle paused by a particularly large copy of *The Mys-*

teries of Udolpho, one of Theo's favourite books, and couldn't resist running her finger down the spine. Without looking at her brother, she said, "Is that not my concern?"

"As your brother—"

"My engagement is none of your business."

His jaw clenched and she could see how urgently he longed to disagree with her. Their father had never been much involved in their lives, being too busy gambling away their fortune, and Henry had quickly assumed the role of heir and protector.

But this was Annabelle's concern. Once, she might have been perfectly happy to let Henry assume control of her life, purely because she did believe he had her best interests at heart. Things had changed since then, however—*she* had changed.

Jacob had changed her.

"I understand the circumstances behind your engagement now," he said. "And I want you to know something—you may feel as though you have no choice but to see it through, but you must know that I will support you if you decide to break it off."

"Henry." She finally dragged her gaze away from the book and to her brother's face. This was unexpectedly sweet. "I appreciate the offer, but—"

"As it happens, I know of some other gentlemen who might better take your fancy," he said, heedless of the way her face fell again. "They are more scholarly, like you, and I think you would like them."

"And if, Henry, I wished to end my engagement and not marry at all?"

He gave her a puzzled smile. "And do what, Anna? Live in

Hardinge's house for the rest of your life? It's not a future you would enjoy, believe me. The spinster aunt?" He gave a short laugh and Annabelle pressed her lips together at the sudden wave of grim shame that overtook her.

As it happened, that had been her plan until recently. To live with either Theo or her mother and fill her days with reading and walking and the quiet joys of life.

But maybe Theo would not want her. Maybe her *mother* would not.

If she *didn't* marry, where would she go?

Her heart twisted at the thought of standing in a church with another gentleman, one who didn't have eyes like midnight sin and a mouth that could tempt even the pure to his unholy ways. How could she ever commit her life to a gentleman who didn't box with his bare fists, who didn't drink to drown whatever pain she still didn't understand, and who didn't touch her as though she was the most precious thing he had ever held?

She inhaled deeply, but the familiar scent of freshly printed books didn't calm her the way it usually did.

The answer was she couldn't. If he continued not to want to marry her, then she would have to find another way through life that didn't involve marriage.

"Are you certain you want to marry him?" Henry asked when she didn't speak. "Is he pressuring you into the match?"

"Pressuring me?"

"I understand Nathanial gave you a generous dowry."

"And you think Lord Sunderland is after me for my money?"

Henry shrugged. "Stranger things have happened. The more money he has, the more he can waste at card tables."

And here she had been thinking Henry was trying to support

217

her. "And if I told you he had no interest in my dowry?"

The corner of Henry's mouth curled in distaste. "You mean to tell me he's in love with you?"

No.

If he loved her the way he had loved Madeline, he would already have married her. Instead, he was doing his best to marry her off to another gentleman.

Her stomach turned and she swallowed back the sour taste.

"I just want you to be happy," Henry said. "And I know what that man is capable of. The lives he's ruined."

"That's enough," Annabelle snapped, unable to listen to him any longer. "If I require your advice, you may be sure I will ask for it."

Henry's brows drew together. "Annabelle, I—"

"Jacob has been kind to me and yes, I'm sure he has done some terrible things in his past, but he has not been terrible to *me*, and I will not be persuaded to change my mind about marrying him or anyone else."

Not that there would be anyone else.

The next time they met, she would ask him once and for all if he would ever marry her, and if he would not, she would end the engagement. Reputation be damned. Now Henry was back, he could keep the family afloat, maybe marry a nice girl, and she could go back to her quiet life in the country. If no one wanted her, she would take an occupation somewhere. A governess, perhaps. Or a companion. That would be enough of what she wanted to be happy.

She *would* be happy.

Henry's face set, but he said nothing as she stalked forward and bought herself a new book with her pin money. But even that didn't soothe the emotions roiling in her chest.

* * *

The next time Annabelle saw Jacob was two days later at the theatre. Unfortunately, her entire family except for Theo, who was claiming illness, was in attendance, so there was little potential for privacy.

The first time she had come to the theatre in a box, she had been captivated by the opera below. Every tiny detail had held her attention, and she had felt her heart soar with the music.

Now, she was achingly aware of Jacob's muscular thigh inches from her own, radiating heat. The last time they had been together, he had done unspeakable things to her, and now she wanted him to do them to her again.

Her cheeks burned and she tried her best to focus on the elaborate staging, her opera glasses fixed to her eyes, her gaze unfixed and mindless.

With him this close, all she could think about was the sight of his head between her legs, and how she wanted him.

This kind of want wasn't pretty—it was a raw, visceral thing that had her fisting her hands until her knuckles whitened.

He glanced across at her; the tiniest movement of his head, one she wouldn't have seen if it weren't for the fact her attention was wholly on him. "Annabelle," he murmured, so low no one else could hear. He took her hand, straightening out her fingers. She was wearing little kitten gloves, and the grooves from her nails were visible in the fleshy part of her thumb. He smoothed over the material the way he might have smoothed over her skin.

She felt it all over.

What she desperately wanted was for the eyes behind them

to vanish. In particular, she felt Henry's glare boring into the back of her head. Before they'd left, she'd made him promise he would say nothing, but there was no need for words when his eyes told a story all of their own.

Jacob retained her hand a heartbeat too long before replacing it on her lap, his eyes down on the opera below.

Look at me, she silently begged as she too pretended to watch the opera.

A muscle in his jaw flexed, but he made no other movement. He could have been a fallen angel in all his dark perfection, and had they been alone, she might have given into her temptation to look at him. Just look, just watch, just wonder what it might be like between them if they were to come together again.

A new ache started between her legs at the thought and she pressed her thighs together. This was a new sensation and not an entirely welcome one.

His gaze darted down to the way her skirts had shifted, and he inhaled. His body tensed for a second, and she half thought he was going to run from the box. Then, the motion looking like a physical effort, he exhaled and relaxed.

"You're missing it, little bird," he muttered when she didn't immediately look away from the tension in his hands.

Frustrated, she stared back at the stage, not taking anything in. A soprano was singing an aria, her voice rising and swelling in accents of agony that reflected in Annabelle's chest. Jacob had insisted on meeting them at the opera house instead of accompanying them there, and now, he looked as though he did not want to be there at all.

Cautiously, for she knew her family were just behind, she reached out a hand and wrapped it around one of his.

Without so much as looking at her, he freed himself from

her grip and placed her hand back on her lap.

The wave of disappointment was crushing. She told herself it was nothing, that he merely would not want to show her affection in public, but it brought back the memory of how he had sent her away immediately after . . . well, after everything they had done.

If that was the case, she already knew what his answer would be when she asked if he would marry her. Her throat thickened. Somehow, inexplicably, things had changed for her, but nothing appeared to have changed for him. She was just his personal history repeating itself, and he was not prepared, it seemed, to let that happen.

Her breath caught on its way out and Jacob's jaw clenched.

A few torturous moments later, the curtain descended for the interval, and Annabelle gathered what tattered remnants of her courage remained. Now was her moment.

"Stay a moment," she said as Jacob made to leave. Behind them, Henry hesitated, then remained with them. She sucked in a sharp breath of frustration. Unmarried, with her family around her, it was impossible to find privacy.

"I must speak with you," she whispered, putting her hand on his arm. His eyes flickered down to the contact. "Please."

"And say what?" His jaw worked. "If you want me to apologise for the last time we met, I—"

"No!" The word was little more than a hiss, but some of the tension seeped from his body. He sighed.

"Then what is it?"

She could hardly tell him here with Henry's eyes on them. "Can I call on you?"

"That's not a good idea, little bird." Jacob tossed a glance behind them at her brother. "Your guard dog might not approve."

"He does not control me."

"Perhaps not, but it would be unwise to provoke him."

He was being infuriating and she set her jaw. "Very well. Be like that."

Jacob offered her a mocking bow, but she noticed his eyes were bleak. "Shall we find the Duke?"

Annabelle had no choice but to accept his arm and let him lead her away, Henry following close on their heels. Evidently now was not the right time to ask him if he would marry her.

The rest of the opera passed in a blur, Jacob still distant for all he played the role of attentive fiance, and by the time she returned home with Nathanial, her head ached and she wanted nothing more than to go to bed.

As soon as they stepped inside Norfolk House, however, she knew something was wrong. The silence was a little too profound, as though the house and all its occupants were holding their breaths.

"Theo?" Nathanial called, his voice echoing in the cavernous space.

One of the footmen stepped forward, his face impassive. "Her Grace was taken to bed earlier, Your Grace."

"To bed?" Nathanial frowned, already taking off his hat and gloves. "What happened?"

"Nothing too extreme, Your Grace, but she expressed a wish to see you as soon as you are home."

"Of course." Without waiting for Annabelle, Nathanial strode for the stairs. Annabelle handed her bonnet to William, the footman, and hurried after him. Theo had looked ill for the past couple of weeks, but she rarely allowed herself to be put to bed.

In fact, the last time she had been, she had been poisoned. Annabelle broke into a run.

Her fear was entirely unjustified; she knew that even as she hurried through Theo's ajar bedroom door.

Theo looked up, exasperated, from where she was reclining on the bed. "You too? Really, the both of you. I am not dying."

Nathanial folded his arms from where he stood by her side. "Forgive me for my concern over the condition of my wife."

Annabelle said nothing, but she could still remember Theo's waxy face and uncontrollable way she had vomited, body shuddering, delirious with fever. She did not think she would ever forget.

"You do not usually take to your bed," Nathanial reminded her.

Theo looked into his face with such soft adoration, Annabelle felt as though she was intruding on something deeply personal. The pain in her chest heightened, reminding her that Jacob had, briefly, looked at her like that, shortly before he had insisted she leave his house.

She made to leave the room but Theo threw out a hand. "Wait, Anna. Stay. This concerns you too, a little."

"How so?"

Theo took a deep breath, glanced at Nathanial, and said, "I'm with child."

Chapter Twenty-Three

The physician who came to visit Theo proclaimed that her ill health had been due to her pregnancy, and he recommended that she leave London. Nathanial made plans to do so immediately, his only concern his wife's health. The only question that remained was whether Annabelle would accompany them or move back in with her mother and Henry.

The answer to that question depended largely on Jacob. She would, of course, travel back to Havercroft, Nathanial's estate, before the baby was due. But the end of the Season was in just two months; if she could prevail upon Jacob to marry her before then, she would stay in London until that date.

If she could not . . . she would leave, and she would break their false engagement.

Her heart hurt at the thought.

Accordingly, because she did not have the time to wait for Jacob to visit her, she took a carriage to Lady Bolton's house, and from there travelled by hackney to Sunderland Place. The butler answered the door with his nose in the air.

"Good day," she said calmly, more collected than she felt. Her heart pounded wildly in her chest. She was almost certain she knew his answer, and she was simultaneously dreading hearing it and waiting in breathless anticipation to see him again without the constraints of society and expectation. "I'm here to see Lord Sunderland."

"Is he expecting you?"

"No, but I wish to see him immediately."

"Without an appointment, I—"

"I am his fiancee," she said sharply. "And I insist upon seeing him."

The butler's face blanked until it might have been made from stone. Then he nodded and stepped back from the door. "Follow me, my lady."

After the last time she had been here, the house now looked familiar. But, instead of veering towards the main section of the house, the butler led her to a small parlour, knocking on the closed door.

"Well?" Jacob's voice came from inside.

"There's a lady here to see you, my lord."

Silence. Then the scraping of a chair and the door was flung open. Jacob wore nothing but a shirt and a pair of buckskins, the soft material clinging to his thighs. His hair was a little wild, as though he had been dragging his hands through it, and he frowned at the sight of her.

"I should have known it was you." He glanced at the butler. "That will be all, Smythe."

"Very good, sir."

Annabelle stepped inside the small room, which she saw now was more fashioned as though it was a study than a parlour. There was a large desk, behind which he had evidently been working, and a separate writing desk. Both were piled high with paper. The curtains were thrown open, welcoming in May sunshine, but candle stubs were visible beside the couch in front of the unlit fire.

"I chose to work here instead of my father's study," he said by way of explanation.

"Why?"

"Suffice to say, the study did not hold fond memories."

"Like the library?" she asked softly, her heart aching for him. The scared, hurt boy he must have been all those years ago.

"Yes."

"I'm sorry."

He gave a careless shrug and strode to the couch as though eager to put distance between them. The tightness around her chest squeezed. "I gather you're here to discuss something important."

"Will you not look at me?" she said as he sat, stretching his long legs out in front of him. "Am I so repulsive to you now?"

His gaze leapt to her face and stayed there. "No," he said quietly. "No, you are not repulsive."

"Then why won't you so much as look at me?"

"Because"—he said each word deliberately, as though he were treading on shattered glass—"neither of us can afford to give in to what we want."

"Why?"

His breath left him in a hard exhale and his eyes burned, scorching through her dress. "Because we should not want it."

She stepped closer. "*Why?*"

His expression hardened, the burning want icing over. "Because you are going to marry someone else, and that should not change." His voice was a lashing whip, but she merely stepped closer again. There had always been something about him that had failed to intimidate her—because he too was an outsider, perhaps?

Dark, dark, dark.

He saw the darkness inside himself as a warning, but for her it was a draw. She'd never wondered what lay behind the light; she had never marvelled at the beauty of the sun. Always, always it was the night sky that held her attention—and she knew that the night had to be dark in order for the stars to shine.

She would be his stars if he would let her.

"And if I don't want to marry another?"

His eyes were tar, sucking her under. "We had a deal."

"The deal was if you cannot find me another husband before the summer is out, you will marry me yourself."

He rose suddenly, crossing to her in two steps and taking her wrist in his hands. He looked down at the contact, his strong fingers against her slim bones. "Look at you. Look at *me*. I agreed to help you, but I cannot marry you." He exerted pressure and she gasped at the almost-pain of it. Any more and— "Do you see?" he said, his voice too low, throbbing with intensity, his eyes tortured and fiercely angry. "I could snap you like a twig. I could break you, and you would throw yourself on my mercy anyway?"

"You would not hurt me," she said, making no move to pull away.

He was carved in marble before her; she wasn't even certain she saw him breathe. "If you think that, you do not know me at all," he said with a bitter laugh "My own family despised me. My brother wished I were someone different, and he died because of me—just like Madeline." His lip curled and she could feel the pain underneath his words. He was hers, and she felt him. She *ached* with him. "He always had a weak heart. I suppose I was just the thing that broke it."

"Jacob, you are not what you think you are."

"I'm *exactly* what I think I am. Yes, that's right, look at me with that disappointment in your eyes. Remember why you ever hated me. I'm a scoundrel, a rake. I ruin everything I touch. That has been my curse since the day I was born."

"I don't hate you." Her voice was a whisper.

"You should," he said, bending so she was drowning in the black fire of his eyes. Only the very rim of the gold-streaked brown iris remained, and she watched the faint glint of it, mesmerised. It would be all too easy to fall into him, to release the last of her inhibitions to the wind.

Maybe he would not marry her as she had hoped, but he wanted her, she was certain of that now, and that would be enough. She would take all she could, even if it was just for tonight.

Even if she would leave London with Nathanial and Theo and never see him again.

The thought was freeing, absolving her of guilt. If she was to leave here and have no one else, at least she would have this. It was not a sin if she loved him.

"I hurt everyone I'm close to," he said, and it sounded like a plea. "I *am* ruination."

She placed her hand on his chest. "You are Jacob. I see you. And I want you."

His eyes searched hers, and she twisted her other hand in his grip—it was loose enough to do so now—so she could link her fingers through his.

"Forget our deal," she said forcefully. "Forget about tomorrow. I want you now."

His fingers were feather-soft as they brushed her cheek. "I can't marry you." His voice cracked on the last word.

"Then don't," she said even as her heart cracked. "Just want me. Just for now."

Still he hesitated, and she thought he would never give in.

Then, with a curse, he tugged her face to his, claiming her mouth with his own. There was nothing tender about this kiss—it was bruising in its intensity, his need a feral thing that fought against her own. His other hand found her waist, sliding along to the small of her back, then down to her backside. He squeezed, pressing her against him, his arousal evident even though her skirts. She was dizzy with want.

So this was what it felt like to fall. When contemplated in isolation, it had seemed somewhat terrifying, but now she knew better: it was spectacular. Because he was falling too, and to be united in this was a delightful thing, like holding hands before taking the jump and knowing the same wind that exhilarated her also stole his breath.

He picked her up, carrying her to the couch before the fire, and deposited her on his lap. Her legs fell on either side of his hips and he dragged her skirts up and away as he continued to kiss her.

Time was suspended.

The only thing that existed in Annabelle's world was Jacob's mouth, his hands, the ridge between her legs that she did her best to rock against. His breath was hot against her neck, and the emptiness inside her grew and grew until she knew nothing but Jacob. He became her world, and she knew with barely honed instinct that only he could sate her. Even if she did marry someone else, no other man would make her feel just as she felt now.

"Annabelle," Jacob said, breaking the kiss and groaning. His eyes were half crazed, dark as the clouded night sky. "We should stop."

"I don't want to." She had never been more certain of anything in her life.

"You deserve better than this. God. There isn't even a bed."

"This is perfectly satisfactory."

"We should—"

If he said they should stop one more time, she would throw something. "Right here is perfectly fine," she said firmly. She wasn't about to have him change his mind on the way upstairs.

Seduction was a step further than mere flirtation, but she put the tips he'd given her to use, biting her lip and looking at him through her lashes. "Please," she said, her voice unintentionally breathy.

His hips shifted underneath her as though he couldn't quite keep them still, and his hands fisted in the back of her dress. "Annabelle—"

"Just say yes."

"This is what you want?"

"*Yes*." She stroked the rough line of his jaw. It looked as though he had not shaved today, and she liked the feel of it against her lips as she brushed them against his chin. "Just you, just me, together in this room."

He groaned. "I can deny you nothing when you ask."

"Please," she said again, kissing down his neck. "Please, Jacob. Show me. I want to know everything."

His palm flattened against her back. "If you change your mind, tell me. We can stop at any time."

"I won't want to stop."

"I mean it, Annabelle. I can't—" He closed his eyes briefly. His throat bobbed as he swallowed. "I can't let history repeat itself."

"It won't," she murmured against his pulsepoint at the hollow of his throat. "My eyes are open. I choose this."

"Then we will do it my way." He took her hands, which had been straying down his torso, and put them firmly on his chest again. "Slowly."

She gave an impatient wiggle. "How slowly?"

He rasped a chuckle and kissed her again, fingers nimble against the laces of her dress, only drawing back to tug it over her head. Her stays and chemise went the same way, and then she was sitting on him wearing nothing but her stockings.

"Keep those on," he said hoarsely, tugging them up over her knees. His eyes were filled with such open admiration, she forgot to be shy even as the cool air caressed her bare skin. "There is one thing I need from you, love."

She held onto his shoulders, digging her fingers in. "Yes?"

"Whatever else you choose, do not regret this." With one thumb, he smoothed the reddened pink of her nipple, coaxing it to stand firm and hard. She sucked in a quiet, helpless breath and he smiled in satisfaction. "Promise me, Annabelle."

"I promise."

"Because I do not think I will ever be able to regret this." His touch turned primal, possessive, as though he knew he was the first to lay hands on her skin. The first to claim her.

That thought, too, sent a rush of wild heat through her. She was aflame, burning in his lap, and he was stoking her higher with every sensual stroke. His mouth followed his hands, worshipping every inch of skin until she was rosy with it.

"Beautiful," he muttered, before sucking her nipple into his mouth. Her head tipped back. "So beautiful."

Annabelle smiled helplessly, because to be considered beautiful by a man who offered compliments so sparingly, was a pleasure so exquisite it almost hurt.

"What about you?" she asked between breaths. "We are not equal."

He looked up at her questioningly. "How so?"

"You are still wearing all your clothes."

"Ah." A smug, altogether too-male smile crossed his face. "So you want to see me naked, do you, little bird?"

"Half of London already has, so you may as well show me."

He gave a bark of surprised laughter and leant back, arms behind his head. His eyes were hooded and lazy as they watched her. "Undress me yourself."

She focused on the task at hand. He was not wearing a coat, so there was just his waistcoat and shirt to remove. As for below . . .

Well. She would cross that bridge when she came to it.

His waistcoat buttons were large and mother-of-pearl, gleaming in the sunlight. It took her shaking fingers an inordinately long time to undo them, and when she came to remove his waistcoat, she had to wrap her arms around him to do so. Her sensitive nipples brushed against the smooth material of his shirt, and she let out a tiny squeak. His breath caught and his hands went to her bottom again, kneading and squeezing as though he needed to be touching her.

Urgency heightened, she tugged at his shirt, up and over his head, and then finally.

Finally.

Smooth skin, bronzed, contoured and toned. She had seen him half naked once before, but she had never dreamt she would be at liberty to touch him. She did so now hesitantly, tracing the ridges of muscle, the dichotomy of soft atop hard. The male body was made up of edges and lines, she discovered.

And so hot, burning under her fingers like the heat of his smouldering gaze.

Exploring him the way he had explored her, she slid her hands around to his back. He stiffened as her fingers encountered a roughness she hadn't expected: a crisscross of lines across the broadest part of his back.

"Not there, little bird," he said, kissing the corner of her mouth and taking hold of her wrists, retrieving her hands.

"Why not there?"

His smile didn't touch his eyes. "Let us focus on you."

"No, wait." Her mission to undress him forgotten, she freed her hands from his grasp and explored with her fingers again. Every muscle in his body tensed, his thighs turning rigid underneath her, his breath expelling from him in a sharp rush. And finally, she understood what it was she was feeling.

Scars.

Lots of them, layered and ridged across his back.

She climbed off him and tugged at his arm, half turning him so she could see evidence of the damage for herself. The lines were faded now, white and wrinkled, some ropy. More of them than she could ever have comprehended.

"Jacob," she whispered.

"Don't. Don't pity me."

"Who did this to you?"

He turned, concealing himself again, and she wanted to cry. "Who do you think, sweetheart?"

"No." Not his father.

He had mentioned hating his family before. Lady Bolton had mentioned that his childhood had not been a happy one. But this—

For him to have been flogged so excessively that the evidence of it was imprinted onto his body. He must have *bled*.

"Many fathers do it," he said. "It encourages obedience. And, as I'm sure you can imagine, I was not an obedient child."

"This is not a mere punishment, Jacob. You were beaten. Viciously." Mere words weren't enough. "How old were you?"

"That hardly matters now."

"I beg to differ." Before she knew what she was doing, she was on her feet in front of him, mindless of her state of dress, the only thing in her mind a scared boy summoned into the library, into the study, and beaten into a bloody pulp.

Tears stung her eyes as she looked at him. "Did he beat you when you were merely a child?"

Jacob's eyes were riveted on her, but after a moment he gave a humourless smile. "My defender. Beautiful and debauched. I like seeing you like this, but you should find more worthy things to defend." He reached for her then, pulling her back onto his lap and smoothing his hand down her back. The answering thrill of desire almost made her forget what had made her so angry that even now she still shook with it.

"Annabelle," he said, cupping her bottom. "Endeavour to forget. I do."

"And do you? Endeavour or forget?"

His hand stilled, just for a moment, before tracing a path up along her side. "You can prevail upon me to forget, love," he murmured. "And I shall endeavour to do other things entirely." He flashed her a wicked smile and leant forward to press his mouth against her breast. His tongue, absurdly hot against her skin, flicked out across her nipple.

So many things one could do with a mouth. Her legs brushed against his buckskins and she realised she had only half completed her task.

"Wait," she said as he kissed his way to her other breast. "I was not done."

He spared her a guarded glance. "In what manner?"

She pushed at his shoulders and, reluctantly, he obeyed, sprawling back against the couch and giving her access to his chest and stomach once more. Straddled like this, her knees on either side of his waist and her core pressed against him, she felt a surge of power. Control. She closed her eyes, savouring the moment, needing to press it into her memory like a flower between the pages of a book.

When she opened her eyes, he filled her vision. Opaque eyes, unreadable expression, looking for all the world like a fallen angel. His chest rose and fell.

When this was over, she would leave and never return.

A log slumped in the hearth, scattering sparks, and agony squeezed her chest. A similar emotion split the opaqueness in his eyes—a response to her pain, perhaps, or a similar reckoning of his own.

His hand came up to touch her face with such tenderness, she thought her heart would break. "Annabelle."

She laid her palms against his chest, feeling the pounding of his heart. Then she slid down, down. Past the rigid muscles of his stomach, which tensed under her touch. Down to the buttons on his buckskins, and the hardness that lay underneath.

"Show me how to touch you," she said.

Briefly, he closed his eyes, his breath harsh. Then he took her hand and placed it against his erection. She shifted back to give herself room, and let herself feel.

He was hot, even through the material. When she experimented, stroking her hand up and down, he made a noise in the back of his throat almost as though she had hurt him. There was no more of that lazy amusement in his eyes now; they were intent, hot, fixed on her with an intensity that brought an ache to the place between her legs.

"What now?" she asked, her fingers stilling.

"When you're comfortable, we can remove these." He tapped at his buckskins.

"I'm comfortable now. I want to remove them."

He twitched under her hand and she shifted back again, this time sinking onto the floor in front of him as he stood and rid himself of his trousers.

She gazed hungrily at his body. Yards of bare skin. Bronzed where the sun had kissed him, paler across his chest, his legs. His muscles tensed as her gaze moved across them, as though she were trailing her hands not her eyes over him, and she pressed her legs together, need burning inside her. A torch, flaring bright, compelling in the darkness.

He bent and drew her up so she was standing too, their bodies flush, the warmth of the sunlight gilding them. "We don't have to do everything," he said, brushing his mouth against the line of her jaw. The places their bodies touched blazed with awareness. "We can do as we did before."

Before, he had focused his attention purely on her.

Today, she wanted more.

"I want to please you," she said.

"Have you not been listening?" He looked at her with pleasure-drunk eyes. "You already do."

"I want to please you the way you pleased me."

His eyes were the dark sea and she drowned in them. Slowly, he sank back down onto the couch, guiding her to kneel before him. The carpet was soft against her knees.

"Your hand," he said gruffly, holding out his palm. She put her fingers in it, and he guided her to his length. His skin was velvet smooth as she wrapped her hand around it. He stifled a groan.

"Like this?" she asked.

"Yes. Just like that, sweetheart." His eyes fluttered shut and his mouth fell half open. The sight of it—her hand working him, his short sharp breaths and the slack, helpless pleasure on his face—was the single most erotic thing she had ever seen. His hips rocked into her hand, and every part of him was drawn tight, pleasure coiling and uncoiling. She had a sense of how it felt, because it had been how he had made her feel.

Only this time, *she* was in control. It was a wild, heady feeling, to have this much power over another person; to know that he was compelled by the single, simple movement of her hand.

Remembering what he had done with his mouth, she bent. He smelt salty, musky, but not unpleasant. It was all unequivocally male, and the ache between her thighs only intensified.

Jacob stilled. "Annabelle, what are you—"

She flicked her tongue across him. At the fleeting touch, he groaned, swore, rocked towards her mouth. His hand found her hair, tangling in the silken tresses, fisting. Holding her away from him.

"This isn't something—you don't have to—"

"I want to," she told him, and the pressure that held her back loosened. She took the moment to lick him again and brought him into her mouth.

The sensation of it was overwhelming. He was too large for

237

her mouth and her teeth threatened to pose a problem, but she worked her tongue across him, concentrating on breathing through her nose. Uncertain of whether she was doing it right, she glanced up at him. His hand was gentle in her hair, but his other hand was tight around the arm of the chair and his jaw was clenched like he was in pain.

"Is this good for you?" she asked, withdrawing briefly,

"*Yes*." The word came out husky and deep. "Good girl. Take me in deep. Just like that. That's right."

Heady from the praise, she increased her pace, and he groaned, every muscle in his body clenched. She explored the hardness of his thighs with her nails as she licked and slaved, and with every eager twitch, every muted gasp, pleasure sank to the gathering heat between her thighs.

She was doing this to him. *She* was the one making him lose control. His voice was ragged as he whispered praises—how beautiful she was, how much he had wanted this, how incredible the feel of her mouth was—and she placed her hand around the base of his shaft to hold him steady.

With a curse, he used the hand in her hair to pull her off. Half dazed, she stared at him, and he reached down to wipe saliva from the corner of her mouth with his thumb. His mouth twitched. "Your enthusiasm is commendable, sweetheart, but any more and this will be over before it has even started," he said with a flicker of self-deprecating amusement. He beckoned her closer. "Come here."

Annabelle did as he requested, allowing him to turn her around so her back was to his chest and his arms wrapped around her. Her legs fell on either side of his and she was bared to the empty room. There was something so frighteningly erotic about the position that she squirmed in restless anticipation.

"That's my girl," he murmured into her ear, and it was as though his voice had stroked all down her sensitive skin. Her nipples peaked in the cool air, her breasts heavy. He cupped them, making a satisfied sound, and she let her head loll against his shoulder as his other hand slid down her stomach. Down, down, past the soft curls that protected her womanhood, to her slick centre. There, right where she needed him. She let out a low moan.

"That's right, sweetheart. Tell me what you like."

"I don't know, I don't know." She tossed her head restlessly as he made small circles. "I liked what you did before."

He pressed a kiss to her shoulder. "I know."

"I just want to feel like that again."

"You will." He stroked her again. Slow, languorous strokes as though he had all the time in the world, seemingly oblivious to the needs of his own body, which had seemed so urgent just minutes ago. And Annabelle lost herself to the pleasure he provoked. It broke over her in hot waves. Gradually at first, then as his fingers became more insistent, it gained intensity, something tightening in her lower regions like pulling on a string.

This was just as it was last time, except it was so much *more* than it had been then. Then, he hadn't teased her with such deliberate, provocative slowness. Then, she hadn't been pressed against his naked body, filled with that strange intimacy that made her heart ache almost as much as her core.

If this was love, then it was unendurable. So sweet it became sharp, panging pain. So much, her body was breaking apart trying to contain it.

"Annabelle," he said against her ear, his voice a low growl.

"You're holding back."

She found his arm, gripping so hard her nails dug in. "No I'm not."

"I can feel it, sweetheart." He licked up her throat then bit, the sharp slice of pain only bringing her closer to that edge. "But never fear. We have all day."

"I just—" She closed her eyes, humiliation burning her cheeks. "I just don't want it to end."

His fingers stilled for a heartbeat. Then he continued, nose nuzzling at the base of her ear. "Annabelle," he said, such unbearable tenderness in his voice that it made her nose sting. "Annabelle."

"Make it last, Jacob. Please."

"There's a delightful fact about women you should know," he said, an attempt at his usual levity back in his voice. He splayed one hand against her stomach, holding her still. "Unlike men, they can do this more than once."

"You mean—"

"Believe me when I say I am not done with you." He slid a finger inside her and she gasped at the intrusion, the sense of fulfilment she'd been craving all this time. But not enough. "So hold back if you wish, Annabelle, but this won't be ending for a long time yet."

It would have been in vain to resist any longer. His low, seductive voice, paired with the innate skill of his hands, was too much. She broke, feeling as though she truly did shatter with the force of her climax. Into shards, tossed by the stormy waves of pleasure that rocked her. Only Jacob held her together again. Jacob, with his strong arms and his reassuring murmurs. Jacob, whose patience in this knew no bounds, because he waited for every piece of her soul to be stitched back together as he eked out every last drop of pleasure.

Only when she sagged limp against him did he remove his hand and just hold her again. This was deeper than a mere joining of their bodies. A sensation that was difficult to put to words, but that made her feel as though the space between them had shrunk.

Before, they had been two people. Now, as he turned her and set her atop him, it felt as though they were one. And it was the rendering them back into two that would cause the pain.

Raising her up a little, he took hold of himself and rubbed against her entrance. His eyes lost focus, and he released a shuddering breath. "This is your first time?"

"Yes."

"I should not like that as much as I do," he muttered, more to himself than her. His hand on her hip flexed and he looked up into her face. "This position puts you in control. If it hurts, and it may, you can stop."

"I don't want to stop," she said, watching the effect it had on him. The way his throat bobbed as he swallowed and he looked at her with such greedy, desperate admiration. She revelled in it, the feeling of power it gave her, that someone could want her this much. Beyond reason.

There was very little reason left between them.

She didn't know her body particularly well, but he did, placing himself right where he needed to be. It was pure instinct to press down, pushing down and down, attempting to take him in despite the tightness and the friction. Delicious, glorious friction that somehow eased the way and sent fire licking up her body. He gripped her hips, muttering obscenities that somehow made the moment sweeter, not forcing her down but guiding her to an angle that had him so deep inside her, she saw stars.

"That's right, sweetheart," he said, voice gravelly when he was fully inside her. She shifted experimentally, and his fingers squeezed her in chastisement. "Just stay still for a moment. Get used to the feel of me."

There had been, briefly, a moment of too-tightness, but that had faded now. The sensation of being filled was almost too much to bear, and yet she could bear it, wanted to bear it, never wanted it to stop.

She raised her gaze to his face and he pulled her in for a kiss as she rolled her hips, experimenting with how best to move. He moaned, gripping her hip almost to the point of pain. Despite the emotion binding her chest, she smiled.

"I've dreamt of this," he said as he pushed into her, smiling at the helpless sound she made. "Not just here—everywhere."

Words were nigh impossible, but she managed, "Tell me."

"Here." His lips brushed her jaw. "Upstairs in my bed. You've done things there that would make you blush."

Annabelle gripped his shoulders as she tried to find her rhythm. His hands on her hips guided, the pressure gentle yet firm. "How long have you wanted to do this?"

"Longer than I should."

That wasn't an answer, but he placed his thumb against her folds and began to rub, and the questions fell away. Her movements became jerky. He smoothed his other hand down her back. "Slowly," he murmured into her hair. "I'm not finished with you yet."

"Jacob."

"When you fall apart, I want my name on your lips."

Such a possessive thing to say, and yet she revelled in it; the gruff note in his voice made her climax closer, closer, closer.

Everything was too bright, too much. And yet not enough. Though it was impossible, she wanted to be closer. She increased her pace, feeling as though fireworks were bursting inside her, bright colour against deep dark.

"Jacob," she gasped. "It's happening."

"I know. Let it happen, love."

Her nails dug into his shoulder and she bent her head, biting down on the muscle between his shoulder and neck. Jacob rasped a laugh as his hand flattened on the small of her back, holding her where he needed her.

"That's right," he said. "I'm yours. Do as you please."

There was nothing that pleased her more than this. She wanted to sink in this moment forever, to submerge and never again break the surface. If drowning meant she could stay here with Jacob, feeling him everywhere, then she would.

Her heart contracted, but before she could recognise the feeling, pleasure swept across her. His thumb grew more urgent, pressing where she needed him, and she cried his name as she fell apart.

His arms were gentle as they cradled her until she shuddered, boneless, against him. Then he shifted her until she was lying on the sofa and he was poised above her.

When he entered her again, it felt like a reckoning. She could summon no laughter as she looked at him now, drinking in the grim beauty of his face. His eyes were dark and lovely. She would never forget them as long as she lived.

Time unravelled. Jacob's thrusts started gentle, little sinuous rolls of his hips that drove her partway insane, and she urged him on with her hands, her nails, her mouth. She kissed and licked every part of him she had access to, kissing his collarbone, licking up the column of his throat. One hand sank into her hair again, holding it just tightly enough; the other came to her throat, and she remembered the way he had wrapped his fingers around her neck in the closet, and the wild rush of heat through her made her skin prickle.

"*Annabelle.*" Jacob's voice was urgent, and she felt it, the way something changed. His movements grew harder, pushing inside her deeper until the pleasure was scalding, blinding, the pressure growing and growing even without his hand between them to urge her on.

This time, when she climaxed, she kept her eyes open, looking at him as she cried out, and he kissed her with a clumsy mouth, not slowing his pace, his body tightening around her.

Too soon, this was happening too soon. She wasn't ready for it to be over.

As though he read her mind, he abruptly slowed, sweat gleaming on his skin and his breathing elevated.

"As long as you need," he said, cupping her jaw.

Forever.

But that was too much. He only meant now; he could give her a few more minutes of bliss now if she needed it.

Conversely, if they'd had more time together in London, she might have asked him to give her a little longer now, but knowing this was to end made every second bittersweet, and there was only so much she could take.

"Now," she whispered.

A shudder rolled through him and his eyes became unfocused. As though her voice alone had undone him, a moan slipped from his lips, and he withdrew from her in a sharp motion, taking himself in hand. Annabelle watched in fascinated amazement as he emptied himself across her stomach.

"So you don't get with child," he explained when he saw her confusion. "At least, the best way I know how without a French letter."

Annabelle was too depleted to ask what that was. He rose and found a rag, coming back to clean her off with tender, gentle movements. She tucked herself against his body and, just for a few more precious moments, let herself just be.

Chapter Twenty-Four

Under usual circumstances, Jacob was not one to cuddle, but when he opened his eyes again, the sun was setting and Annabelle was tucked against his chest, her breath flowering across his skin.

He could live a hundred lifetimes and never deserve her.

But he wanted to. And he closed his eyes against the strength of that desire, because it was crumbling his every resistance. The scars on his back ached, and he was reminded yet again that he had removed his shirt. She had seen all of him, even the unpleasant parts, and she hadn't run screaming from the room. She had wanted to *defend* him.

He pressed a kiss to her temple, waking her. She stirred sleepily, and then her eyes widened as she took in the passage of time. She sat, reaching to cover herself. He caught her wrist and kissed her shoulder.

"Don't be ashamed, little bird." *And don't regret this.*

He could bear her marrying another—he thought. That was the punishment he had chosen for himself, and he would find a way to endure her being happy with another gentleman. But if she looked at him with disgust now this was over, he didn't think he could ever endure that.

"No, I should just—I should return home."

"Let me send you back in a carriage," he said. That was one point he was determined to be firm on. History *could not* repeat itself. No matter what, he would protect her reputation.

And her reputation would be better protected by another man, one whom her brother didn't despise and actively speak out against.

She blinked several times, and he realised with belated horror that her eyes were glassy with tears. Helplessness swamped him, and he swiped under her cheeks with his thumb. "No, don't cry," he said softly. "Not over me."

"I just don't want to say goodbye." She shook her head and pushed away from him, finding her discarded clothes. "But we must."

"This doesn't change anything." He watched her, unable to look away although he knew he should. The imprint of her naked form would be forever etched in his mind. He would never be able to escape her, no matter how far he ran. "I will still find you a suitable husband."

She snorted, a not unreasonable response. "I don't want a suitable husband," she said, sliding her chemise over her head.

The temptation to ask her to marry him, damn the consequences, was almost overwhelming. He gritted his teeth. The Devil of St James didn't have a heart; everyone knew that. Annabelle had known that going in. *He* knew that.

Whatever obsession he was in the throes of, it would fade with time.

If he married her, they would have children. The Barrington line would continue despite his every effort to the contrary. The family he had grown up to hate would live on in their children, and that felt like a betrayal.

"What do you want?" he asked.

She gave him a sad smile as she turned, offering him her back. "Would you do up my stays and dress?"

His fingers were not as nimble as they should have been, and they fumbled with the laces. "What was your purpose in coming here?" he asked when he was done and she was fully clothed—and he was still naked.

"For two things." She looked into his face and he was startled to see heartbreak there. "To see if you would marry me as agreed at the end of the summer."

"We still have two months left."

"I don't *want* another husband, Jacob." Her bottom lip trembled and he fought the urge to smooth his thumb across it. "I would have married you, but I have no wish to marry anyone else."

The one thing Madeline had never said. And though Madeline had hurt him, it had never felt quite like this. That had been the dream of a boy who knew no better, who mistook attraction for love. This was something wholly sweeter, more obtainable, and yet he still felt her slipping through his fingers.

He knew he needed to let her go, but watching her leave was the hardest thing he had ever done.

"Annabelle—" he started, hardly knowing what he was going to say.

"Hush." She reached up and brushed her lips over his. "You don't want to marry me."

"I can't," he whispered, and something broke inside him.

"Then this is right." Her smile was sad, her eyes were shimmering with tears, and there was a crack in her voice, but her hand was soft as it lingered on his cheek. "You gave me this, and that is enough, Jacob."

It was a peculiar kind of pain, to watch her slip from the room knowing he had denied her. But though she wanted him, it was only because he had been the one to touch her first. One day, and one day soon, that would not be the case.

The thought made him want to hurt something—or perhaps just himself. His heart ached in a way he had thought it could not, and it was agony. *He* was agony. But this was for the best. Even if, in the aftermath of a joining that had shaken him to the core, it did not feel like it.

* * *

Jacob,

My sister is with child and by the time you receive this, I will have left London. After our meeting, I think it's only fitting I end our arrangement and engagement now. Fear not: no one will think you mistreated me or behaved dishonourably.

Thank you for teaching me what it meant to be wanted. I will treasure that all my days.

Yours,

Annabelle

Jacob stared at the missive in his hands with unarticulated shock, his gaze lingering on the small scrawled 'yours' for far too long. She had messy handwriting, elegant despite the chaos of her uneven letters and the blotches of ink she'd left at the bottom of the page. There was a thumbprint on the back from when she had folded it up.

She was leaving.

This was everything he had been looking for, the escape he had been searching for. And it had come at very little cost to him; she was the one to break their agreement and she would announce she had ended their engagement. People would whisper, because they always did, but his reputation would not be significantly damaged.

She was leaving.

He should be celebrating. What a painless end to an engagement he had never intended to uphold.

She was leaving.

Blindly, he sank into a chair, an iron ball in the pit of his stomach. Yesterday, she had come to him for pleasure, and now she was gone. Absurdly, he felt used and discarded, though he had been the one to insist he could not marry her. Shock punched a hole straight through him, and the resulting emptiness made him dizzy.

With every loss he suffered, he thought he would grow accustomed to the bottomless sink of it. The way grief clawed up his insides and raked bloody gashes across his emotions until he bled out.

Empty.

But no, this was not grief. He had not loved her. He did not love—that was the nature of the devil. That was everything he had promised himself all those years ago when Madeline had ripped out his heart and replaced it with the blackened, ruined thing he'd carried in his chest all that time. This could not be heartbreak.

She had come to say goodbye. When she had cried, it had been over leaving him forever, but he had just thought she hadn't wanted to leave him *then*.

Unbidden, he looked at the couch where they had slept

together after he had taken her virginity, the very thing he had sworn he would never do.

He cursed, but nothing eased the heavy weight that was sinking him further into the chair.

Thank you for teaching me what it meant to be wanted. I will treasure that all my days.

She wrote as though she would never see him again. Whatever they had shared was over.

He did his best to convince himself it was better this way. Mere hours ago he had held her and never wanted to let go, but he told himself that he did not care for her.

He cared for nothing.

And he never would again.

Chapter Twenty-Five

"What do you mean you ended your engagement with the Marquess of Sunderland?" her mother demanded, hands on hips, feet planted in the middle of the drawing room. All four of them had arrived at Havercroft, Nathanial's ancestral seat, the previous day, and Theo still looked faintly green from the travelling.

"We were not well suited," Annabelle said with a calmness she didn't feel. At least Henry wasn't here; she didn't think she would be able to bear his vindication.

Her mother's jaw dropped. "But you were *engaged*. And may I remind you of the circumstances behind your engagement?"

"There is no need," Annabelle said, gritting her teeth.

Theo pushed Nathanial's restraining arm away and sat up straighter. "Anna, look at me," she said. "Was he cruel to you?"

"Cruel?" Annabelle didn't have to feign her astonishment. "No, he was—" *Helping me to find my poise and confidence. Occasionally unspeakably kind. The only man I have ever wanted.* "He was nice," she finished lamely.

"Never mind nice—he was a marquess." Her mother narrowed her eyes, and the familiar feeling of being too small swept over Annabelle. "You had no right."

"I had every right," Annabelle said.

Theo's eyes narrowed, and Annabelle had the uncomfortable impression she was seeing too much. She had lost her virtue and she feared it was written across her face.

"Do you dislike him?" Theo asked.

Annabelle tried to keep her expression blank. "No."

"Then why have you ended an engagement that had a good chance of saving you from ruin?"

"Because he never wished to marry me in the first place." *And he still refuses to marry me.* Her head ached.

"Did he talk you into ending it?" Nathanial asked, his voice tight with anger.

"No." Annabelle clasped her hands behind her back and clenched until her fingernails bit into her palm. "He didn't know I was going to do it until I sent him a note the day of our departure." She forced a smile. "The Season is almost at an end, and by late autumn people will have found new things to gossip about."

"It's true," Theo said. "It won't be so bad, Nate. It won't, Mama."

Annabelle kept her decision not to marry to herself. There was no point agitating her mother even more. Of everyone in the room, only Theo would have a chance of understanding, and she was somewhat distracted.

"Is there any way of reversing this?" her mother asked, apparently not listening to anything anyone else said.

"Unfortunately not," Theo said before Annabelle could. "There has been enough scandal around the engagement already. Like Anna said, we should let the rumours die of their own accord while we're in the country."

Their mother's eyes narrowed. "Very well. But come next

Season, Annabelle, I *will* find you a husband."

Unfamiliar stubbornness bloomed in Annabelle's stomach. Her experience with Jacob had taught her two things: what it was like to want without reserve, and that it would never happen to her again. She sucked in a long, deep breath and escaped through the side doors onto the lawn.

The garden at Havercroft was an ambitious affair. The kitchen gardens were growing enough vegetables to feed an army, the grand lawn was interrupted by hedges cut into intricate patterns, and there was a walled lavender garden where bees congregated with a low hum.

Annabelle's favourite part of the garden, however, was the wilderness that adjoined the lawn. There, wildflowers were allowed to spring up with abandon, and benches were placed along small, enclosed walkways, and—her favourite—there was a swing attached to the bough of a great tree.

When she and Theo had been younger, they had come out here with Nathanial to play on this swing, laughing when he pushed them too hard. Annabelle had fallen off, once, and Theo had yelled in his face.

Now, Annabelle perched on the swing and let the toe of one slipper graze the grass underneath as she looked out across the rolling English countryside. Already, it promised to be a hot summer.

A year had changed so much. Theo was married and with child, and Annabelle finally knew what she wanted. She had finally discovered what it was to breathlessly want someone, and that had merely solidified her desire not to marry. A year ago, her decision to remain unwed was because she didn't want a man.

Now she wanted the wrong one.

CHAPTER TWENTY-FIVE

She had not known love could hurt that much.

She did not even know when she had begun to love him; she had landed before she had ever known she was falling. But if he would not marry her, she could not marry another. There was no other man who could take his place.

Better she leave and make her own way in the world. Henry was right: she could not remain living off the charity of others, but that was a bridge she would cross when she came to it. For now, Theo needed her and she would for the foreseeable future. Later, she would decide on her course of action. A governess, perhaps. She could play the pianoforte, she could sing, she could paint, and she was the younger daughter of an earl; if she needed to find work as a governess, she was certain she could. Yes, it was not the done thing, and it wouldn't be easy, but she could do it.

She *would* do it.

And somehow she would contrive to forget Jacob.

* * *

With nothing better to do with her time, Annabelle read through Nathanial's library. Her days passed within the pages of one book or another, and by the time a month had gone by, she had finished all the novels she could find—which were sadly few. She was reading an uninspiring tome about duck husbandry on the swing when she heard footsteps behind her and turned to see Henry approaching, his hat in his hands.

"Henry," she said in surprise, shutting the book with some small relief. Theo was sleeping and the duck book was better than nothing, but any distraction was welcome. "I wasn't expecting to see you here."

"I arrived a few minutes ago. I found I had some business on the estate and so I thought I would drop by." He nodded at the swing. "Do you remember we used to play here as children?"

"You mean you and Nathanial used to run off and play, and left us at home to trail after you?"

He rubbed his chin, which had a slight graze of stubble. "I suppose I do."

"You pushed me off when I was six," she mused. He had been sixteen and lanky then, not having grown into the man he'd become.

"I was a brat back then. But I picked you up and brushed you down and apologised."

"That's only because you were worried I would run to Mama."

"Well, was I right?"

She conceded the point with a slight smile, and tilted her head. "The fault is yours for pushing me off in the first place."

"I'll accept that." He leant against the tree and looked at her with those weary eyes. "I heard you ended your engagement with Jacob Barrington. My congratulations."

And the peace of the moment was dashed. Annabelle glanced at her book, wondering if it would be rude to openly ignore him. Unfortunately, she concluded, it would be.

"It's hardly something to congratulate," she said. "And if you have come here to gloat, you may leave. I have no interest in discussing my former engagement with you."

"Anna, I wouldn't gloat." He sounded a little hurt. "You know I just want the best for you."

If Jacob had wanted her, he would have been the best for

her. Or at least, the only thing she wanted, and she could not find a difference between the two.

"The Season is not yet over, and Theo's child is not yet born," Henry continued. "I came here to request you come back to London with me. We still have a month or two left, and I have a few friends I would like to introduce you to. If you marry before the Season ends—"

Annabelle held up a hand, slipping off the swing, her feet landing on dusty ground, the grass having been scraped away. It was June; the sun was hot and the days long. "You want me to marry one of your friends? That is your grand plan?"

A muscle in his jaw worked. "I have mentioned them before. They are scholarly and kind and would treat you well, and if you were married, your future would be assured."

"I have already mentioned I have no wish to marry."

He made an impatient gesture. "And what, Anna? Have you truly thought this through? Theo and Nathanial are forming a family of their own. Perhaps you can look after the children, but they will employ a nanny for that. And think of the scandal if you remain unmarried. Yes, I am prepared to support you, but you need to help me. I'm trying to save us *all*. Do you realise how close to ruin we are?"

"And marrying me off is going to solve that?"

"It will certainly help. I will take other measures."

"Such as marrying someone yourself?"

He held her gaze. "That is certainly a consideration."

Shivering despite the warm air, she crossed her arms. "And what if I don't love him? This man you've selected."

A dark expression crossed Henry's face, too fast for her to read. "Marriage is not always about love. Sometimes it is about security."

"I don't want security if it comes with misery."

"Perhaps you don't understand the reality of our situation, Anna." He blew out a frustrated breath and began to pace. "Thus far we have stayed afloat because of Nathanial's generosity, but that cannot continue. We must find ways of standing on our own two feet and making our own way in the world."

"I see, and I am the sacrifice to your ambitions?"

His eyes glinted with anger. "You will thank me when you are old enough to understand just what a precarious position you are in, and how our reputation must suffer as a result."

Guilt pressed into her, but she kept her head high, the sting of tears in her nose. "I don't want to go back to London, Henry. And I don't want to be passed around your friends until one of them decides Nathanial's dowry is worth his time."

"Passed around my friends?" He snorted. "If you hate him, there is no obligation to marry, but as it happens I think you will *like* him. He is bookish like you, and he has a kind heart. Do you think I would commit your future to any less of a man?"

"Well how should I know?" She threw up her hands, furious at both him and herself. "You come back from the war a stranger and demand I marry a man of your choosing merely because he is *bookish*."

"I had not thought you would be so choosy," Henry said coldly. "After all, you consented to marry Jacob Barrington."

"Yes, and he treated me well." *I loved him.*

"If *that* is what you consider goodness, then you will have no problem with marrying a man far superior in character."

Annabelle stared at her brother, who was now a stranger, a man she barely recognised. "Who *are* you?"

"I am your brother and the head of this household, and I am

trying to save us all." He slammed his hand against the trunk of the tree. "You will accompany me to London tomorrow and you will do my friends the honour of meeting them."

London, to where Jacob was. To meet a man she had no intention of marrying. But if her brother was this determined to see her married—an aim shared by her mother and the Dowager Duchess, she was sure—then her refusal would hardly be taken seriously.

"And if I refuse?" she asked quietly.

His mouth pressed into a hard line. "I will request for your things to be packed tonight."

Annabelle sucked in a breath, but Henry's expression did not ease as he turned and strode back to the house. Her thoughts churned and her fists clenched. If this was how he was going to be, then he left her with no choice.

She would make her own way in the world. And she would leave that night.

Chapter Twenty-Six

Jacob reclined in his armchair, a glass of scotch—or was it brandy?—in one hand, a lady somewhat drunkenly playing the piano at the other end of the room. A few gentlemen cheered as they competed to see who could drink faster. More of an Oxford pastime, but Jacob hardly cared. They could do what they wished. And if they spilt wine on the carpets, fine by him. Other gentlemen perched ladies on their knees. Courtesans, mostly. A few wandered the room with pitchers of wine or decanters of brandy.

Everything had sunk into a delightful haze that numbed the pain in his chest.

In the month that had passed since Annabelle left, Jacob had fallen back into all his old habits with abandon. He sought ruination.

And if he sometimes lay awake, his body missing a woman it had only just begun to know, he shut down all awareness of it. Time would erase her from his life, and he threw himself into forgetting.

His friends, if he could call them that, cheered him on, and he fell further into the pit he had been digging since the moment he was born.

Smythe handed in his notice. Jacob told himself he didn't care.

There was nothing in the world that could affect him now. No mother would ever want him for her daughter; no moneylender would grant him the sum needed to clear his debts. And Jacob Barrington, reluctant Marquess of Sunderland, told himself he was happy.

"My lord?" came a husky voice. She had striking dark curls that tumbled loosely down her back. No doubt she had just exited a bed with another man. He found he didn't care. And, although she was objectively extremely pretty, he had no interest in seeing what skills she had learnt as she had worked her way up the courtesan ranks.

He trailed an absent finger along her shoulder and then flicked her away. "I already have a drink."

"I thought perhaps you could do with some company, my lord," she said, not shifting from where she was bent over him, breasts visible through her gaping neckline. "You haven't had any entertainment all night."

He gave her a sharp smile. "I'm not looking for entertainment, my dear." Even inebriated, he knew that much.

The only lady he wanted had left London because he had chased her away. And now she was gone, he was beginning to understand just how much of a hold she had on his heart. The only thing that kept him from chasing after her was the knowledge that she would be happier without him. And even that certainty was losing its allure. Once he'd thought *he* would be happier without her, and he'd been drunk for three days and nights now, drowning the pain the only way he knew how.

The woman pouted at him, no doubt intending to showcase

her plump bottom lip. "Then why are we here?"

"For everyone else." He gestured.

"You would like it, my lord, if I could show you how to relax."

"I am certain you are skilled." He caught her hand as she attempted to walk it up his thigh. "And yet your beauty leaves me indifferent."

Her eyes flashed with irritation. No doubt that wasn't what she was accustomed to hearing. And in the past, he had been very generous with his mistresses. No doubt she wanted a bite of his estate.

Too bad.

"You'll be paid for your troubles," he said, taking another long drink. It was scotch after all. "And if it concerns you, you may tell whoever you please that you were with me. Say whatever you like."

She frowned. "Don't you care?"

"I care for nothing."

"Barrington," one of the other gentlemen called. "Have you tried this wine?" He laughed drunkenly as the woman on his lap poured it into his mouth, the burgundy liquid splashing down his shirt. "Imported directly from France."

"I'll bring you some, my lord," the girl in front of him said quickly, rising to fetch a jug of it. While he waited, he tossed back the remainder of the scotch in his glass and put it unsteadily on the table.

When had this ceased to be fun? When he was younger, he had revelled in the parties, the women, the drinking. Now he just felt tired.

The dark-haired girl returned with the jug of wine and straddled his lap, one hand holding the jug and the other skating along the side of his jaw. He didn't have the energy to remove her.

Perhaps the wine would be enough to help him forget. Finally.

It was as the wine was being poured down his throat that pandemonium broke loose. The door slammed open and a familiar voice rang loud and disgusted.

"What the devil is going on here?"

"Louisa?" Jacob blinked, pushing past the girl to look at his old friend. She strode into the room as though she owned it, and was looking around with her lip curled. Her eyes flashed when they met his, and he gave her a lazy grin. "I'd invite you in, but it seems you've dispensed with the necessity."

She gave him a poisonous glower. "Send them away."

"But they're having so much fun."

The girl on his lap gave him a frown, clearly expecting him to remove Louisa, but if that was what she hoped for, she had misjudged. He valued Louisa far more than a nameless girl. He shrugged, pushing her off, and the wine clattered to the floor, staining the carpet. Scowling, she picked herself up.

"Leave," he said before she could protest at his treatment of her. Yes, he was an unmanageable bastard; yes, she should hate him. Everyone else did. "Get out. I don't know or care how you do it so long as you leave."

The music faltered to a halt. Conversation and laughter dimmed. A few hastily rebuttoned their trousers.

Jacob clapped his hands. "You heard me," he said. "The party is over."

Under Louisa's glower, no one dared argue, and the room slowly emptied. Jacob felt no twinge of remorse. It was hardly as though he had been enjoying himself, and if Louisa was going to flay him with his words, well then she could do her worst.

Villiers clapped a sympathetic hand on Jacob's shoulder in passing, and offered Louisa a bow. "My lady," he said. "A delight."

"Leave," she said with icy finality.

Finally, they were all gone. Jacob wiped the last few drops of wine from his chin. His head spun and he knew the moment he tried to rise, he would lose his balance, so he stayed where he was, narrowing his eyes on his unwelcome guest.

"What in the name of all that is holy do you think you're doing?" she demanded.

He gestured around with a slightly clumsy hand. "What do you think, my dear? I'm having a party."

"You are destroying this house and yourself. Half your staff have left. Loyal retainers, Jacob." She flung her gloves onto a table before making a face and picking them back up. "I've stood by and watched as you've done your best to ruin yourself, but enough is enough."

"You sound like my brother."

"Perhaps one of us should. For God's *sake*, Jacob." She began pacing, skirts rustling around her ankles, and he attempted to see the drawing room through her eyes. One of the sofas was upturned; glasses were abandoned on the floor where they had been left. Candle stubs were left on every available surface, and the light was now a little dim. He was probably out of candles and would have to send for some more.

"Oh, look at you." Louisa stopped before him. "This is pathetic. Do you think I lost myself when the man I loved allowed me to marry another?"

"I don't care."

"Yes you do. This is all because you care. Too much." When his eyelids barely flickered, she snorted. "Oh, go stick your head in a bucket. Then maybe we can talk." She took hold of his wrist and dragged him out of his chair with surprising strength. "Outside, now."

"Why are you here?" he asked as he made his unsteady way to the front door. "You weren't invited."

"As if that means anything to me," she said impatiently. "You know I've never been one for convention."

He wrinkled his brow in ponderous confusion. "Did you come here alone?"

"Considering no one knows I'm here, it hardly matters, does it?" She led him into the courtyard to where a pump sat. She pointed underneath it. "Head."

"Now then, Louisa." He attempted a charming smile, though his face was a little numb. "We should talk about this."

"*Now*, Jacob."

He eyed the pump. The evening was cool, though the day had been extremely warm, and he knew the water would be cold. He swayed on his feet. "I could refuse."

Muttering curses under her breath, she took a handful of hair and dragged his head down. Before he could protest or regain his balance, she doused his head with water. It was shockingly cold, so icy it immediately made his bones ache.

"There," Louisa said as he staggered back. "Now we can talk."

He shook his head like a dog. An element of sobriety fell back into place and he frowned at Louisa with fresh understanding. "What has happened? Why are you here?"

"*There* we go." She eyed him for a long moment. "Annabelle has run away from home."

The words rang dully in his ears and he heard the sound of his breath as he dragged it in. "Impossible."

"If that were true, I would not be here. She sent me this letter." There was a note of hysterical amusement in Louisa's voice as she drew a slip of paper from her reticule. "Asking me to pretend I'm concealing her if her brother comes asking. Ridiculous girl. Thinking I would not object to this plan of hers."

He ran a clumsy hand over his face, struggling to make sense of everything Louisa was saying. Annabelle had no *reason* to run away from home. "Why?"

"That *idiot* Henry thought it would be a good idea to force her into matrimony, but she refuses to marry." Her laugh was slightly wild. "But do you know who she would have married, Jacob, if you had just asked her? That girl is head over heels for you."

"But—"

"And if you mention anything about your family or your name or this ridiculous notion in your head that no one can love you, or that you destroy everything in your life, I will duck your head back under there." She whirled and stormed back to the house. "We leave in half an hour, so get your valet to pack for you—if you still possess one. In fact, never mind. *I* will ask your valet to pack." She paused at the doorway and glared at him. "And if you refuse, Jacob Barrington, so help me they will never find your body."

* * *

Jacob had never been so hungover in his life. The rattling, swaying motion of the carriage was doing nothing good to his stomach, and after travelling through the final hours of night, the sun was beginning to rise, sending sharp shafts of pain directly through his eyeballs.

Coffee. He needed coffee. Then, preferably, sleep for a few days. After that, he could perhaps manage some dry toast.

His stomach rolled again and he gritted his teeth against the wave of nausea.

"Only another few hours now," Louisa said, entirely too cheerfully.

He shot her a dour look. "You don't have to enjoy my suffering quite so obviously."

"Oh but I do, Jacob. You've been enjoying yourself for far too long."

"I'm merely doing what I swore I would always—"

"Enough." She waved an impatient hand. "That story is old and you don't believe a word of it, anyway. All that progress I saw when you were courting Annabelle . . ." She sucked in a breath. "Well, I suppose it is a good thing you're going to ask her to marry you."

"I never said I would," he grumbled, though his skin heated at the words. Marry her. Annabelle would be *his*. Such a primal word—such a primal feeling. Better his than anyone else's. Every piece of darkness in him rose at the thought of her marrying another man. *Being* with another man. Submitting to his caresses.

To marry her, he had to accept he would not be the end of the Barrington line. If he married her, he was setting aside a lifetime's worth of hatred in exchange for . . .

Annabelle.

For years, he had thought he did not have a heart, but the truth of the matter had become too pressing to ignore: he had a heart.

And it belonged to Annabelle.

"You *will* ask her to marry you. And then you will clean up your act and figure out what it means to be happy, because I don't suppose you've ever encountered happiness once in your life."

"History is repeating itself," he said.

Louisa glanced at him sharply. "No it isn't. For one, Madeline was a conniving hussy who wanted all she could get without paying the price. She was greedy, Jacob. She wanted your love and she wanted Cecil's position and she was willing to relinquish neither." She shrugged. "Madeline would never have gone to a boxing match to see you."

The tightness in Jacob's chest only increased at the memory of seeing Annabelle in that awful place—the urgent, all-consuming need to get her out. His anger she was putting herself in danger, and his anger that she was seeing the worst part of himself. But she had not run from him even after he had sent her away, she had come to his home to apologise. To *him*. Even after she had learnt of Madeline and all the mistakes he had made.

He didn't deserve her. But by God he wanted to learn how to.

"When did she send the letter?"

"Two days ago," Louisa said. "She intended to leave shortly after, so I expect she's already gone."

"And you don't know where?"

"If I did, I would hardly be involving you in this state," she said tartly.

His head ached. His nausea was a clawed beast climbing up his throat, and more than anything else, he couldn't stop thinking of what might have happened to Annabelle. When Madeline made her way from Cecil's house to his, she had never arrived.

Fear raked its way along his insides. Ignoring his pounding hangover, he gripped the seat and leaned closer. "Can this thing go any faster?"

Chapter Twenty-Seven

Jacob arrived at the Shrewsbury estate, which bordered Havercroft, just as the sun had fully risen above the horizon. The old house had blank, hollow windows and ivy crawling up the walls, and, hopefully, would contain some coffee inside.

"Why are we here?" Jacob asked, finally putting the pieces together. "I thought Annabelle was staying at Norfolk's estate?"

"So she was, but I thought it might be judicial to confront Henry in his own home. The houses are close enough that you will be able to go after Annabelle perfectly well from either."

Jacob pinched the bridge of his nose. "How will I know where to find her?"

Louisa tossed him a scornful glance. "Are you incapable of making enquiries? She is a high-born lady travelling alone, or at best with a servant. Surely she should be easy enough to find."

If she is still well.

The thought would not leave him be, filling him with restless energy as they entered the house. Henry was not yet there, having no doubt travelled to London to see Louisa, if Annabelle had told him she was staying there. Louisa had then left him a note to return here.

"Better we confront him here," she said comfortably, sitting herself down as though she had been here countless times before. "Then you may pursue Annabelle more easily."

"What about Henry?" Jacob paced rather than sit. "Will he not insist on accompanying me? Or going without me?"

"I shall keep him here."

Jacob ran a hand through his hair, which had seen so much of the same treatment no sign of his Brutus style remained. "You seem extremely confident of that point, Louisa."

"That is because I am."

"And there is no potential for doubt?"

"Not when he sees that you are in love with her," she said placidly, and at the sound of footsteps, she nodded, a hard glint in her eye. "He is here."

Henry stalked into the room, baulking at the sight of Jacob standing by the window. Jacob did not so much have time to adopt a fighting stance before Henry had him by the collar, his cravat crumpling irreparably under his fist.

"Where is she?" he spat.

Jacob quirked an eyebrow, his own anger burning in his gut. On the way, he had resolved to put their differences aside for Annabelle's sake, but this was the man who had chased her away.

If he wanted a fight, he was more than happy to oblige.

"I might ask you the same question," he said.

He didn't even see the blow coming. It cracked across his brow, hard enough that his head rocked back and he saw stars.

Good, it felt good to be fighting again.

"It's not enough for you, is it?" Henry demanded. "First you need to corrupt Louisa and now this. My *sister*."

Jacob tilted his head back up, curling his lips in a smile that felt more like bared teeth. "If you think Louisa needed any corrupting, you don't know her as well as I do."

The next blow caught him across the cheek, sending pain splintering back into his head, and he smiled, the pain a balm. "Excellent form," he said conversationally. His pulse pounded in his ears, all the frustration he'd tried in vain to tame with debauchery finally finding an outlet. "Go on. Show me what you think of me. Beat me to a bloody pulp in front of Louisa. That is what a future earl does, is it not? Comports himself with a lack of dignity?" He grinned, feeling blood on his teeth. "Or is that my job?"

"Really," Louisa drawled from where she was still sitting. "You should both be ashamed of yourselves."

Henry dropped Jacob and whirled, taking Louisa in for the first time. Jacob straightened, taking perverse enjoyment in what was about to happen.

"If you've finished brawling like schoolboys, perhaps you might sit down so we may discuss this like adults," she said, sparing Jacob a cutting glance that was enough to assure him of her irritation at his having used her to taunt Henry.

Well, it wasn't his fault that this staid, duty-obsessed man had loved rebellious Louisa, or that he had done his best to turn Annabelle against Jacob. Or that he had tried to force Annabelle into a marriage with another gentleman.

Suddenly, he wished he had punched Henry in return.

"Louisa," Henry said blankly. "Why are you here?"

She narrowed her eyes. "Sit down. And I hope you have an excellent explanation for trying to force Annabelle into marriage."

Henry stiffened. "I hardly see why that's any of your

272

business."

"I rather think the fact she wrote to me in order to ask me to cover for her makes it somewhat my business," Louisa said icily. "And you did not answer my question."

Henry scowled, but finally sat. "I was trying to protect her. The world is not kind to an unmarried lady and she would be happy with Mr Comerford if she gave him the chance. I made it plain I would not force her into matrimony."

Mr Comerford? Jacob swallowed the absurd burn of jealousy and flexed his fingers.

"And did you ever ask her what she wanted?" Louisa asked, and before Henry could speak, she answered for him. "Of course not. If you had, we would not have been in this mess."

Henry scowled, sitting a little too upright, his fists clenched. "I was doing what I thought best for my family and for her own happiness."

"Then you should have been promoting the one marriage that would have *made* her happy."

Henry looked faintly nauseated at the thought. "Barrington?"

"Who else has she been engaged to for all this time?" Louisa threw her hands into the air. "I'm dealing with a pair of idiots."

"That's all very well," Jacob said, "but you can berate us another time. I need to go after her."

Henry looked at him now, the anger drained from his face. The silence was uncomfortable, filled with a thousand things Jacob could say and none he wanted to give voice to.

"Good God," Henry said after a long pause, his voice faint as he looked at Jacob. "Are you in love with her?"

"Of course he is," Louisa said impatiently. "And she's in love with him, only he's too much of a damned idiot to ask her to marry him even though it's the only thing that would make him happy, and from what I can tell, it's the only thing that would make Annabelle happy, too."

Henry looked between them with an expression of vague horror. Jacob glowered at them both. "Do something useful and tell me whether she took a maid. And I will need a horse."

Louisa's glare could have set fire to the upholstery. Henry looked as though he wanted to argue, but eventually said, "She did not take her maid. I only waited to ascertain the barest of essentials before setting off, but it seems she rode a horse into the village. We found it at the local inn."

The foolish, foolish girl. Jacob nodded curtly. "I will find her."

"I will come—"

"No," Louisa said sharply. "You will remain here. The last I heard, the Dowager Duchess of Norfolk is preparing to leave London, and you may be sure she will visit the Duke at Havercroft. She cannot know that Annabelle has fled. Spread the story that she has taken ill and is recuperating here." Louisa raised her eyebrows. "You see how your presence is required. Jacob will find her."

"But the impropriety," Henry protested.

"I can be discreet," Jacob said. "And I will ask her to marry me."

"An enlightened conclusion," Louisa said, her tone biting. "Did you come up with it all by yourself?"

"I might be a damned idiot, but you're a damned harpy, Louisa. I pity the man who loves you." He strode to the door and turned back to face them. "And Beaumont—you have probably guessed this by now, but Louisa and I aren't lovers. Not even close. God help me if we were."

CHAPTER TWENTY-SEVEN

With that, he left the room.

* * *

Curled up before the fire in a small inn parlour, Annabelle read and reread her application letter. She had little experience with these things, but Mrs Hampshire sounded nice, if a little busy, and she wished to give her daughters a lady's education. That was one thing Annabelle was certain she could provide.

She had to find a position soon. Although she had a fair amount of pin money left, she could not remain here indefinitely, and she had no intention of returning to Havercroft only for Henry to drag her away again. And if the thought of entering a strange household as a governess made her stomach twist uncomfortably, that was just something she would have to get used to. A governess would not be expected to attend parties and make polite conversation with people she didn't know. A governess would have a job to do, and no one would bother her so long as she did as she was asked.

Annabelle could do that.

A shudder ran through her and she pushed away her doubt. Leaving had been easier than she'd anticipated. After Henry had ordered her to return to London with him, she had left the house early the next morning. But instead of catching the stagecoach south, she had gone north towards York. She had been in this small inn for several days now; there was no chance that no one had discovered her missing, but hopefully Lady Bolton would be covering for her. At least until she reached her new employer and could send them all a letter explaining what she had done.

Five days away from home and she felt as though her future was finally unfolding. Not the future she had hoped for, admittedly, but better than marriage to a man she could not love.

She put her letter aside and picked up the book of sonnets. Really, she should have known better than to bring it, but when she had gone to leave it behind, her heart had given another pang, and she had been unable to let it sit there.

This book had been loved once. And she would love it now.

She had just begun rereading her favourites when the sound of a disruption reached her. The inn was a large, bustling one, and she was accustomed to the sound of coming and going after two nights in this place, but this was different. A scurrying subservience that made her skin prickle with anticipation. Closing her book, she rose and moved to the door, pressing her ear against it.

"A private parlour," a familiar, drawling voice said. "And a meal, if you would."

She shrank back from the door, eyes wide, her hands shaking.

Jacob.

It didn't seem possible for him to be here. *Here.* In a small coach house in the middle of nowhere. How could he have known that she was here?

He should not have even known she had left home.

She pressed her ear to the door again. "Are you quite well, sir?" she heard the innkeeper ask solicitously.

"Got the devil of a headache."

Yes, that was Jacob all right. Terser than she remembered him, with less of that lazy drawl. Here, it seemed as though it

276

was on a tight leash.

She kept listening, but what remained of their exchange was lost to the general sound of the inn, and eventually she gave up, pacing the small room. *Had* he come for her? The thought took root, growing in her until it was inescapable, large and flowering and unbearably sweet.

Before she could think better of it, she strode to the door and wrenched it open. And there he was, casting the innkeeper into obscurity by his height and his devastating handsomeness. His hair was a trifle too long, falling into his face, and his expression was a little rumpled, like a piece of cloth fisted in one's hand until the creases became part of the fabric itself.

He looked up at the sound of her quiet gasp, and his expression turned razor-sharp. "Well met, little bird," he said in a voice of anger and want like curling smoke. "May I come in?"

Chapter Twenty-Eight

The innkeeper frowned, and Jacob waved a dismissive hand. "My sister," he explained, giving Annabelle a distinctly un-brotherly smile. "No doubt she neglected to tell you she had run away from home. Never mind. I'm here to collect her."

Annabelle's spine stiffened. So he *had* come after her, but not for *her*. It was just so he could drag her back home and Henry could walk her down the aisle to a gentleman who would restore her reputation.

Well, if Jacob wasn't willing to marry her himself, he could hardly expect her to go along with his ridiculous plot to keep her from ruination.

It was a little late for that.

She glowered at him, and he waited as though he knew she would be forced to claim the relationship. The innkeeper's frown was deepening, and this was not a place where she wanted to draw attraction to herself or cause a scene.

"That's right," she said as he gave a satisfied smile. "He's my *brother*."

"Thank you," Jacob said, tossing a careless coin to the innkeeper and striding towards Annabelle. Before she could even attempt to shut the door in his face or turn him away, he was inside, looking around the small space, his gaze landing on the folded newspaper, the letter, and the book of sonnets. An unreadable emotion flashed across his face.

"Why are you here?" she demanded, folding her arms and forcing herself not to be swayed by the dangerous glint in his eyes, or the stubble that marked his chin, or the worn quality of his face, as though he had aged five years in the month they had been apart.

Her heart gave a traitorous leap.

"Did my brother send you? Did he think that I might be more likely to return home with you than him?"

Jacob gave a short, hard laugh. "Your brother was ardently against me finding you, little bird."

"Then why are you here? And how did you *find* me?"

"Why do you think?" He stepped up to her, closer, closer, too close, until her nose was level with his chin and his scent wrapped around her. Horses and leather and that amber scent she always associated with him. "Because you ran away from home and could be in any amount of danger. Do you suppose I would sit indifferent in London when I discovered you were missing?"

"But how?"

"Louisa," he said shortly. "As for how I found you—that was a challenge, I'll admit, but a lady travelling alone is somewhat singular. And you are pretty enough that people remembered your face." He reached out to tug at one of her curls. "Then it was merely a matter of checking the inns along your route until I found the one you were staying at." His jaw clenched and he looked abruptly away. "What were you thinking?" he asked in a quiet, intense voice that made her skin prickle. "Coming out here alone? Anything could have happened to you."

"I can take care of myself." As she had admirably proven thus far.

"Can you now?" He gave a harsh laugh. "So long as no one takes advantage of you. What of your future plans?"

"I have been accepted to a very respectable position."

His eyes narrowed. "A position?"

"As a governess."

"And you think working as a drudge in someone else's house would be preferable to marriage?" He cursed, the sound so explosive she flinched. "Do you think you would be safe and cared for there? Did you truly believe you would have the life you always wanted while subservient to others' children?"

"What does it matter to you?" Annoyingly, tears stung her nose, and she scowled to ward them away. "The last time we met, you told me you would not marry me, and I accepted that. I ended our engagement, and—"

"I was *wrong*." He dashed a hand through his hair, looking wicked and debauched and everything she had ever wanted. Her heart twisted and pounded and she forced herself to look away before her hopes could rise. "For weeks, I have been able to think of nothing but you, Annabelle," he said, his voice quiet like the eye of a storm. "I thought it would be the greatest mistake of your life if you married me, but now I know it would be the greatest mistake of mine if you did not."

Annabelle's mouth dropped open, but she found herself at a loss for words. Jacob gave a crooked smile that rent her heart entirely in two.

"I thought that might get your attention, darling."

Her hands shook and she looked at him more closely, realising there was the ghost of a bruise on his cheek. She raised a shaking hand to touch it and he held perfectly still, his eyes devouring her.

"What happened?"

"I caught your brother by surprise." His mouth quirked in a wry half-smile. "It transpires he doesn't like me."

"Are you all right?"

He caught her hand, bringing it to his mouth and kissing the tips of her fingers. "I am now I know you're safe."

She remembered that Madeline had died when she had fled Cecil, and her chest squeezed.

"You may think I am wicked," he murmured against her fingers, "but I am nothing compared to the cruelty of the world."

"I didn't think you cared," she whispered, and her breath shattered at the thought. She had been running from Henry and his threat, but perhaps she had been running to escape the terrible hurt that had followed her after leaving Jacob.

He rested his forehead against hers. "I always cared, Annabelle. Even before I wanted to. I did my best to convince myself to leave you alone, but that was a futile effort."

"What changed your mind?"

"Because I woke up and I realised that my life means nothing without you in it." His hands found her waist, holding her closer. "And because, little bird, I am madly in love with you. If you are foolish enough to want me, then I am sensible enough to never let you go."

His gaze drifted from her eyes to her mouth, and lingered. His eyes darkened still more until they were almost wholly black.

The colour of the devil.

The colour of desire.

She had to grip his arms so she didn't fall.

"Annabelle," he said, her name music from his lips. "Annabelle. Be mine. Be my wife. Make demands of me and I shall endeavour to fulfil them. If you want books, you can have them. I will buy you a whole library so long as I never have to lose you again."

Annabelle meant to tell him he was the only gentleman she could ever marry. She *wanted* to tell him that she loved and hated him in equal measure, and her heart was his in its entirety.

Instead, she burst into tears.

Chapter Twenty-Nine

Jacob held Annabelle close, cradling her head against his shoulder, his stomach coiling into helpless, desperate knots. She fisted her hand in his waistcoat, gripping so tightly the fabric would be forever ruined, and he pressed his mouth to the side of her head.

"Annabelle," he said against her hair. "Annabelle, tell me how I can make it better. What will make you stop crying?"

If anything, she merely cried harder. He could feel her tears soaking through his waistcoat, and he wished he could transport them away from this dingy, awful tavern with its straw-lined floor and bawdy dining room filled with drunken patrons. Once, he might have revelled in the quiet, underlying threat of violence, but as soon as he had stepped inside and heard that there was a young, fair-haired lady staying there, his stomach had sank.

So long as she consented to go with him, he would order a post-chaise and four to take them back to Kent tonight, or at least as far as a more salubrious establishment. And if she did not consent to marry him, he would do his best to at least persuade her to leave with him.

The thought he had done too much damage for her to still

love him would not leave him. He was a creature of pain, but he had never, never wanted to hurt her. But she was crying over him again. Again. The sight and sound of it flayed him inside out. Seared through him. She could brand him with her tears—but as long as she needed him to hold her, he would be there.

"There has not been a moment since I first met you when I have not wanted you," he said, because he needed to fill this space between them. Her body was flush against his, but he couldn't shake the feeling that the distance grew further with every shaky breath she took. "I may have been born wicked, but you make me want to be good, Annabelle. You make me want to find a way to deserve you. You make me want to fight for the one thing in my life that is worth having." He tightened his hand in her hair, wishing he could reach through her and whisper his words directly against her heart. "I don't care that my father beat me or that I bear his name, or that if you marry me, our children will bear his name. Because they will have your eyes and your kind heart, and God, Annabelle, I haven't wanted anything in my life the way I want to be with you. Losing you almost killed me. I can't do it again." He found her ear with his mouth. "So if you make me work to win you back, I will. I am here to stay." His arms tightened of their own accord. "Tell me you hate me if you must. Tell me you never want to marry me. Tell me whatever is on your heart, and give me the chance to learn how to make you love me."

Her shoulders shook with the force of her sobs, but she said nothing, and the silence disturbed him more than anything else ever could.

"And if you can never love me, at least let me protect you by marrying you," he said. "I will give you space, give you books, everything you ever wanted, and I won't disturb you if that's truly what you want. Just let me do this one thing for you."

Finally, she leaned her head back to look at him. His Annabelle, her face shiny with tears, her eyes red-rimmed, her eyelashes damp and clumped together, more beautiful than a fallen star.

"Tell me again," she said, her voice thick. "Tell me you love me."

He smiled and smoothed away the tears on her cheeks. "I love you with every broken piece of me. My heart is a blackened, imperfect thing, but it is yours to break if you wish. You have that power, Annabelle." He searched her shimmering eyes, needing her to hear him, to understand him. "With just a word."

"You love me," she whispered, her fingers finding his lapel and holding him in place.

"I never stood a chance, darling." He smiled down at her. "I did my best to hold out, but it was a fruitless effort." Holding her gaze, he took both her hands, freeing them from his lapels so he could look down at her properly. "Marry me, Annabelle Beaumont, and save a man from a misery of his very own creation."

Her answering smile was a little watery. "You might have saved us all this pain by coming to this conclusion earlier."

Hope flared to life in his chest, and he bent his lips to brush against her damp, salty ones. "Am I to take that as a yes, sweetheart?"

"If I loved you any less, I would tell you to leave," she said, her voice cracking. "I hate you almost as much as I love you, Jacob Barrington, and you are the only man on earth I could be prevailed upon to marry."

285

No force in existence could have stopped him from kissing her then.

* * *

"I have a room," Annabelle gasped out as soon as he gave her time to breathe. Privacy, they needed privacy—and as soon as possible.

He brushed his mouth against her forehead, then both cheeks. They were still wet from her flood of tears, but she could not bring herself to be embarrassed when he held her this tightly, as though one or both of them would shatter if he released her. "Not here," he murmured. "Much as I would love to have you here—and in a bed, no less—I insist you find a more suitable establishment. Then we can claim to be married and share a room without fear of a maid walking in and disturbing us." He kissed the top of her nose then took her mouth again as though he could not help himself.

"But it's dark," she said in surprise, drawing back. "Are you proposing we travel at night?"

"That is precisely what I am proposing, little bird. There is a remarkable invention—you might have heard of it—called the lantern, and it will suffice to cast a light that—"

She slapped his arm and he broke off with a smile that touched his eyes. One of the first she had seen since he had found her. The sight of it filled all the cracked places inside her.

How quickly hurt could be soothed when the right balm was found.

286

How ironic that her most effective balm was a man known for his violence, his carelessness, and his reckless seduction.

Nothing about him now seemed reckless, however. He was all tenderness as he kissed her once more, promised that he would hire them a coach, and bid her not to leave the room should something befall her.

There was nothing careless about the measures he took to ensure her safety. Despite the hour, he procured them a chaise and four, and settled matters with the innkeeper regarding dinner.

Before she had time to collect her wits, she was sitting opposite Jacob in the shabby carriage, a lantern swinging from the side, sending inconsistent light grazing over them both. The hour was late and although the days were warm, the nights were still cool enough he had requested a blanket to cover her knees.

She felt a little dazed at the speed by which everything had happened.

They were engaged. She had agreed to marry him. Jacob Barrington was in love with her—and not just that, but he was prepared to marry her. Prepared to fight for her.

Part of her had been tempted to make him fight to win her back. But while she was angry, there had been devastation in his voice, and he loved her.

There could be no fighting that.

"Does my brother know you had intended to propose?"

"He did," Jacob confessed, the uneven light casting shadows across his face, gilding him in gold and night. "I think perhaps he might not have opened the conversation with his fists if he had known. Although," he added with a wry grin that made her blood heat, "I can hardly blame him."

"He should not have hurt you." Staggering a little from the motion of the carriage, she moved to take the seat beside him, smoothing her fingers again over the bruise on his cheek. "He hit you."

"In his defence, I provoked him."

"How can you justify it?"

He chuckled, his fingers coming to her cheek and pulling her down for a kiss. "My little defender," he murmured against her mouth. "Hearing you leap to my defence does things to me, little bird."

"Good things?"

His lips moved to her earlobe, giving it a nip that sent heat through her. "Oh yes," he said, his voice so low she barely heard it. "I would say they are good things." When he drew back, she saw yearning flicker across his face as clearly as she felt it melt her bones.

The feeling inside her was too big to be contained. A rabid, possessive need to make this man hers, to ensure he never looked at anyone else the way he was looking at her now.

Every movement awkward, she rose and half collapsed on his lap, straddling him the way she had on the sofa, her knees pressing against the leather.

"Annabelle." His hands caught her waist, drawing her down onto him, and then he was kissing her. Kissing her as though his world had ended and she was the light that beckoned him on; as though the only thing that existed in his world was her.

He sucked her bottom lip into his mouth and bit down, just hard enough for her to gasp with the sting and pleasure of it. Her body went molten, sinking into him. His hips moved and she dragged at her skirts, moving them out of the way, raising them to her chest until her legs were bare.

CHAPTER TWENTY-NINE

There. *There.*

He groaned, a sound that skimmed across her senses, pressed against her skin. With one hand, he gripped her hip; with the other, he ran a hand up her calf to the crease of her knee, tickling the sensitive skin there until she moaned and wriggled against him.

"Careful, love." His eyes were bright when he broke away to look at her, so bright she could hardly bear to meet them. Heat and want that burned her inside out. Such a delicious ache. "We're in a carriage."

"I don't care." She kissed him again, coaxing his tongue with hers until he returned her caresses with an enthusiasm that bordered on filthy. His hand cupped her bottom, grinding her against him, and she laughed. *Laughed.*

"One of these days," he said between kisses, "we will find a bed. And when we do, I won't let you leave it for days."

"Days." The word sounded dreamy. She could stomach days in a bed with Jacob and his wicked mouth, his capable hands, his seductive voice as he told her how much he loved her.

His hips thrust up into her and although he was still wearing trousers, the friction of his erection against her core was enough to make her dizzy. This alone could bring her to that bright peak, but she was still aching and empty inside.

Her need tightened at the thought of him sliding inside her the way he had before.

"Jacob—"

He met her gaze blindly, lust clouding his eyes, and she cupped his face in her hands. "Tell me what you want, love, and I'll give it to you," he rasped. "Tell me how you want me, and you can have it."

"I want all of you."

"Christ, Annabelle." His eyes were unfocused as she rubbed herself against him again, emboldened by the way he responded to her, as though his control was barely hanging on. As though *he* was barely hanging on. His fingers squeezed her bottom in a silent plea, asking for the thing he would never beg her for.

"I want all of you," she repeated. "Because I love you."

His mouth was on hers, and he tasted like desire, like need. She wanted to capture this moment for her memory forever, so she would always know what it was like to be wanted more than life itself. The feeling of being loved was in the shape of his lips, the gentle scrape of his fingers, the taste of his tongue. If ever she had doubted it, she could not now, not while he worshipped her mouth and her body as though she were made out of precious gold and diamonds.

As though she were an angel and he were a shepherd guided by her light.

As though he was lost and she were the path to salvation.

As though she was Annabelle and he loved her.

"Annabelle." Desire was thick in Jacob's voice, and he raised his gaze again, looking at her with eyes that had become more familiar than her own. "I want you to look at me. I want to see your face."

When she looked at him, he urged her up with his hands at her waist, and obediently she lifted herself free of him. He unbuttoned his breeches, freeing his length and positioning himself in preparation for her.

"Here," he said, his voice rasping a little as she sat back on his lap, letting him find the place she needed him to be. "You might need a little—" he started, then as he slipped easily inside, he groaned. "No, I should have known. You're ready for me."

It was a reckoning between them, this moment. A beginning of something new, the end of what had come before. Yesterday, she had thought she would never see him again; now they were tipping headfirst into the future, and that future was wrapped in each other.

There was no mirth in his face, no wicked seduction or gentle mockery. Gone was the teasing, the easy smile that felt as though it had grown on his face the way muscles had wrapped around his arms. Now he was serious, deadly so, everything about him tensed as she sank all the way down.

Deliciously full. Deliciously his.

This is what I was made for.

She'd been foolish to think love somehow beneath her. Because when love looked like this, stripped bare of pretence and malice and artifice, only beauty remained. Soul-deep beauty that had them silent as they watched one another, the rattling of the carriage fading into the distance until there were only their mingled heartbeats. His and hers. Theirs.

Jacob leant forward, pressing a butterfly kiss to her forehead, her nose, her cheeks, her eyelids as she closed her eyes over tears that refused to stay inside her chest.

She turned her head, finding his lips with hers, and for another deliciously extended moment, they were still in everything except their breathing. He linked his fingers through hers and brought them to his chest.

Home.

She shifted against him and his attention focused razor-sharp on that point of contact. The carriage bench gave her more room to spread her legs, take him as deeply as she could, and experiment with angles. Shallow, rising and lowering herself, the sensation not quite enough, more of a tease than a relief. Need spiked, but she forced herself to remain slow, tilting her hips and angling herself so he brushed the spot inside her that sent her vision dimming.

"Annabelle . . ."

"Say my name again."

"Annabelle." It was a plea, a prayer, a blessing. "Annabelle. Annabelle, Annabelle, Annabelle."

Her climax came so quickly upon her that she didn't have time to prepare; it slammed into her in forceful waves. Endless, weightless. She was soaring, she was tumbling, she was suspended in glorious, wild, overwhelming pleasure.

"Annabelle." Jacob's voice was hoarse, and when she collected herself to look into his eyes, they were dark and wild. He was breathing heavily, on the brink of control.

"Arms around me, sweetheart," he said, guiding her arms from his shoulders to his neck. "Hold on tight. Tell me if it's too much."

At his words, her body, which had been languid after her climax, heated once more. Her core pulsed, her need almost agonising.

"Yes," he murmured. "Just like that." His hands gripped her hips, lifting her, setting his own rhythm. Her weight seemed to mean nothing to him, and it was all she could do to hold on.

* * *

Jacob had once thought that he would never again fall for a

woman's charms.

That had been before he'd met Annabelle.

She consumed him and he drove into her with single-minded purpose. He was lost to the demands of his body and hers. They were in a moving carriage for heaven's sake, but he was animal first, man second.

No matter what she deserved, she had chosen him despite his flaws. He would endeavour to be worthy.

Her arms were tight around him, her breath hot against his neck, the tiny gasps and moans that escaped her lips driving him closer to the brink.

He slowed, not wanting it to end so soon. He was alive with desire, every nerve singing a song that sounded like her name.

Her fingers found his hair, nails scraping his skull, hands tugging, and the shock of it, bordering on pain, spurred him on.

All his life, he had been searching without realising; he had been an empty vessel, rejected by a family he could barely consider his own, and she had been the one to fill him.

For her, he would learn to be the man she had always wanted. It felt like a blessing to be finally free of his family's curse—not because he had destroyed the family name, but because through Annabelle, he would turn it into something good, something beautiful.

Underneath her skirts, his thumb found her slick centre, pressing and drawing slow circles. She tightened around him and his vision darkened. The pressure at the base of his spine tightened.

"Annabelle." He raised her and brought her back down on him, loving the little gasped moan she gave. "Annabelle, sweetheart, I need you to look at me."

Her eyes tilted up to his again. Blue, such a stark, lovely blue, like the sun against the clear sky. It reminded him of those hot summer days when he was a boy, before he knew how hard life could be. It reminded him of innocence, of happiness, of barely acknowledged joy.

He would acknowledge it now.

"One more time," he urged her. "For me, little bird. For me. Once more."

"Jacob." Her voice cracked.

"That's right, love. Say my name. Come apart for me."

The command was enough and she shuddered, gasping his name. He held on just to see her climax through before he broke, his fingers entwined with hers, her body cradled against his.

Mine.

The thought was primal, but for once, it didn't feel out of place. He was hers and she was his, and everything was right with the world.

Chapter Thirty

After spending the remainder of the night at a coach house, posing as man and wife, they made the final leg of the journey to Kent. The closer they got, the more nervous Annabelle became. She fidgeted so much, he captured her hand with his own.

"If you're scared of what Henry will say, don't be." He gave a brief smile. "Louisa will have taken him well in hand. If anything, he will be the one grovelling for your forgiveness."

She gave a delicate snort. "Henry doesn't grovel."

"For Louisa, he might." Jacob had no doubt that part of Henry's dislike of him stemmed from the rumours that he and Louisa were lovers, and that, if nothing else, proved there were still lingering feelings between them. Add that to Louisa's disquiet when she had discovered Henry was returning to London—well, the conclusion was plain.

Not that Jacob had any intention of involving himself in their business. They could conduct themselves as they pleased so long as it did not hurt Annabelle.

The Shrewsbury house came into view, and Annabelle's grip on his hand tightened. "Did you write ahead to say we were coming?"

"No, but he knows I had every intention of coming back here once I found you."

As they pulled around the fountain to the front door, the door opened and Henry stepped through. Even Jacob could appreciate the man was not at his best: his stance was all military bearing, but his eyes were bloodshot and his cravat was creased.

"Oh, he's angry," Annabelle whispered. "I knew he would be angry."

"Peace, little bird. I shan't let anything happen to you."

"What about you?" She eyed the bruise on his cheek with more of that protective spirit he found so captivating. In all his life, no one had tried to take care of him. For all Louisa's friendship, even her idea of care was submerging him in cold water. Necessary, he granted, but it was not nearly as appealing as Annabelle's hot defence.

"If it devolves into fisticuffs, this time I will return the favour." The carriage came to a halt and he squeezed her hand before letting her go. "I doubt that will happen, however. Your brother will almost certainly be eager to make amends."

A footman opened the door, and Jacob descended first, nodding at Henry before turning to assist Annabelle. Thankfully, she looked perfectly presentable, and nothing about her appearance suggested he had taken her slowly in the dawn air that morning, his mouth on hers, her legs wrapped around him.

Henry released a shuddering breath at the sight of his sister. "Annabelle," he said, with such heartfelt relief, her eyes filled with tears. "I thought for certain something terrible had happened to you."

"Have some faith, brother," she said, dashing one gloved

finger under her eye. "I can take care of myself."

Jacob resisted the urge to snort. Annabelle was many things, but she was not worldly wise, and he would not have wanted to know what might have happened to her if she had remained in that grimy inn.

Henry turned to him and gave a stiff bow. "Thank you for bringing her back. You have my gratitude."

The temptation to make a quip almost overcame Jacob, but he merely managed to nod once, curtly. "With respect, I did not do it for you."

Henry's answering nod was equally short. "I know."

"Wouldn't it be wonderful if you were friends?" Annabelle piped up, looking between them both. Jacob did his best not to rear back, and Henry concealed the horror that crossed his face with a cough.

The first thing they had been united in.

Jacob took Annabelle's hand and dropped a kiss on her knuckles. "You should really learn how to not push your luck," he murmured, giving her a look through his lashes that made her blush. "We will learn to tolerate each other, but don't ask for more."

"Even for me?" she asked hopefully.

Jacob groaned and broke away. "I'll make my way inside. Join me once you've had a chance to talk. You may tell him our news." As he passed Henry, he said too low for Annabelle to hear, "She needs an apology, Eyresham. Don't let her down."

* * *

As Jacob disappeared up the steps and into her childhood home, Annabelle switched her gaze back to Henry. He looked just as tired as Jacob had.

Because of her. With everything that had happened, she could not feel sorry that her absence had prompted Jacob into declaring feelings she had only ever guessed at, but she did regret making Henry worry. Whatever his methods, she knew it had come from a place of care.

"I'm sorry—" she started, but he held up a hand.

"This apology is mine to make," he said, and scrubbed that hand across his jaw. "I made a series of mistakes, and I made you feel as though you couldn't talk to me about how you felt, and although I do not condone your actions—running away is not the answer, believe me—I'm sorry you did not feel as though I would listen to you."

Any desire Annabelle had felt to rake her brother over hot coals vanished in a rush of sympathy. "I'm sorry you were worried. As soon as I was in my position, I intended to write to you and let you know of my safety. But there is something else I must inform you of."

Henry cleared his throat, his shoulders sinking with resignation. "I have a suspicion, little sister. You are engaged?"

Annabelle did her best not to beam too widely. "I am."

He heaved a breath and nodded to the gardens. "Would you do me the honour of walking with me?"

She accepted his arm and they walked slowly across the large lawn to the wild rose garden. Some had yet to bloom, but the soft perfume still hung in the air, and she took a deep breath. "Is Theo well?"

"Except for the fact the Dowager Duchess came to visit two days ago," Henry said wryly. "She heard about the end of your engagement with Barrington."

Oh no. That could only mean—

"Hardinge said you were convalescing with me," he said before the panic could settle too firmly on her. "He said you have pneumonia. It does mean you can't visit your sister until the Dowager leaves, but I'll let her know you're back and well."

This meant she would have to wait to be married again, but that was hardly too much of a hardship. Annabelle chewed her lip and nodded. "Does she know we are still engaged?"

"No, but I'll make sure she discovers it." Henry ran a hand through his hair. "Do you truly love him?"

"I do," she said simply. "I know you don't like him, but he has been nothing but kind to me."

"And that is why you did not want to marry anyone else?"

She spared him a sharp glance. "I never *wanted* to marry. And in particular not a man anyone else had chosen for me. You might think that marrying someone you don't love is part of your duty to this family, but it is not mine."

A muscle in his jaw twitched. "I would not ever have asked you to do something I would not do."

"And if you decide to marry a young lady for the sake of her money and your reputation, then that is your decision, but it was never mine."

He gave a short nod. "I only ever wanted the best for you, Annabelle."

"I know," she said, laying a hand on his arm. "But your best is not my best."

"Then," he said, heaving a sigh, "I hope you will be happy."

Annabelle could not stop the smile from spreading across her face. "Do you know, Henry, I believe I will."

Chapter Thirty-One

Jacob's ancestral seat, Belcourt Hall, was located in Cheshire, and after securing Annabelle's hand in marriage, he travelled there for the first time since his father had died. While Annabelle kept her sister company in Kent, he set about the task of setting his estate in order.

He flung open the windows to let light and air into the musty rooms; he ordered everything to be cleaned in preparation for the new marchioness; he spoke with the groundskeepers and the steward to establish what he would need to do to revive the land.

If they were going to spend the majority of their time here in the future, as Annabelle preferred the quiet of the country to the bustle of the city, he had every intention of learning how best to run his estate.

This was the role his father had never thought him capable of. Even Cecil had never believed he could make anything of himself, for all he had wished it. But Jacob found himself enjoying being a landowner. Politics was not something he was cut out for, but he could do this, at least.

And he took great pleasure in ordering all his father's portraits to be burnt.

Then, he turned his attention to the paperwork that had mounted during his inaction.

The door to his study creaked open and Annabelle crept in, shutting the door carefully behind her. She had arrived a few days ago with Louisa on a visit that was, on the surface, largely above board. He had suggested she see her future home before they married, and Louisa had offered to act as chaperone.

Sometimes, when he was alone, the memories of what had been done to him in this room were overwhelming, but when Annabelle was with him, all the darkness within him gave way to her light.

"You really do have a lot of debts," she said, peering over his shoulder at the papers.

He laughed under his breath and snaked an arm around her waist. "That is hardly the surprising part."

"Then what is?"

"The fact I'm going to pay them off." He tapped the end of her nose. "As soon as you marry me, that is."

"I knew you were only marrying me for my dowry," she said mock-teasingly.

"Guilty as charged."

She laughed, a slow unfurling of sound that made his stomach tighten. He wasn't sure why—probably because he'd heard her laugh so rarely over the course of their acquaintance. Now, she was laughing freely and without restraint, and he would never tire of hearing it.

"Where's Louisa?" he asked, tugging Annabelle onto his lap.

"Distracting your housekeeper." Annabelle wiggled against him with deliberate provocativeness, and he hardened against her backside. "She requested a tour of the gardens and I claimed a headache."

"Little minx," he said affectionately, holding her in place. His teeth grazed her earlobe and she bit back a gasp. "I suppose you came here looking for polite conversation."

"I thought we might discuss your investments." She arched against him as he splayed his hand against her stomach.

"Well *that's* an offer I can't refuse," he murmured, drawing her more firmly against him. "Although why is it you always find me when there's no bed?"

"There are very few opportunities to find you when there *is* a bed." Her voice dissolved into a sigh, and he smiled against her neck. "It will be a relief when we are finally married."

"Only one more week." The thought filled him with an almost possessive pride. "I'm sure you can hold out that long." He slid his fingers through her hair, gripping the silky strands and tugging her head back. She made a low noise of approval, and he reached up to cup her breast.

She was tinder; he was a match. The conflagration was inevitable.

"Are you nervous?" she asked, her head tilted back to his shoulder.

"About marrying you?"

"About the concept of marriage."

"To anyone else I would be." He licked up the column of her throat. "Then again, I wouldn't be marrying anyone else."

"No, nor would I." She let out a long, shuddering breath. "I thought I would be nervous."

"Of what, love?"

"Marrying the Devil of St James."

"I *do* have a terrible reputation," he said, taking hold of her earlobe with his teeth and tugging.

"People will whisper." She took his hand and guided it to her

302

throat, which she bared as an offering. Trust—he had never had anyone trust him the way she did. "But I don't think I mind."

"Let them whisper. Let them envy our happiness from afar."

She twisted so she was facing him, her summer eyes now the violet of approaching autumn. "I have never cared less what other people think."

"Long may that continue." He leant forward and kissed her, drawing her bottom lip into his mouth and sucking. "Although for what it's worth, I shall comport myself with the *utmost* dignity when we are in Society together. No one shall be able to fault my behaviour."

"Liar," she said, laughing, her cheeks rosy pink. "You'll shock all of the matrons with your outlandish comments."

"Well, I will flirt with you *outrageously*."

"That's not done," she said primly, but a smile tugged at the corner of her mouth. "A husband and wife should not show each other undue affection in public."

"Then I take it back: I shall not comport myself with dignity. I shall be slavishly devoted to my wife and break every rule of convention."

"The world will be amazed."

"The world can go hang. I want what will make you happiest."

"You," she whispered, looping her arms around his neck. "You, Jacob. That's all."

He kissed her forehead. "And books."

"Well, yes. Of course."

"I would expect nothing else."

"But they do come second," she said, considering. "I think."

"I'm flattered."

Her laugh was low but it still tingled up his spine as though she had put her finger to his skin. "I hope you are. *That* is a concession I never thought I would make."

"Then I'm not only flattered but honoured," he said, kissing her again because he could not quite help himself. "How long do we have?"

"Until dinner, I think."

He rose, lifting her and placing her on the desk. To hell with his paperwork. "Wait there," he instructed as he strode to the windows and shut the curtains. There was no point offending the staff when Annabelle would soon be their mistress.

Annabelle was flushed, her eyes shining like stars, and he took a moment to appreciate her shy beauty. Pointed chin, full mouth, large eyes, soft freckles across her nose which she confessed to hating and he adored. Cheeks that were more frequently red than pale, as they were now. Sometimes with embarrassment, but more recently, with pleasure.

"You," he said hoarsely, "are a wonder."

She gave a shy smile. "High praise coming from a man who has brought Society to its knees."

"There's someone else I would like to see on their knees."

Her cheeks glowed a deeper red. "*That* would be scandalous, my lord."

"It would be delectable, sweetheart." He stepped closer, taking his time. "But that's not what you're here for."

"And what *am* I here for?"

He picked up a book from his desk and handed it to her. "Reading is your love, is it not? Open a page and begin."

She eyed him over the top of the pages, her flush sinking down her throat to her chest. "What will you do?"

He sank to his knees and pushed her skirts back. "Distract

you."

* * *

Jacob's hand was warm on hers as he led her out through the gardens. July had eased into August, and the grass was dry underfoot. Tomorrow morning, they would travel to London for the wedding. Then, to her relief, instead of parading her to Society like she had feared a new husband might, Jacob seemed perfectly content to whisk her back off to the country. A honeymoon in Yorkshire then back to her new home.

Heaven.

Of course, now she was able to retreat from Society, she found she didn't fear it the same way she had. There were still expectations—rather alarming ones, given her forthcoming rank and consequence. But she had Jacob by her side, and although his reputation was not altogether savoury, he was at least now a rich and influential man, and he looked at her as though she had hung the moon and every single one of the stars.

"Given you already have me, body and soul," Jacob said, a languid drawl in his voice, "what do you want most in the world?"

She raised an eyebrow at him. "You presume you come first."

"You informed me only the other day that you prefer me to books."

"I said *I think*, and my opinion can quickly change. Especially when you're arrogant and obnoxious."

He gave her a hooded, lazy smile and her heart quickened in anticipation. Really, she was insatiable when it came to him, and although it wasn't precisely unwelcome, it wasn't always *convenient*. "Ah but, little bird, I am *always* arrogant and obnoxious. I have it on the best of authority."

"Then I suppose I prefer books," she said tartly, twinkling up at him. Past the pretence at indifference, his eyes glowed back, all heat and seduction and something deeper, warmer.

"A timely conclusion." They turned a corner to see a small stone cottage overlooking a lake. Havercroft was beautiful, but here, Jacob's estate embraced the land, wilderness and all, and Annabelle loved it with a fervour she'd thought she'd saved exclusively for Jacob.

Apparently it extended to all of his worldly possessions, too.

"It's beautiful," she said, taking in the white wooden porch and the curving wall that overlooked the lake. The windows on that side were especially large and would catch the afternoon sun. "Is this the summerhouse you've been building?"

"It is and it isn't."

She frowned. "Then what *is* it?"

"You'll see." There was an enigmatic smile on his face as he strolled forward, apparently in no rush to explore the building he had kept from her the entire duration of her stay. He pulled a key from his pocket and handed it to her. "This is for you," he said. "Consider it yours hereafter."

"Mine?" With slightly shaking hands, she put the key in the lock and turned. There was a *clunk* and the door slowly opened. Annabelle stepped inside, into a . . .

A *library*.

The entire building was one large library, a curved wall with two enormous windows, complete with window seats and towering bookcases on every wall. The shelves were not yet filled, but there were many books here already. Some she recognised—her favourites.

"Jacob." She turned to him with tears in her eyes. "Jacob, what is the meaning of this?"

"I'm sorry it's not yet fully stocked; I have to be mindful of my debts." He shifted a little uncomfortably. "And I confess I had to write to your sister to discover all your favourites. I know you particularly like my London library—and I confess I dislike the room far less now, for some unaccountable reason—but we'll be spending a great deal of the year here. So I thought you should have a library of your own that you can make into whatever you wish."

Annabelle mouthed the words *library of my own*. She'd thought she'd been happy before, but this transcended everything.

"You love me," she said in wonder, turning back to look at his beautiful face. "You *love* me."

"If I'd known the library was what it would take for you to believe me, I would have bribed the workmen to build it faster." He laughed down at her, cupping her face in his hands. Then his smile pressed softly to hers, and her heart was so full of adoration that it hurt. A sweet, indefinable pain she would spend a lifetime untangling. None of the books she'd read had prepared for the tumultuous reality of loving a man more than the rest of the world put together.

"I love you," she said, needing to say it aloud. Around them, the library was silent and cool, and she took his hand, dragging him to the window, from which the lake glittered under the stone-grey sky.

He cradled the back of her head as he kissed her the way

he had done that first time, with the lazy arrogance of a man confident his kisses would be well-received. Annabelle held on tight, certain she would never need anything else.

Their story was in motion, the pages turning, and she was loving every single word.

He pulled away, looking at her with that ferocious hunger in his eyes. Oh, the way he wanted her; she would never be used to it.

"You," he said, his voice a midnight purr that made desire coil in her belly, "are Annabelle Barrington."

Annabelle Barrington. Her name sounded impossibly good in his mouth.

"And you," she said, reaching up to kiss him back, "are mine."

THE END

Epilogue

The autumn light glowed in softly through the windows as Annabelle woke in her husband's bed.

Her *husband's*. That would take some getting used to—but in the delicious, decadent way one accustomed oneself to a rich dessert. Chocolate. Jacob Barrington, Lord Sunderland, was chocolate to her unsophisticated palette, and she found herself taking great delight in savouring it. And him. Frequently.

She stretched out her limbs, gilded in the hazy morning light. A frost lay across the lawns, crisping the grass, and the sky was a clear, arching blue. Beside her, Jacob did not even stir as she rolled away from him and slid out of bed. One arm was flung to one side, where it had been wrapped around her before she had wiggled free. They had stayed up late all last night, talking about their plans for the future, talking and giggling until he had lowered himself over her body and all conversation had been exchanged for something that was no longer new but just as wonderful. Her body felt stretched, full. She was replete.

Throwing a robe around her nightgown, Annabelle slipped from the room, walking through the silent house. It was still early enough that only the scullery maids were awake, lighting the fires and warming the cold rooms, but Annabelle had no intention of remaining inside—although she had come to love every single tiny part of this house.

Her home.

Something else she had yet to accustom herself to. She, little Annabelle Barrington, nee Beaumont, was the Marchioness of Sunderland, and she had a host of responsibilities placed upon her head. Once, she might have thought herself unable to fulfil them, but now she knew better.

She had Jacob.

But while he was not an early riser, she often found her heart and mind too full to sleep much past dawn, and so she had taken to crossing across the gardens to the lake, which today was still and soundless under the November sky, trees dyeing the surface with shades of orange and red. There lay her personal library.

Jacob had given her the only key, but she'd had several more made—one for him, one for the housekeeper, and one in case of emergency. As always, however, the door was locked, and she took great delight in unlocking it.

Inside, it was dimly lit. Bookshelves rose through the gloom, more in them than before, although they were far from full. That would take a while, for books were not cheap, but Annabelle hardly minded. This was *her* library, to fill as she would, with novels and stories about adventure and chronicles of life abroad under hot suns that did not resemble her own.

For many newly wedded couples, it was customary to visit Italy or Spain, but they had only spent a few heady days in Yorkshire before turning home.

Perhaps, though, she would suggest a trip to one of the places she read about in her books. They could write their own stories there, of love that transcended every obstacle that was flung their way.

Although, she was more than happy with the life they were forming together. He was becoming the man he had always secretly wanted to be, and through his strength, she was finding her own. She was unafraid to defy convention occasionally in favour of happiness.

She was not afraid to let the world know she loved a rake.

Selecting *Sense and Sensibility*, one of her favourite novels, she sat by the window to read, time passing in fits and starts every time she looked up. Dawn gave way to day, birds chirped, the world came alive around her, and the last of the frost was banished by the November sun.

After an indeterminable amount of time had passed, the door creaked open, and she looked up to find Jacob's tall figure leaning against the doorjamb, a tray in his hands.

"You could wake me, you know," he said, still adorably tousled as he made his way into the cold room. He had dressed, but not fully, with a waistcoat and coat but no cravat, and his hair imperfectly brushed. A crooked grin crossed his face at the sight of her in her nightgown and robe, reading by the light of the windows. "Though I should have known you would hardly have noticed my absence."

"You like to sleep," she said, placing a silk bookmark in her place and closing the book. "And I like to read."

"Then read in bed." He prowled closer, placing the tray—hot chocolate and toast and fruit, by the looks of it—to one side. "So I am not obliged to find my wife every time I wake."

***

If you would like to find out what happens next, sign up to Copperplate's newsletter where you can read it, plus other freebies and goodies, for free! You can find it at: https://copperplate-newsletter.beehiiv.com/subscribe

And please, if you enjoyed reading, consider leaving a rating or review on Amazon or Goodreads (preferably both!). Reviews are authors' lifeblood, and I appreciate every single one from the bottom of my heart. Thank you!

Author's Note

As many modern authors do when writing historical fiction, I took some liberties with historical accuracy to make the book what it is. Aside from the characters having somewhat modern viewpoints, and an earl's daughter considering throwing away her position merely to avoid marriage (which would never have happened), I also took some liberties with Jacob's boxing.

Gentlemen did box during this period. Gentleman Jackson made it into a gentleman's sport, and he had a saloon on St James's Street. However, while boxing matches were legal, they were frowned upon and often held outside the city to prevent magistrates finding them. It would take perhaps a day on the stagecoach to reach many of them. In an earlier draft, I did have Jacob travel out. However, the time necessary for the travelling disrupted my timeline, and so I chose instead to have him fight in London instead.

It was also not customary for gentlemen to fight these boxing matches. They often bet on the outcome (as Cecil urges Jacob to do), but while practicing the sport could be a gentleman's pursuit, fighting them was not. I wanted to use this as a way of showing the way Jacob felt about himself—how, while he was technically a part of the aristocracy, he did not consider himself a gentleman. It was also a way of demonstrating the way he released all the darkness and

313

hurt within himself without causing any permanent harm to another. It was a difficult line to walk, showing where he began and his personal growth without making him inherently dislikeable. I hope my portrayal of boxing, whilst not strictly accurate, helped do that.

However, they did employ knee men (!) for the boxers to sit on between rounds, and a bottle man to provide water and a sponge. The boxers were also allowed an orange, or a bite of one, for a burst of energy.

Boxing could be dangerous, and rounds could go on for quite some time, only ending when an opponent was knocked to the ground. For obvious reasons, I had my boxing rounds quite a lot shorter!

I took some other historical liberties in the writing of this book, but I truly hope it held a flavour of Regency England while still being fun, pacy, and full of tension. And I hope you fell in love with poor, hurting, boxing Jacob the way I did.

Acknowledgements

I have so many people to thank who were involved in this book in one way or another.

Firstly, my biggest thank you has to go to my incredible betas: Charlotte, Kelsey, and Rachel. You three transformed what was, frankly, a mediocre book into something special, and you patiently bore with my numerous drafts, my unhinged ramblings, and my frequent despair. Thank you. Always, thank you.

Thank you to my mother, who supported my dream of writing from when I was a child and beyond. You always believed in me, and that encouragement turned me into an adult who never stopped trying.

A huge thank you to my husband for allowing me to ignore him to write books he will never read. You are the Jacob to my Annabelle (if a little less tormented and anguished, but no one's perfect).

A big thank you to every single member of my writing group—your wild encouragement has provoked me to keep going when I feel like a slug (which is a lot). You are all wonderful people, and I feel very lucky to have such accomplished writer friends in my life.

And finally, thank you to everyone who has read, rated, reviewed, signed up to my newsletter, ARC read, or basically interacted with my book in any way at all. Every author needs readers, and I love you all.